BORDER FIELD BLUES

BORDER FIELD BLUES

COREY LYNN FAYMAN

Copyright © 2020 by Corey Lynn Fayman

Published by Konstellation Press, San Diego

www.konstellationpress.com

Copyeditor: Lisa Wolff

Cover design: Corey Lynn Fayman

Author photo: Bruce Fayman

ISBN: 978-1-7346421-1-7

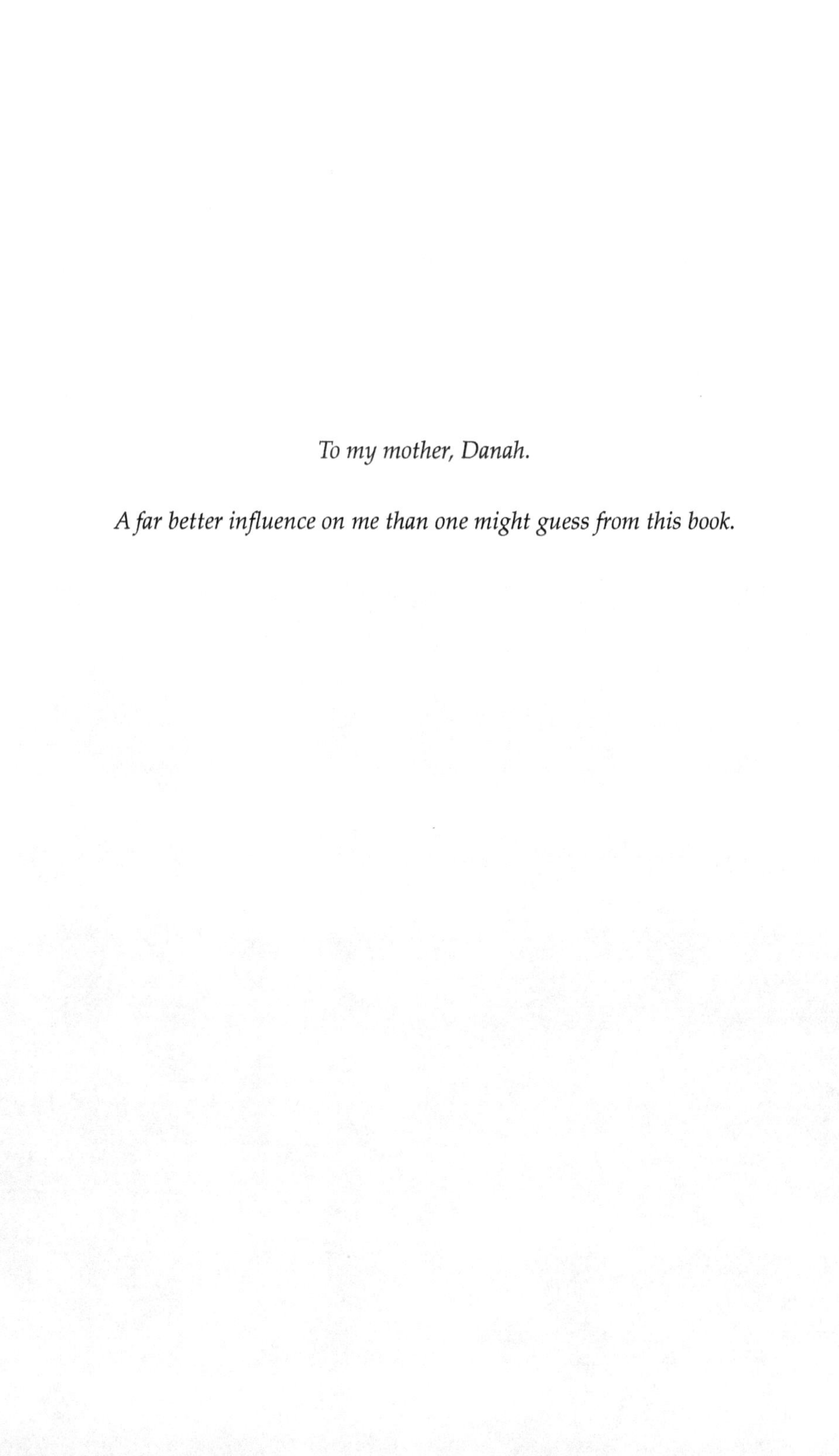

To my mother, Danah.

A far better influence on me than one might guess from this book.

1

EL MUCHACHO (THE BOY)

The men departed as the last of the sun dipped into the ocean, but the boy waited until the darkness was complete, when the great bullring was a dark purple shadow above the roaring ocean. He did not fear darkness. He did not fear anyone. He had a knife. A rattlesnake head hung from his belt. That was enough for a man to protect himself.

The guitar on his back shifted as he slipped under the wire fence. A knot in the strap caught on the cut wire. He dropped his shoulder and slipped off the strap, let it go slack, pulled away from the fence and got free, then pulled the guitar through after him. One of the coyotes had offered to take him across in exchange for the *vihuela*, but he refused the man's bargain. His mother had given the little guitar to him when he turned eight. It was his father's guitar. Or so she claimed. He could not always believe what his mother had told him. Many times she had lied.

She wished for him to become a *guitarrista* one day, that he would learn musical skills from the men who worked in that place. He did not wish to be like them. Guitar players drank too much tequila. They were drug addicts and degenerates, little better than the whores. He would not be surprised if one of them was his father, but he did not care which man it was. They were all whoremongers. He had seen what they did to his mother, what all the men who came to her did. When she died, it was nothing for him to leave that place. He hated the smell of it.

He slipped the guitar onto his back and climbed to his feet, staring into the dark land between the two cities. Behind him the lights of Tijuana glowed closely, a sickening yellow haze. Ahead of him, many miles away, a cold blue line floated above the dark land. San Diego, the first American city he would come to. The sidewalks were scrubbed clean there. Every house had a toilet. And glass walls. A man could live there, free from the sulfurous stench of sewage and whores.

The night folded in on him as he moved down the canyon, feeling his way along the worn dirt path. He listened for voices, but the land was silent. He had only his breathing and footsteps for companionship. A tentative breeze filtered up through the canyon, bringing a pleasant perfume. He had traveled only a quarter mile into the new land, but already it smelled fresher, an ambrosia that lifted his spirits. The air smelled of *mandarinas*, the little orange fruit his mother gave him each Christmas, the one without seeds. The air was a promise, wrapped in its skin.

Soon the land leveled out under his feet. The canyon widened. The shadows of trees rose around him, aligned in perfect order, laid out in a grid. The trees gave off the perfume. He walked up to one of them, searched its branches, found the dark little globes hanging there. He reached for one of the globes, tugged on it. The fruit fell loose and dropped to the ground. He grabbed another, removed it more carefully and held it up to his nostrils, gorging on the aroma. He tore off the skin and devoured its sweetness. He picked three more and ate all of them. He felt rich.

He continued down the canyon, snatching the outermost fruit from the trees as he passed, stashing them in his pockets until they were full. A glimmering azure light beckoned from the end of the orchard. He stepped out from the trees, then in behind a group of boulders that stood above a large house. The house was dark inside. The light came from the pool of water behind it. He'd never seen a real swimming pool, only the ones on TV, in the *telenovelas* the whores watched in the daytime when business was slow.

There was a girl in the pool, paddling from one side to the other. She was naked. He'd seen women naked before, many of them, but they were all whores. They had scars, and bad teeth. Even the young ones had sagging breasts. This girl did not. She climbed out of the pool and sat on the edge, splashing her feet in the water. There was a roundness to her belly, like the Madonna. The girl looked up at him. He stepped farther into the shadows, against the rock. He did not know if she had seen him or only looked up at the place where he stood. He continued to watch her through a gap in the rock. A feeling came over him, unlike any before. The girl was his destiny. She was a vision, like *Coatlaxopeuh,* she who gave the roses to Juan Diego in the desert. The girl's hair glowed orange, like the *mandarina* skins; even the hair of her *concha* had the same color. Her skin seemed translucent, glowing with soft light.

"You like what you see?" came a voice from inside the rocks. The boy jumped.

"*¿Quién está allí?*" he called to the darkness.

"She is temptation," the voice continued. "She has married the serpent."

"*Muéstrese,*" the boy said, demanding to see the man's face.

"Will you renounce the serpent?"

"*No le entiendo,*" the boy said. He reached for the knife in his pocket. "*No lo sé.*"

Something moved from the darkness into the half-light. He saw a man's face, a glint of metal. Two barrels of cold steel jammed into his neck. It was a shotgun. He'd felt one before. The *chulo* who ran the house kept one behind the bar.

"*¡Renuncie la serpiente!*" the man whispered. "Or I'll blow your head off."

"*¡Lo renuncio!*" the boy said. It was nothing for him to renounce the devil. He'd made no contract with Satan, or the

Cristo. They were both for the foolish and weak. His only contract was with himself, with his knife and his rattlesnake head. He had cut the old *chulo*. He would cut this man too.

"Don't move!" the man called. The boy paused. He touched the knife handle under the bulging tangerines. He waited.

"Show your penitence," the man said. The boy didn't move.

"On your knees," said the man, kicking the boy's feet out from under him. The boy fell to the ground, tasted dirt in his mouth. He pulled the knife from his pocket. He would not let this man make him unclean.

"To renounce the devil, you must deny the serpent," the man said. "Only those who have shown penitence may pass through his kingdom."

The boy did not understand.

"*¡Su dinero!*" the man said. The boy understood. The man was a thief, a common bandit, like the other insects who scuttled these hills. The boy had six hundred pesos, but he would not give the man any of it. The man pressed the gun barrel hard against the boy's cheek.

"Your money or your immortal soul," he said.

The boy twitched, grabbed the barrel of the gun and pushed it away. The shot blasted against the hard ground, a bright explosion that lit up the rocks with a split-second flash. Hot pebbles burned the side of his face. He swung his knife, catching the man full in the groin. The man screamed. The boy pulled the knife out and stabbed him again. The man fell on top of him, flailing his arms. The boy grabbed the man's shirt, twisting the cloth in his grip. He slashed his knife across the man's throat. The warm smell of blood engulfed him as it sprayed across his face. The man gurgled and twisted in a great spasm, like a chicken, an alley dog. He grabbed the boy's shoulders. And then he was still.

The boy pushed the man's body away and climbed to his feet. It was the first time he'd killed a man. Others had turned away at the sight of his blade or run away with the first cut. He felt the side of his face. There were little holes where it burned. He felt dizzy.

"Daddy?" a voice called. He looked through the hole in the rock. It was the girl, the Madonna. She stood near the fence, looking up at the hill.

"Daddy?" she called again. "Is that you?"

The boy stepped out of the rocks and walked down to the fence where she stood. He did not care what she thought of him, if her father was dead. She watched him come down to her. She looked unafraid. He walked to the edge of the thick metal fence, reached a hand through the iron railing and beckoned her. She stepped toward him.

"Is he dead?" she asked. The boy nodded.

"I knew you would come for me," she said. She took his bloody hand and placed it on the cool skin of her belly.

"You are the serpent," she said. "And I am your concubine."

"Game Over" flashed in yellow letters on the television screen. The computerized characters froze in place.

"Who won?" asked the fat man on the sofa.

"Nobody won," said the boy. "We have to play again."

"Sure. I guess. I got nothing better to do."

The fat man pulled a cell phone out of his pocket.

"I'm gonna order some Mexican," he said. "You want anything?"

The boy punched a button on his controller, rebooting the game. He didn't say anything.

"How do you win this game, anyway?" asked the fat man.

"Somebody kills The Ancestor. That's how you win."

"That's the shadow thingy?"

"Yes."

The fat man found the number he wanted and tapped on his phone.

"Sure is a weird freakin' game," he muttered to himself as he waited for someone to answer his call.

2

EL PARQUE (THE PARK)

Two men stood on the hill above Border Field State Park, surveying the terrain that led out to the beach. A low ceiling of gray clouds hung over them like smudged cotton.

"Whattya think?" said Max Gemeinhardt, scratching his beard.

"What am I supposed to be looking at?" asked Rolly Waters.

"There. That's the preserve," said Max, pointing to the area just below them, a boundary of short wooden posts connected by low-hung steel chains. "You see those tire tracks?"

"Yeah. I see 'em," Rolly replied. Beyond the posts and chains, ground-hugging plants scrabbled across low mounds of damp sand. Tread marks crisscrossed the area, making it look like a large, sandy doodle pad. In the history of environmental crimes, it probably didn't count for much, but that hardly mattered to Max. For Max this was personal.

"The least terns lay their eggs down there," he said. "I want to nail this bastard."

Rolly had no idea what a least tern was, or what made it least, but he'd seen the signs posted by the park service, warning visitors to stay clear of their nesting area under penalty of fines.

"You sure those tracks are new?" he asked.

"They weren't there yesterday. I've been down here the last three mornings. Audubon Society's doing a census this week."

"Oh."

"I thought maybe you could get an imprint or something, before the wind covers them up, use plaster of Paris or something like that?"

"I guess that might work," replied Rolly. He didn't know how to make imprints of tire tracks, or what to do with them if he did. That was advanced stuff, for specialists, for TV detectives with their high-tech laboratories. He was a private investigator, and a part-time one at that. His resources were limited. Even that was an understatement.

"What about the Border Patrol?" he asked.

"I talked to a guy up here earlier," said Max. "He said it wasn't their jurisdiction. Hell, one of them probably did it. They drive around here like they own the place."

"Whose jurisdiction is it, then?"

"He said it was Parks and Rec. California State Parks."

"Maybe we should talk to them."

"You see any rangers around?"

"It's still kinda early."

"Say the ranger shows up today, which is unlikely as I haven't seen a single one here in six months. Maybe he files a report. Whattya think happens after that?"

"I don't know."

"Well, in case you haven't heard, the late great State of California is broke. Cutting back hours, putting workers on furlough. They gotta prioritize."

"Uh-huh."

"Best scenario, they get around to dealing with this in six months, maybe a year. Probably never."

"How about the police?"

"The cops won't come out here unless someone's dead. That's why I need you to look into this."

Rolly checked his watch. It was six forty-five in the morning, too early to look into anything but the back of his eyelids. He turned away from the scene, looked across the parking lot at the border fence.

"That's the new fence, huh?"

"There's two of 'em now," Max said. "Ninety feet in between. No-man's-land, like we're in a war zone or something. You see that little stone obelisk there in the middle?"

Rolly nodded.

"Nineteen seventy-one," Max continued. "I came to the ceremony. Pat Nixon was here. She dedicated that monument. Now you can't even get close enough to read the damn thing."

"What's it say?"

"Commemorates the Treaty of Guadalupe Hidalgo. Eighteen forty-eight. End of the Mexican-American War. That's where they set the border. She made 'em cut a hole in the fence so she could go over there."

"Who?"

"Pat Nixon. There was a big crowd on the Mexican side of the border. She made the Border Patrol cut a hole so she could go through and talk to them, made a nice little speech about taking the fence down someday. Seven presidents later, we got two fences."

"I remember you bringing Mom and me down here once, after the accident. There were all those families over there, having picnics, trading stuff through the fence."

"Yeah, this place used to give me hope for humanity. Might as well be Berlin now. Except this wall's going to last even longer."

"That's why they call it Monument Road, huh?" said Rolly, recalling the road signs on the way in.

"The excuse now is Homeland Security," Max continued. "We went to court, tried to stop it."

"Who's 'we'?"

"SOCK. Save Our Coastal Kingdom. I'm their counsel. We got an injunction, on environmental grounds, but the judge threw it out."

"Oh."

"You see those tractors back at the entrance?"

"Yeah. I thought maybe they were fixing the road."

Max snorted.

"Nah. That would actually be useful. Did you know more species of birds pass through this spot than any other place in North America?"

"No. I did not know that."

"First it's new fences, then a new road, a couple federal trailers, the next thing you know they've paved over the whole thing, put in housing developments, shopping centers. Pretty soon there won't be any birds out here, just another set of suburbs and cul-de-sacs with bird names on the street signs."

Rolly grinned. Retirement hadn't slowed Max down. It had only given him more time to hack at the gorgon-heads of government bureaucracy.

"Well, it's your dime," Rolly said. "I'll take a look around if you want me to."

"You need any help?"

"Nah, I'm okay."

"I'm heading home, then," said Max. "I've been here since sunrise."

"How's your census going?"

"Pretty good. I saw a spotted grackle and a pair of western tanagers this morning."

"Can I go in there?" Rolly asked, indicating the area inside the posted boundary.

"I guess you might have to," said Max. "Keep an eye out for the eggs, though. The nests are just these little divots in the sand."

"You're sure there's no rangers around?"

"I'll pay any fines, if that's what you're worried about."

"The thought crossed my mind."

"I'll cover any and all expenses. Just don't make things any worse."

"I'll be careful."

"Your mom doing okay?" Max asked, patting his pockets.

"She's fine."

"You want to go to the game tonight?"

"Got a gig tonight," Rolly replied. "At Patrick's. You should come over and hear us after the game."

"I'm too old for that shit. How about tomorrow?"

"You mean the game?"

"Yeah."

"Sure."

"Starts at one," Max said, still searching through his pockets. "Maybe you'll have something for me by then."

"Maybe. What're you looking for?"

"My keys. Here they are. Meet in the lobby? Twelve thirty tomorrow?"

"I'll be there," said Rolly.

"I bet it's one of those AFA assholes," said Max.

"Who's that?"

"I'd love to nail them."

"What are you talking about?"

"Those tracks, in the park. These AFA guys think they're allowed to do the Border Patrol's job. We sued them too."

"Did you win?"

"Not exactly. At least we got 'em to give up their guns."

"Should I worry about these guys?"

"You got a California driver's license?"

"Yeah."

"Then you don't need to worry. I'll see you tomorrow."

Rolly watched Max walk down the hill to the lower parking lot and drive away, then turned back to survey the upper parking lot. On the ridge of hills across the border stood middle-class suburbs of Tijuana, well-kept houses and apartments, a motley architecture painted in bright shades of yellow and blue, pastel greens. The Tijuana suburbs ran out to the bullring. It sat on a promontory overlooking the ocean, directly across the border fence. The Coronado Islands slumbered offshore, shapely female figures half-immersed in a bed of liquid blue. He wished he were in bed, with a woman, or without. It was too damn early to be out in a place like this. It was too early to be out anywhere. He turned back to the bird preserve, looked at the trash and tire tracks.

His private investigator training had taught him a lot about looking up names, searching through public records. It provided lots of information on legalities, how to cover your ass. It even taught him how to set up a stakeout, but he couldn't remember any lessons covering tire treads. He'd have to figure those out on his own.

A cloud of dust swirled across the least tern preserve. It blew up into his nostrils, arid and warm, a reminder of the approaching dry season, the hot Santa Ana winds that came in from the desert. He sighed, anticipating a morning of parched defeat.

A twinkling reflection caught his eye, a sparkle of light winking out at him from inside a tangle of low-growing plants. He walked to the bottom of the hill, then stopped to check for any potential witnesses to his intended trespass. No one appeared. He stepped over the low-slung chain links and into the least tern breeding grounds, walking toward the blinking reflection.

Something screamed, flurried up from below him. A scrambling brush of feathers whirled up in front of his eyes. He raised his hands to protect his face. The feathers twisted away from him, catching an updraft. A gray and white bird floated above him, screaming, calling him names. He looked down at his feet and saw two brown-speckled eggs nestled inside a shallow depression of sand. He stepped around the nest and moved on, keeping a careful eye as he followed the tire tracks. Pieces of eggshells and their dried-up contents littered the tread marks. He leaned down and looked closer. The screaming bird flew away. Embedded in the edge of one tread mark was a mashed chunk of crushed feathers, a tiny yellow beak. At least one tern chick had been lost to the driver's recklessness.

He pulled out his cell phone, switched to camera mode and

snapped some photographs of the treads and crushed feathers. Slipping the phone back into his pocket, he saw the blinking light again, inside a patch of ice plants. He walked closer, spotting what looked like a CD case clutched in the plant's tentacles. The square plastic case quivered in the wind as if trying to escape. He leaned down and picked it up. On the front cover of the album, an alluring young woman stared out at him. She was naked except for the strategic cover of a few jungle vines across her breasts. A large snake, a cobra, curled around her upper leg and spread across her hips, covering her womanhood. *Jungle Love* was the title of the album, by a band called Serpent. Rolly flipped the case over and tried to read the back credits, but the type was too small for his aging pupils. He opened the case and found a blank CD inside, sans label.

"Attention, Attention," a distorted voice blared across the morning air.

Rolly jolted, turning his head in the direction of the voice. A black pickup truck sat next to the ranger's booth, just inside the park entrance.

"Attention. You are in a restricted zone," the voice blared from the truck. "You must return to the trail. Attention. Return to the trail."

Rolly waved in acknowledgment.

"Attention," called the voice. "Return to the trail or you will be placed under arrest."

Rolly waved again, slipped the CD case into his jacket pocket and walked back toward the trail.

3

EL CAZADOR (THE HUNTER)

Rolly walked along the road toward the truck. As he drew close, the driver's-side window slid down, revealing a man wearing a camouflage shirt, baseball cap and reflective sunglasses.

"You can't read signs or something?" the man said.

"Just picking up some trash," Rolly said, tapping his pockets. "I hate litterbugs."

"I guess that makes it okay to break the law?"

"Are you a ranger?" asked Rolly. The truck was fully rigged for off-roading, with jacked-up shocks and big tires, a crossbeam of racked headlights over the cabin and some sort of winch or tow structure in back. No government seal adorned the exterior.

"No, I ain't the ranger," the man said. "I'm a private citizen, trying to make a difference down here."

"You're an avian enthusiast?"

"An A-V what?"

"A bird-watcher."

The man laughed.

"I don't know shit about any birds. I'm hunting for Mexicans."

"You're with the Border Patrol?"

"Do I look like BP?"

"I don't know."

"Well, I'm not."

"I'm not Mexican, either."

"No. I guess you're not. There's a fine, you know, for being out there, in the bird area."

"You're not the ranger."

"No."

"I guess we're done then," said Rolly, turning to leave.

"If that's your Volvo station wagon in the parking lot, I got the license plate," the man said. "I can call the Parks people, tell 'em you was out there."

Rolly sighed and turned back to the driver.

"What do you want?"

"I wanna know what you're up to. And don't give me that litterbug shit. Nobody crosses the chains just to pick up trash."

"A friend of mine called me this morning. He asked me to come down here."

"What for?"

"I'm an investigator."

"What kind of investigator?"

"Here, I've got a card," Rolly sighed. He pulled a business card out of his wallet and handed it over.

"Rolly Waters," the man said, reading the card. "Private Investigator."

"That's me."

"The Rock 'n' Roll Dick. What's that supposed to mean?"

"It's a joke," Rolly said. "I play guitar in a band." He regretted letting Moogus talk him into adding the tagline to his card. There were four hundred more cards in a box at home, so he'd have to live with it for a while.

"Real cute," said the truck driver. "So what're you investigay-tun, Mr. Dick?"

"Somebody drove through the least tern nesting area last night. That's why I was out there. There's some tire tracks, big ruts all over the place. Looks like some birds got killed."

"This friend, he's your client or something?"

"Yes."

"What's his name?"

"I can't tell you that."

"You gotta protect his confidentials, huh?"

"Confidentiality."

"Yeah. This friend of yours, he's paying you to investigate?"

"He was very upset."

"About the birds?"

"He likes birds."

"Sounds kinda gay."

"Can I go now?"

"Depends. Can you tell me anything about the tire tracks?"

"Like what?"

"What kind of treads? Cross-country or street?"

"I don't know much about tires. I took some pictures."

"Can I see 'em?"

"Why?"

"Well, Mr. Rock 'n' Roll Dick, you said you didn't know anything about tires. I do. Maybe I can help you out."

Rolly pulled his cell phone out of his pocket, scrolled through his photos until he found one of the tire tracks, then flipped the phone around to show it to his interrogator.

"Regular treads," said the driver, studying the photo. "Pretty skinny, too, two-hundreds I'd guess."

"What's that mean?"

"It means they weren't driving some jacked-up sand-crawler like mine. Some underpowered putt-putt, or maybe a sedan. That's what I'd guess."

He handed the phone back to Rolly.

"That help?"

"It might. Thanks."

A radio squawked from inside the truck cab.

"Breaker three-ninety. Checking in. Smuggler's Canyon."

"Roger, three-ninety," came the reply. The truck driver punched a button on the radio. It went silent.

"Who's that?" Rolly asked.

"Border Patrol."

"You can listen to them?"

"Sure, if you got short-wave."

"Don't the bad guys listen in, too?"

"The frequency's scrambled. You gotta have the code."

"So how'd you get it?"

"I got friends."

"Doesn't exactly sound legal."

"He said it was cool."

"He's with the Border Patrol?"

"Nobody's gonna give me a hard time for just listening in. I'm not making calls on the thing. It just lets me know how they're situated so I can fill in the dead spots, stay out of their way."

"You weren't out here last night, by any chance, were you?"

"Those aren't my tire tracks, if that's what you're getting at."

"Yeah, that's what you told me," said Rolly. "What'd you say your name was?"

"I'm pretty sure I didn't tell you before."

"No. You didn't."

"People call me Nuge."

"You mean The Nuge, like Ted Nugent?"

"No, it's just Nuge."

"Cat Scratch Fever? The Motor City Madman?"

"Hey, you're the rock 'n' roll dick. I'm Nuge. You got a problem with it?"

"What are you doing out here?"

"Just hanging out."

"You said something about hunting Mexicans."

"Did I?"

"You meant illegals, right?"

The man nodded.

"That's right," he said.

"Isn't that the Border Patrol's job?"

"We're here to help."

"Who's 'we'?"

"A-F-A," the man said. He pointed at the cap on his head, with the letters embroidered in red, white and blue over a black silhouette of the lower forty-eight.

"What's that stand for?"

"Americans for America," the man said. He grinned. "Mom, Guns, and Apple Pie."

"Do you carry a gun?"

Nuge stared Rolly in the eye.

"You tell me first."

"What?"

"Are you carrying?"

"I might be."

"What kind of gun?"

"It's a Glock."

"What caliber?"

"Um, forty-four."

"Glock only sells forty-fives."

"That's what I meant."

"You're one lame-ass liar," said Nuge.

"Yeah, I used to be a lot better," Rolly said. He smiled, trying to defuse the situation. Nuge chuckled.

"You ain't much of a detective, if you ask me."

Rolly shrugged.

"Yeah, well, I don't have my gun either," said Nuge. "Not with me. Some fag-ass judge said we couldn't have 'em if we wanted to be down here."

"I think I heard something about that," said Rolly, recalling Max's lawsuit.

"Said it created a toxic situation. Typical liberal bullshit. We only had 'em with us for defense. Anyway, that's how I got the paintball idea."

"What's that?"

"Got my gear in the back," Nuge said, nodding his head

toward the back of the truck. Rolly looked in the truck bed. Two paintball guns lay there, along with a visored helmet and two cardboard boxes marked "Paintballs–1000ct."

"What do you do with those?" Rolly asked.

"Shoot Mexicans. To mark 'em."

"You sure that's legal?"

"The judge said we couldn't carry real guns. So we use paint guns. Until he says otherwise. It's not lethal force. I checked with our lawyer."

"Doesn't it hurt, when you shoot somebody?"

"Kinda stings, if you hit 'em right, but there's no permanent damage. Mostly, it makes them easy to pick up. We only shoot the ones that try to get away."

"Oh."

"I mean it's kinda hard not to be noticed when you're walking around with big splats of red, white and blue paint all over you. It most definitely leaves a stain."

"Yeah, I guess it would," said Rolly. "What about drug smugglers?"

"What about 'em?"

"I figure there must be some down here."

"You looking to score some dope, Mr. Rock 'n' Roll?"

"No," Rolly said, rolling his eyes. "I was just wondering how you'd deal with someone like that. Last I heard, those guys carry real guns."

"We could take 'em," the man said. "There's ways to do it. The drug guys don't mess around here much, anyway, not anymore. They just bribe people, put stuff on a plane or a boat, hide it inside a big rig. They like to bring the stuff in at peak hours, hide out in a crowd and hope it gets missed."

"Low signal to noise."

"Hmm?"

"Nothing. It's not important."

Rolly looked over the items in the truck bed again, noticing a child's lunch box with the words "Family Act" written in cursive pink letters, with sparkling gold stars around them.

"You got kids?" he asked Nuge.

"Huh?"

"I thought that might be your kid's lunch box back there, with the guns."

Nuge gave Rolly a funny look.

"What's it to you?"

"Nothing. Just making conversation."

"Fuck you. What else did you find out there?"

"In the bird preserve?"

"Yeah, in the bird preserve, butthead."

"I just took some pictures. Like I showed you. The tire tracks. And some dead birds."

"I saw you pick something up."

"Just some trash. Like I said earlier."

"Don't fuck with me. It was some kind of evidence."

"Maybe."

"So what was it?"

"I just had a thought."

"Pretty exciting for you, huh?"

"Maybe one of your AFA buddies was out here last night."

"Oh yeah?"

"That's why you're giving me a hard time. Maybe it wasn't you, but maybe you want to protect your buddies, make sure that judge doesn't find out about this."

"Why would I help you out with those tread marks if I thought that?"

"Were any of your buddies out here last night?"

"No."

"How do you know? Is there a schedule or something?"

"No."

"People just show up when they feel like it?"

"No. I mean, sure, there's a schedule. But I only know about my own hours, man."

"Who keeps track of the schedule?"

"It's on a website."

"How do I get to this website?"

"You gotta have a password to get in."

"How about a phone number? Is there somebody I can call?"

"None of our guys is gonna be out here with treads like that."

"How do you know?"

"I don't have to talk to you. You aren't a cop."

"No. Neither are you."

"Fuck off."

"That's helpful."

"I'm out of here. Good luck with your freaking birds."

Nuge put his truck into gear, hit the gas and took off. Rolly caught the spray of damp sand kicked up by the slipping rear tires.

"Good luck hunting Mexicans, shithead," he muttered, wiping himself off as the truck pulled away. He turned and walked back to his car, half-expecting Nuge to spin a U-turn and try to run him down. He made it to the parking lot, and his old Volvo wagon, without incident. He opened the door of the Volvo and climbed in, pulled the CD out of his pocket and looked at the woman on the cover again. She had long red hair, like a billowing fire. A trace of desert wind, the Santa Ana, drifted over his face like hot dog's breath. He licked his lips. They felt dry and ready to crack.

4

EL VAQUERO (THE COWBOY)

A rattling noise caught Rolly's attention. He looked up from the red-haired temptress on the CD cover to see a dilapidated green Chevy pull into the parking lot, hauling a long horse trailer behind it. A man in a cowboy hat climbed out of the truck, walked to the back of the trailer, guided a horse out and saddled it. The man's easy demeanor suggested he'd done this before, his hands as sure with a saddle and halter as Rolly's stringing an electric guitar. The cowboy retrieved two more horses from inside the trailer and prepared them for riding as well.

Rolly climbed out of his car and trudged toward the trailer. The three horses stared at him as he approached, looking less than thrilled their morning had started this way. A crashing sound came from inside the trailer. A voice cursed in Spanish. The rear end of another horse appeared, kicking its hooves at the hardscrabble ground. The front half of the horse exited the trailer, along with the cowboy, clinging to its reins. As the horse reared back and pawed at the air, the cowboy slipped to one side, narrowly escaping its sharp hooves. The horse dropped back to the ground. The cowboy shortened its reins, looped them twice around a hook on the back of the trailer and pulled them tight. The horse tried to rear up again, but the reins held. The horse shook its head, snorted twice and settled into a pose of resignation like its trailer mates. The cowboy tied off the reins, then ducked down between the horse and the trailer.

"*Buenos días, Señor*," he said, doffing his hat when he spotted Rolly. He took a seat on the trailer's rear bumper and pulled a red handkerchief out of his pocket, wiping his brow.

"*Buenos días*," said Rolly.

"You like a ride?" the cowboy asked, nodding in the direction of the saddled horses.

"No, thank you," Rolly replied.

"I give you good price."

"It looks too dangerous for me."

The man laughed.

"They are good horses," he said. "But they no like the trailer. Every day, it is like they never see it before."

"Are you out here often?"

"*Sí*, every day, in the summer, I am here, with the horses."

"You rent them out?"

"Yes. The people, they like to ride on the beach."

Rolly nodded, stepped toward the trailer. The horse on his right shook its mane and stomped the ground. Rolly stopped.

"Do not worry, my friend," the man said. "She will be fine now. You know what is the difference between horses and women?"

"No," Rolly replied, shaking his head.

"Women, they only break your balls after you ride them."

The cowboy laughed, put his hat back on and tied the hand-kerchief around his neck. He pulled a bottle from his back pocket, took a shot and offered the bottle to Rolly.

"No thanks," Rolly said. He recognized the green label—Herradura Reposado. Tequila. "Were you here yesterday?"

"*Sí.*"

"How late did you stay?"

"After the sun was gone. My people stay out late."

"Seven, seven thirty?"

The cowboy shrugged.

"I do not know the time," he said. "There was still light, over the ocean, but the sun was below. Why do you want to know this?"

"Someone broke into the park last night, drove through the bird reserve, ran over some nests. I'm trying to find out who did it."

"You work for the government, no?"

"I'm a private investigator," Rolly said, pulling a business card out of his wallet. He handed it to the cowboy.

"You no look like you work for the government," the cowboy said. He glanced down at the card.

"You are Roy-ee?" he said.

"Rol-lee," said Rolly, offering a handshake. "Rolly Waters."

"I am Jaime," said the cowboy, grasping Rolly's hand in his leathered brown grip. He looked older than Rolly had first thought, at least sixty, his face dark and wrinkled from a lifetime in the sun.

"This is your work?" Jaime said. "To ask questions?"

"Yes," Rolly replied.

"What will you do if you find these men, the ones who drive over the birds?"

"Someone hired me. He'll decide what to do with 'em."

"He is with the government, no?"

"No," Rolly said, shaking his head. "He's a private citizen. Was there anyone here when you left last night? In the parking lot? Any cars?"

"No. I was the last."

"The gate was closed then?"

"It is closed all the time now."

"Did you see anyone up near the bullring?"

"I do not think so. Except for *La Migra*. I do not look for anyone, though."

"And you left after sunset?"

"Yes, it was dark by the time I get home. After I put the horses away."

"Where do you live?"

"Near the river. Across from the canyon. That is my home."

"Did you pass anyone on the road? Anyone headed into the park?"

"No. I did not see anyone."

Rolly pursed his lips. He had a nine-hour window to work with, sometime between eight last night and five this morning, when Max arrived.

The growl of an approaching engine came to his ears. He looked back toward the park entrance and saw Nuge's accessorized pickup squeeze around one side of the entry gate and pull onto Monument Road. The truck honked, picking up speed as it went by, kicking up a hazy cloud of dust, though the air remained clear enough for Rolly to note the middle-finger salute offered by Nuge as he passed.

"That was for me," he said, turning back to Jaime. "I talked to him earlier."

"He did not like you asking questions."

"No. I guess not."

"I would like to have a truck such as that one. Mine is old now. I must work on it always."

"Have you seen that truck before?"

"There is a truck that is like that one, in the canyon sometimes."

"What canyon is this?"

"The one across from my land. Smuggler's Canyon it is called."

"Sounds like a place he'd hang out. Do illegals come through there a lot? Border crossers?"

"In the past, yes. Not so many now," Jaime said. He pointed at the tractors in the parking lot. "There are machines there, like these. They make the new fence."

"Smuggler's Canyon," Rolly said, repeating the name.

"I do not call it that," said Jaime. "It is just the canyon, to me."

"I found something while I was out there," Rolly said. "In the park."

"What is it you find?"

Rolly pulled the CD case out of his pocket and handed it to Jaime.

"For the music, yes?" said Jaime. He opened the cover and inspected the disk.

"Yes. It plays music."

Jaime closed the case, stared at the picture on the cover for a moment, then handed the case back to Rolly. He took the tequila bottle out of his pocket, unscrewed the top and offered the bottle to Rolly again. Rolly shook his head.

"You no like the tequila?" said Jaime.

"I like it too much," Rolly replied.

Jaime nodded, took a drink.

"The tequila is good for you," he said. "But not too much."

He put the bottle back in his pocket and stared at the ground. The sun broke free of the morning's haze, a delirious light bending over the eastern mountains that warmed Rolly's skin. A choir of birds sang in the fields. Their calls danced on the air in a lazy, pulsating rhythm. Rolly listened to the sound of their natural counterpoint, no note out of tune, all connected. He rested his own voice, a full measure, then two.

"*Me atormentará*," Jaime said.

"What's that?"

"It is Xtabay," said Jaime. "The woman, there, with the music. She is Xtabay, the seducer of men."

Rolly looked at the CD cover again and saw no reason to disagree with Jaime's assessment.

"In Yucatán," Jaime continued. "That is where I was born, the old men tell of Xtabay, the woman who lives in the jungle. She will show herself to the young men, the ones who go into the jungle alone. They will desire her. She will lead them far into the jungle, give them pleasure. The young men will die. They will not find their way back."

"It's a story, a myth?"

"I think yes. That is what you call it. I, too, think this as a young man."

"You don't think so now?"

"She has been here, with me. She came to me last night, in a dream."

"Xtabay?"

"Yes. I surrender this time, in my dream. I take pleasure in her. I think now I will die soon."

"It was only a dream."

"I find something, too," said Jaime. "When I wake up from my dream. *Anoche.*"

"What did you find?"

"I will give them to you."

Jaime pulled something from his front pocket and handed it to Rolly. It was a pair of pink satin panties, with the word "Serpent" on one side and "Jungle Love" on the back.

"Where did you find these?" asked Rolly.

"*En mi casa.* My house."

"You found these in your house?"

"*Sí.* When I awake this morning."

Jaime took another hit from the tequila bottle. If the morning's intake was any indication, he would make it through the whole bottle by noon. His memory, and his dreams, would be drowning in it. Rolly thought about the dreams he used to have, the drunken nightmares. They had seemed real then, his pickled brain transmuting unconscious thoughts into winged furies and soul-stealing spirits, the vivid manifestations of an uneasy mind drowned in alcohol. The dream-furies disappeared two months after he became sober.

A blue minivan appeared on the road, headed in toward the park. It slowed, then came to a stop across from the two men. The driver's window slid down. A round-faced woman with a tall blond hairdo poked her head out.

"Do you rent those horses?" she asked.

"*Sí.* Yes," replied Jaime.

"Can we ride on the beach?"

"Oh yes, that is fine. They like the water very much."

"How much will it cost?"

"How many horses?"

"Three. Just for a couple of hours."

"*Muy bueno*. Three is good. I give you good price."

The woman looked doubtful. She turned back to talk to someone in the car before returning to Jaime.

"All right," the woman said. She turned the car into the lot, parking between Jaime's trailer and Rolly's Volvo.

Jaime stashed the tequila inside a small cabinet on the side of the trailer.

"I have customers now," he said. "I must go with them. For the insurance."

"Wait," Rolly said. "You said something, earlier, when you looked at the picture. *May tormenta?*"

"*Me atormentará.*"

"Yes. What does that mean?"

"She is a curse."

"The woman in the picture? She's the one in your dream?"

"It was not a dream. She is Xtapay."

"She looks like Xtapay, the picture, that's what you mean?"

"I have seen her, that one."

"Who is she?"

"She is a ghost."

The doors of the van opened, disgorging the chubby woman driver and two preteen females.

"C'mon, girls," the woman said. "This will be fun."

The girls didn't look convinced. Jaime collected his horses, helped the woman and her daughters mount up, then led his own horse over to Rolly.

"You want these back?" Rolly said, indicating the panties.

"Take them to her," Jaime said. "Then I will be free."

"I don't understand."

"You stop drinking the tequila, *sí?*"

"Yes."

"You have great strength, *muy fuerte*. She will not seduce you."

Jaime mounted his horse.

"Where do I take them?" asked Rolly.

"It is an old house. Back down the road, where the white earth spreads out from the canyon. Smuggler's Canyon. That is the house. You will see the machines there for moving the earth. They are next to the house. On the other side of the road, there is land that opens out to the river. That is my house, down by the river. *No le atormentan.*"

"This woman lives there?" Rolly said. "Xtapay? Is that what you mean?"

"*No me atormentará más,*" said Jaime, again. He clicked at his horse, waved to the woman and her girls. They followed him out toward the beach, where California ended and ran into the Pacific.

5

———————

LA CASA (THE HOUSE)

Rolly drove back along Monument Road, searching for the house Jaime had described, passing tall grasses and reeds, tough thickets of plants that thrived in the briny mud marsh of the river plain. To his right, dusty round hills swept up to the border. Long, winding ruts creased the crests of the hills, tracks of Border Patrol vehicles that paced the fence like caged jaguars.

Ranchers and farmers had settled the land long ago. Their inheritors still lived here, but the slumped barns and rusted tractors he saw didn't bode well for an agrarian future. The farmhouses looked worn, in need of repair and a fresh coat of paint. Weather stains under drooping windowsills made the windows look like fatigued eyes. Rolly slowed the Volvo, negotiated a set of sharp curves and entered a long straightaway. A motionless flow of white earth spilled down toward the road from the canyon above. He slowed the car and pulled in next to a pair of large yellow tractors. The Volvo's aging shock absorbers rattled as the wheels caught the dirt shoulder, bouncing him around like seeds in a pair of maracas. The car stopped. He climbed out, surveying the scenery. A line of smoke trees fronted a black metal fence. Beyond the fence, a house stood on a small hill.

Smuggler's Canyon, Jaime called it. It wasn't much of a canyon, more a wide gulch, or an arroyo. Whatever its geologic appellation, the place was a garbage dump. Bits of consumer flotsam dotted the flow of dried runoff that ran down its spine. A weather-beaten sofa sat between the two earthmovers, surrounded by a half-circle of discarded tires and crumpled beer cans. As the canyon receded toward the border, the earth closed in on it in a series of irregular hills. At the top of the farthest hill ran the dark line of the border fence; above it, bleached sky. At what point the sky became Mexico, Rolly couldn't tell.

He checked his watch, wondering if Jaime's seductress was awake yet. He walked down to the road, until he could see the front of the house. It sat on a small rise of ice plant, fifty feet back from the road. A cracked blotch of asphalt indicated the drive-way, traversed by a heavy mechanical gate. A spiked fence encircled the property.

The house looked like it was built in the sixties, perhaps early seventies, California-Modern-Hippie, flat and rectangular, the exterior covered in weathered wood stripping. He imagined the interior as it once might have been—the smell of incense, fern plants in hand-stitched macramé hangers, enthusiastic pottery efforts displayed on the dining room table. The house had been a free spirit once, but someone had wrapped it in chains. Metal bars covered the windows like rusted scars, bolted on at odd angles, broken hopes scrawled on a once hopeful face.

He spotted a plastic intercom near the hinge of the gate, set into a large blob of dried glue, painted flat black to match the iron bars. He pushed the button next to the speaker. There was no reply. He tried again, holding the button down as he spoke.

"Hello," he said. "Is anyone home?"

No one answered. He waited, pulled a business card from his wallet, wedged it into a crack in the speaker's grill and headed back toward his Volvo.

Passing the corner of the fence, he spotted a garbage can

tucked in between the fence and the smoke trees. He slid in next to the container and lifted the lid. A raft of smells wafted out of its depths. The food wasn't rotten yet, but it would go soon in the heat. An adrenalized shot of digestive acid shot up his esophagus, burning the back of his throat. He dropped the lid, stepped away from the garbage can and bent over, hands on his knees. The nausea passed without incident. He stood up and swallowed. The taste of acid-washed pepperoni slid down his throat, a reminder of the pizza he'd shared with the bar staff last night, after closing time.

He looked to make sure no one was around, then pulled out a handkerchief, covered his nose with it, opened the lid again and looked in. A polystyrene container sat on top of the pile, emblazoned with the logo of the Villa Cantina, a well-known eatery in the East Village. He grabbed the greasy paper receipt that clung to the top of the container and slid it into his pocket. Someone at the restaurant might remember who ordered takeout. They might have a phone number.

"Get away from there!" someone shouted at him.

Rolly jumped, catching his foot on the bottom corner of the garbage receptacle. As he fell, he reached back for something to break his fall and caught the top corner of the container, bringing it down on top of him. The voice squawked again. It came from the speaker attached to the gate.

"What are you doing?" the voice said.

Rolly climbed to his feet, wiped a blob of guacamole from the leg of his pants and looked up at the house. A woman stood in the front doorway, wearing an orange paisley robe. One slender leg peeked out from below the robe's loosely tied satin, arched as if on toe-point. A luxuriant tumble of hair surrounded her face and poured down onto her shoulders. It glowed in the morning light, golden orange like her robe.

Rolly waved.

"Hello," he said.

"What do you want?" the woman called down to him, her breathy voice cracking like a Keith Richards falsetto.

"I rang the bell earlier, but no one answered," Rolly continued. "I wanted to talk to you."

"What about?"

"My name's Rolly Waters," Rolly said. "I'm an insurance investigator. I'm looking into an accident last night at Border Field Park."

"What are you doing in my trash?"

"I thought I might find your name, or a phone number."

"Why?"

"So I could call you."

"I'm not interested."

"I'd like to talk to you."

"No."

"I just have a few questions."

"Please go away. I don't feel well."

"I'm sorry. Were you here last night?"

"No. I was out."

"What time were you out?"

"That's none of your business."

"Yes, you're right. It's none of my business. I think this accident happened sometime after eight last night. Did you see or hear any cars go by?"

"Cars go by all the time."

"At that time of night?"

"All the time."

"Oh. Really?"

"If you don't leave I'll call the police."

People rarely called the police the first time they threatened to, especially when they had something to hide. That was Rolly's experience, anyway.

"Can I show you something?" he said, reaching into his pocket.

"You're not one of those, are you?"

Rolly pulled the panties from his pocket and held them up for her perusal.

"Jaime asked me to give these to you."

"Who?"

"Jaime," said Rolly. He pointed across the road, toward a house by the river. "He lives over there, I think. Older fellow, a cowboy? I don't know his last name."

"What have you got there?"

"It's a pair of women's panties. They've got the words 'jungle love' and 'serpent' on them."

The woman laughed, a harsh cackle.

"You want an autograph or something?"

"Jaime gave them to me," Rolly said, not sure what to make of the question. "He seemed to think they were yours."

The woman crossed her arms, staring down at Rolly.

"I don't know any Jaime," she said.

"Could you just take a look?" he asked. "He asked me to give them to you."

The woman stepped off the porch and walked down toward Rolly, negotiating the steep driveway in her high heels as if she'd been born in them. She paused a few feet from the gate, pulling the orange silk robe tight against her skin. At close range, she looked a bit older than fabulous. There were signs of collagen desperation in the shape of her lips, an age-inappropriate lift to her tits.

"What's your name again?" the woman asked.

"Rolly Waters. I'm in insurance."

"What do you really do?"

"What do you mean?"

"You don't work in insurance. You don't have the right eyes."

"What kind should I have?"

"Your eyes are too soft. You've got deep eyes that let everything in."

"What kind of things?"

"They let me in, didn't they?"

Rolly cleared his throat.

"I look people over," he said.

"You certainly do."

"It's part of my job."

"I saw the look in your eyes. It's not insurance. An artist, perhaps?"

"Well, I used to play guitar for a living."

"Oh. You're a snake."

"Excuse me?"

"Guitar players are snakes."

"Oh."

"Slithery, slidy snakes."

"Some of us aren't so bad."

"I like playing with snakes."

It was too early in the morning for Rolly to play the whoopee hustle. He reached in his jacket and pulled out the CD case.

"Is this you?" he asked, pointing to the girl on the cover.

The woman took a step closer.

"What do you want?" she hissed.

"I want to find out who drove their car through the least tern preserve last night."

"The what?"

"Least terns. They're birds. Over at Border Field Park."

"This is all about birds?"

"Yes."

"You were going through my garbage."

"I needed your name."

"I thought you were stalking me."

"Jaime said you were the girl in the picture. He asked me to give you these panties."

"Why?"

"He says he'll die if you don't take them back."

"That's a new one. Some men would die just to get them from me."

"There's this legend from where he grew up in Mexico, about a goddess, Xtapay. She lives in the jungle."

"I see."

"She seduces young men and lures them to their death."

"I like her already."

"Jaime said you were with him last night. That you left him the panties."

The woman laughed again, deeper throated, more relaxed.

"Oh dear," she said. "What have I done?"

"What?"

"There's been someone, up in the rocks. A man. We've been playing a little game."

"What's that?"

"You're not a prude, are you, Mr. Waters?"

"I've been around."

"You've enjoyed a little variety in your sexual life?"

"Like I said."

"Well, I like to go 'au naturel' on occasion, out back. There's a pool. It's not entirely private, if someone's positioned in the right place. Lately I've had a feeling that someone might be watching. He's been up there, more than once."

"Why didn't you call the police?"

"Why should I? He wasn't threatening me."

"Did you see him?"

"No. But I knew he was there. I'll admit to giving him a little show sometimes. I'm a bit of a free spirit that way."

"What's that?"

"Well, if some man's up there, hiding away, taking his pleasure in looking at me, what do I care? It's a compliment, really. I flirted a little. He never showed himself."

"What would you do if he had?"

"Well," the woman giggled, "that would depend on the man. If he was a snake . . ."

The heat from the asphalt driveway blew up into Rolly's brain. He changed the subject.

"Have you ever been to a restaurant called Villa Cantina?" he asked.

The woman inspected one of her fingernails, chewed on it a moment.

"No. I don't think so," she said between bites.

"I found some take-out containers in your trash."

"People put things in my trash all the time."

"What kind of people?"

"The men who work over there, in the canyon."

"You mean the construction crew?"

"There's all sorts of men over there, tearing things up, making noise."

"Maybe it was one of them, up there, looking at you?"

"Construction workers are heavy breathers. This man was quiet, a gentleman, you might say."

"Oh," Rolly replied. He looked at the panties again. "You're sure these aren't yours?"

"I need to go now," the woman said. "Give them back to your friend."

"I don't think he'll want them."

"They're yours then, I guess. Enjoy."

"I don't think I got your name, by the way."

"No, you didn't."

"I'd love to know it," Rolly said, flashing his friendliest smile, the one he used to seal the deal women thought they'd made with his eyes. "Maybe we could talk again sometime."

"My name's Tangerine," the woman replied.

"Tangerine," Rolly repeated. "What's your last name?"

"Just Tangerine," she replied, turning away from him. "Like those sweet little fruits."

Rolly watched the robe swish across Tangerine's bottom as she sauntered back to the house. The heat from the asphalt blew up into his brain again. If he was a snake...

6

EL DESAYUNO (THE BREAKFAST)

Hector Villa walked out from the kitchen of the Villa Cantina, carrying a rack of water glasses. He'd shaved his head since the last time Rolly had seen him. Hector stood about five-foot-six in his huaraches and had two silver rings in each ear, a gold stud in his tongue. When not attending to restaurant duties, he played congas with local salsa bands or DJ'd at the underground club next door. The nightclub was his parents' concession to Hector's bohemian enthusiasms, a carrot they'd dangled to keep him close to the family business. They'd opened the restaurant over thirty years ago, a homespun lunch place on the edge of the barrio, frequented by longshoremen and city bureaucrats. These days slews of young urban night crawlers swarmed the eatery, especially on weekends, fueling up between club hops and gallery openings. East Village gentrification made the place hip.

"*Buenos días, amigo,*" Hector said, squatting down to stash the drinking glasses under the counter.

"*Hola,*" said Rolly.

"I just talked to some lady on the phone, Alicia Waters? She any relation to you?"

"Sort of."

"We're catering a party for her next Saturday. In Coronado."

"She's my dad's second wife. His birthday's next week."

"You gonna be there?"

"I'm the entertainment," said Rolly, reminding himself to call his stepmother later. She'd asked him to come by the Coronado house this weekend, pick out a corner of the patio where he could set up and play.

"You still playing with the band?" Hector asked.

"Couple of nights a week. We're at Patrick's this weekend."

"Ay, yi, yi. That's like playing in a sardine can."

"We're doing the early shift tonight, four to eight. It's not bad."

"If you say so."

Rolly shrugged, relieved he wouldn't be out late. The only people on the streets after closing were speed-balling ravers or drunken frat boys, prostitutes, meth addicts, pushers and cops, each of them problematic in their own way. The later a gig went, the more dangerous it became.

"Menu?" Hector asked.

"Sure. I'll take a look."

Hector grabbed a menu from under the counter and passed it to Rolly.

"Club soda, right?" Hector asked.

"Yeah, with a lime, please."

"You got it."

Hector walked to the soda machine and drew a tall glass of bubbles. Rolly surveyed the room, noting the upgraded decor. Empty bulk coffee bags covered the opposite wall in rough burlap. A long wooden shelf had been installed along the top of the wall. On top of the shelf, Frida Kahlo self-portraits served as bookends to a display of vintage tequila bottles and colorful ceramic plates. In the corner of the room, by the front window, some sort of thick, green-leaved tropical thing sat in a large clay urn. Three young women sat at a table next to the urn. They laughed as Rolly's gaze settled on them, but they hadn't noticed him. They never did anymore. He'd become invisible to all females under thirty-five.

Hector returned with a club soda.

"I thought you'd be busier this morning," Rolly noted.

"Yeah, I guess everyone's out at the beach or something, Labor Day weekend, you know. It's cool by me. I gotta finish my costume for Monday."

"What happens on Monday?"

"There's a protest. I'm going as Pancho Villa."

"What're you protesting?"

"The AFA's holding a rally," Hector said.

"You mean the guys with the paint guns, that AFA?"

"Yeah. You know about them?"

"Americans for America, right?"

"Asshole Fucking Anglos is more like it."

"Where's this rally going to be?"

"Border Field Park. Across from the bullring."

"I was down there this morning."

"Oh yeah? What were you doing down there?"

"Bird-watching."

"Yeah, right."

"You don't believe me?"

"No offense, but you don't seem like the type."

"I'm full of surprises."

"So, what kind of birds did you see?"

"Least terns."

"Everybody sees them. They got a preserve there."

"I saw a spotted grackle."

"Hmm, I think we might've had one of those in here last night. Skinny girl with freckles. Had a really sexy laugh."

"This is a real bird."

Hector laughed.

"Yeah. And I'm a real hound dog. Anyway, the AFA's having a rally down there on Monday. MENCIA's staging a counter demonstration."

"Who's MENCIA?"

"*Movimiento Estudiantes Nuevos Chicanos Independientes de América*. It's a Chicano student political organization."

"You're not a student."

"No. I'm Chicano, though. I gotta protect my people's rights."

"You grew up here. You're not an illegal."

"Listen, those AFA fuckers are breaking the law," Hector said, his voice rising. "They're nothing but vigilantes."

"I ran into one of them this morning. He said it was legal. The paint guns, I mean."

"Yeah. Technically. That's how they're getting around the court ruling. The judge said they had a right to be down there as long as they didn't carry firearms."

"Paint guns don't count, I guess."

"It's bullshit. You ever been hit by one of those things?"

"This guy said it stings a little."

"Roberto, my lawyer, he plays with some friends on the weekends. He's always got these big welts. And he wears protective equipment."

"I'm just telling you what the guy told me. I'm not signing up with 'em."

"You sure?" Hector said, raising one eyebrow. "I thought all you white boys turned Republican in your dotage."

Rolly shrugged. He didn't remember the last time he'd voted for anyone—Republican, Democrat, Libertarian, Whig.

"You ready to order?" asked Hector.

"The usual, I guess," Rolly said. He pulled the receipt from his pocket and handed it to Hector. "Can you tell me anything about this? I was hoping to get a name, or maybe a phone number that went with it."

"What for?"

"Just looking into something."

"*Ay caramba*," said Hector. "This is that day job of yours, isn't it?"

"It's related. I thought you could help me."

"You want your Mexican amigo to help you find some bad

pachucos?" said Hector, channeling Alfonso Bedoya.

"Well, one bad *pachuco*, at least," said Rolly.

"What'd he do?"

"Killed some birds."

"At the park? That's why you were down there?"

Rolly nodded.

"Don't you detective guys usually pass out some *dinero* for this kind of information?"

"Only in the movies. I'm on a budget."

"So, what do I get for my labors?"

"My continued patronage of your establishment."

"Sweet. I'll start planning my retirement."

"You know, it could be one of your AFA buddies."

"You think one of them did it?"

"Don't know. Could be. You could help me find out."

"Now you got me," Hector said. "I'll grab the credit receipts from last night. I'd love to nail those bastards. You know what you want yet?"

"The usual, I guess."

Hector retreated to the kitchen. He returned with a small bowl of sliced cucumber, avocado, and shredded jicama and plunked it down in front of Rolly.

"I can't find the order," he said. "They must have paid cash."

"It was a take-out order, I think."

"You should talk to Vera. She worked front of the house last night. I had a catering gig."

"Is she here?"

"She's at the bank. She walks over there every Saturday. Deposits our cash receipts for the week."

"Isn't that a lot of money to carry around?"

"She's got a gun. I bought if for her. Nice little pearl-handled .22, silver engraved with her name."

"That's sweet of you."

"No one fucks with Vera."

"I know *I* won't."

As if on cue, the front door opened and Vera stomped in,

wearing a yellow bandana and short shorts, her feet strapped in high-heel glory.

"Hey, Vera," Hector called, "come over here."

Vera plopped down on the stool next to Rolly, placing an oversized straw purse on the counter. She undid the bandana and shook out her frizzy black hair.

"What's up?" she said, snapping her gum.

"Rolly's got a receipt from last night. He thinks it has something to do with this case he's on."

"What kind of case?"

"He's a private eye."

"Really? I thought you played guitar for a living."

"Pays the bills," Rolly said, shrugging. He handed the receipt to Vera. "I was hoping to get a name or address that went with this order."

"Oh, yeah," Vera said, "I know this one. It's the same order, every Friday, around ten."

"You're sure?"

"Yeah. It took me a few weeks to notice. Always Friday night. Two six-packs of Mountain Dew. The food order changes, but there's always two six-packs of Dew."

"Sounds like a party."

"I might have the name on my notepad."

"I'm gonna check," Hector said, hoisting himself over the counter. He knocked Vera's straw purse off the counter as he scurried away.

"Hey, watch it," said Vera. She bent down to retrieve her purse.

"You got a girlfriend, Rolly?" she asked, placing the purse back on the counter.

"Not at the moment."

"You want one?"

"I'm too old for you, Vera."

"I'm thinking I might prefer someone more mature."

"Compared to what?"

"Mr. Piñata Pants there, bouncing off the walls, throwing his candy all over the place."

Rolly looked down at his salad, picked at a chunk of jalapeño pepper with one tine of the fork.

"I don't mean other girls," said Vera. "If that's why you're getting squirmy. I been with worse guys, that way. It's just that goddamn crazy energy. He's always got some new project, running out to the next thing. Sometimes I'd just like him to slow down a little. You know what I mean? I can't keep up."

"Like that MENCIA rally he was telling me about?"

"Oh, God, MENCIA," Vera said, rolling her eyes. "If they're so on fire about being Mexicans, why don't they move back there? Know what I mean?"

Rolly wasn't sure what Vera meant. He nodded his head anyway.

Hector returned, waving a yellow stationery pad.

"Is this the order?" he said.

Vera grabbed the pad from Hector and read the marks on the page.

"Yeah. That's it. Two packs of Mountain Dew. Paul Barrere. That's the name."

"Is that his phone number?" Rolly asked, indicating the number next to the name.

"Should be. I always ask for a phone first if it's a take-out order, in case we get cut off."

"I'm calling the guy," Hector said, flipping open his cell phone.

"Hold on," Rolly said.

"What?"

"I don't want to make him suspicious."

"Don't worry. I got a plan," said Hector. He punched in the number and held the phone to his ear. "Check this out."

Rolly looked over at Vera. She opened her palms and raised her eyebrows as if to say, "See what I mean?"

"*Hola,*" said Hector, speaking to whoever had answered the

phone. "I'm trying to reach Mr. Barrere? Paul Barrere. He ordered take-out from the Villa Cantina last night. Uh-huh. Who's this? James? Well, James, I guess you're our winner, then. That's right. You've been selected to receive a fifty-dollar gift certificate for free food and beverage from Villa Cantina, the Mexican restaurant where fresh ingredients and old family recipes get a new start."

Hector paused for a moment, listening.

"Sure, you can use it anytime," he said. "Just come by and pick it up . . . Oh, I see. Well, normally we don't deliver . . . Yes? What's that? Sure, I can have somebody bring it over. What's that address?"

Hector looked at Vera, making a writing movement with his hand. Vera reached in her handbag and pulled out a pen. She scribbled down the information as Hector repeated it.

"Twelve-zero-two Tenth Avenue. In the lobby. Two carne asada burritos. Okay, give us about twenty minutes. Yes. Yes. All right then. Goodbye, and have a great day!"

Hector flipped the phone shut. He laughed.

"See?" Hector said. "I told you I could take care of it. No problem."

Vera tore the address from the notepad and handed it over to Rolly.

"It's like four blocks away," Hector said.

"Who's James?" Rolly asked.

"I don't know. He answered the phone."

"What about Paul Barrere?"

"James never heard of him. I figured you could scope it out when you get there."

"What do you mean?"

"You can be our delivery boy. Take him his lunch."

Rolly frowned.

"I guess that would work."

"Nobody gets suspicious when you give them something for free," said Hector. "I'm a genius."

"Yeah, you're a genius," said Vera. "Except we don't carry any gift certificates."

7

EL RASCACIELOS (THE HIGH-RISE)

Rolly opened the glass front door of the high-rise condominium located three blocks up the street from the Villa Cantina and walked into the lobby. A gigantic security guard sat behind the front desk. It looked like the guy weighed at least three hundred pounds, most of it fat.

"Hello," said Rolly.

"Good morning," said the guard. A large red rash ran across the guard's left ear, along his pink, porcine cheek and down his neck, where it tapered away into the overstuffed collar of his blue shirt.

"I'm looking for someone named James," Rolly said.

"That'd be me."

"You're James?"

"That's what I said."

"I'm from the Villa Cantina."

"You got my burritos?"

"Yes," said Rolly, placing the take-out container on the desk.

"They said something about a gift certificate?" said the guard.

Rolly reached in his pocket and pulled out the printed certificate Hector had cobbled together on the computer in the Villa Cantina's back office.

"Here you go," he said, placing the envelope on top of the take-out container. "Fifty dollars minus this order comes to thirty-seven-fifty."

"Now how 'bout that twenty dollars you owe me?" said the guard.

"What?"

"You owe me twenty dollars."

"How do you figure that?"

"Sir Roland owes me twenty bucks."

"Do I know you?"

"You're Rolly Waters, right?"

"Yes."

"Also known as Sir Roland the Stratomaster?"

"I haven't heard that one in a while," Rolly said, studying the man's face, trying to place him. The appellation, Sir Roland, went back to his earliest days, when he'd set out with his guitar every night of the week, on the lookout for any band that would let him sit in, any gig he could find. Moogus had crowned him with the title one night after Rolly wielded his six-string in especially noble and wondrous style.

The guard flipped open the take-out container, leaned down and inhaled the aroma of the burritos.

"That's a Royal Tingler, for sure," he said.

"Jimmy?" said Rolly. "Big Jimmy?"

The guard laughed. The sound of his laugh was as big as the man and confirmed Rolly's reckoning. James Bodeans, aka Big Jimmy, had been the bouncer at Pelicans bar in Imperial Beach twenty years ago, maintaining order, rousting bikers, surf bums and swabbies with equal prejudice, back when The Creatures were Pelicans' house band, when malfeasance buzzed around the band like a swarm of human flies.

"Had you going, didn't I?" said Jimmy.

"You shaved your beard," Rolly said. "You look different."

"Yeah. Cleaned up my act."

"What's this twenty bucks I owe you?"

"I loaned it to you my last night on the job. Before that guy stabbed me."

"Somebody stabbed you?"

"Yeah. I still got the IOU. Signed by Sir Roland."

"With a knife?"

"Yeah. With a knife. Punk-ass little Mexican dude. I can't believe you don't remember."

"What happened?"

"This little beaner started hassling some girls in the line, so I kicked him out, told him to go back to his own country. Guy comes back in a couple of minutes with a switchblade. Sticks it in me. Four times. Woulda stabbed me some more, but these jarheads standing in line jumped the guy, beat the crap out of him."

"It was your last night?"

"Well, it didn't start out that way, but that's what I decided after I got home from the hospital. Something like that kinda makes you reconsider your way of living, got me started on the straight and narrow, if you know what I mean."

"We were playing that night?"

"Sure. I remember the song you were playing, right after I got stabbed, that Madonna thing you used to do—'My girl's a sad-eyed Madonna . . .'"

"Every night she's praying for me," Rolly said, completing the couplet.

"Yeah. That's it. The ambulance is there. The lights are flashing, and the paramedics are trying to talk to me, but all I can hear is that damn song. And I saw her, you know. Madonna. I'm sure I'm about to die and I see her floating there in front of me. She had that pointy metal bra on."

"It wasn't about that Madonna."

"Oh yeah? I always thought it was about her. Well, that's who I saw, anyway. I must've been hallucinatin' or something. That was your song, right?"

"Yeah. I wrote it."

"Well then, you must have been there."

"Sorry. I don't remember," Rolly said. "I wasn't always . . . sober in those days."

"Nobody was sober in that place. That's why I had to get out."

"I can pay you," said Rolly, reaching for his wallet.

"Forget it. Like I'm going to care now."

"No. I want to give it back."

Rolly pulled a twenty out of his wallet. He handed the bill to Jimmy.

"Square?" he asked.

"Square," said Jimmy, taking the money. "So what're you doing? Working as a delivery boy or something?"

"Just this once. As a favor. You eat over there much?"

"I been a couple of times. Seems a little pricey when I can go to Roberto's and get three burritos for less *dinero*."

"Yeah. I hear you. Were you working here last night?"

"What time?"

"Around ten."

"Nah. I was on the road then. What's going on?"

"Somebody called in an order from your phone number. The phone you answered."

"Uh-huh."

"The guy who called you, from the Villa Cantina with the gift certificate. He did it for me."

Big Jimmy gave Rolly a blank look.

"You know, I'm not the smartest guy in the building," he said. "And there ain't nobody here except you and me."

"Someone called the restaurant last night. About ten. With a take-out order. Paul Barrere?"

"Never heard of him."

"This guy calls every week. Same order. That's how I got your address, when the guy from the restaurant called you about the gift certificate."

"Okay. I get it. I think."

"You weren't on duty last night?"

"Not at ten. Wasn't my shift."

"Is there a guard after you?"

"Sure. I don't remember his name, though."

"Does anyone else use that phone?" Rolly asked, indicating the phone on Jimmy's desk.

"No one, as far as I know. There's nobody here."

"No one else uses it?"

"That's what I'm trying to tell you. Nobody lives here."

"Really?"

"Yeah. Really. This place is empty. Some kinda lawsuit or something. All the buyers backed out."

"The whole place is empty?"

"Like I said. Why's that restaurant sending you over here? Didn't this guy pay or something?"

Rolly reached in his pocket and pulled out a business card. He handed it to Jimmy.

"I'm looking into a car accident. Whoever picked up the order last night might know something about it."

"No shit," Jimmy said. He leaned back in his chair, perusing Rolly's business card.

"Rolly Waters. The Rock 'n' Roll Dick."

"Moogus came up with that."

"Figures. How's that work with the ladies?"

Rolly shrugged for an answer.

"Not like the old days, huh?" said Jimmy.

"No."

"You guys must've collected more panties than Elvis."

"I doubt that."

"Not that I'm complaining. Peons like me got to pick over the leftovers. Moogus is still around, huh?"

"I'm playing with him tonight."

"That guy cracked me up. Where you playing?"

"Patrick's. Fourth and F."

"Man, I can't believe you guys still play together, the way you fought all the time. I'm surprised you're both alive."

"I'm surprised too. Just lucky, I guess." He and Moogus had been lucky. Matt, The Creatures' lead singer, hadn't been.

"Those were good times, though, huh? While they lasted."

"Sure. Listen, you know any way I might be able to get this guy's name?"

"What guy?"

"The security guard. The one who worked here last night. After you."

"You think he's your guy?"

"I'd like to talk to him."

"Have you espied the Royal Tingler?"

"Hmm?"

"That's what you and Moogus always asked me when you went on break."

"Oh."

"You don't remember, huh? I used to spot for you. Pick out the best-looking girls in the room."

"The Royal Tinglers."

"Yeah."

"How could I forget?"

"Big Jimmy took care of things for you guys. I kept that place under control."

"You sure did. Listen, about this other guard, is there someone I can call? This company you work for, they'd have the schedule or something?"

"Sure. Pantera. Give them a call."

"Pantera?"

"Yeah. Pantera Security. That's who I work for. Google 'em."

"I'll check it out."

"Say, this gift certificate. It's legit, right?"

"Better be. I paid fifty bucks for it," Rolly said. Fifty bucks he'd have to charge Max.

"They got good food there. I don't go much 'cause it's expensive."

"You should get a few meals outta that."

"Takes a few meals to keep this body going."

Rolly smiled.

"Sorry I can't stick around longer, but I gotta see somebody. Good to see you again."

"You too."

Rolly walked to the front door and pulled it open.

"Hey Rolly," said Jimmy.

"Yeah?"

"I took care of you guys, didn't I?"

"Yeah, you sure did."

It was true, Rolly thought to himself, as he walked down the sidewalk. Big Jimmy took care of them, treated them like they were special. It had been a long time since he'd thought about Pelicans, the notorious beach dive where the band learned its trade, when sex, drugs and rock 'n' roll were his holy trinity. Drugs, by necessity, disappeared from his life. Sex was rare. The music he played now was more subdued—straight blues, country swing, New Orleans second line, the smaller capillaries feeding into the big rock-and-roll heart. No one took care of the band now, not like Big Jimmy did then, making sure the good-looking girls, the Royal Tinglers, sat up front. Jimmy would bring drinks for the girls, too, compliments of the band, on the house. He'd been the band's spotter, their confidant, and their protector. In the language of recovery Rolly learned in therapy, Big Jimmy had been their enabler.

8

LA TIENDA (THE STORE)

Norwood's Mostly Music sold used guitars and old vinyl records, a smattering of related items. It was the kind of place aficionados loved—a dank cavern, hostile to dilettantes. Norwood's Mostly surrendered its secrets to customers who weren't in a hurry, who could see past the dingy carpet and poorly labeled displays. Parents didn't bring their teenagers into Norwood's to slap down nine hundred bucks for a shiny new Kramer or to pick up the latest CD from Lady Gaga.

"You got some money for me?" said Rob Norwood, looking up from the back counter as Rolly walked into the shop.

"I just need some guitar strings," said Rolly.

"D'Addarios okay?"

"Yeah. Just one pack. Nines."

Norwood squatted down behind the counter and searched through a drawer. He'd played the same clubs as Rolly had, many years ago. Norwood's band released two albums on Mercury before the label dropped them. The band broke up soon after. Norwood cut his losses and married rich, to a woman he could tolerate. Their union had produced one precocious daughter who kept her father wrapped around her finger like a tourniquet. The shop was more a hobby than a business for Norwood, a place where he could hang out with musical friends, reminisce on the past, discuss the relative merits of Kings—B.B., Albert and Freddie. Ignorant customers were treated like unworthy intruders. Rob Norwood was an encyclopedia when it came to classic guitars and collector's vinyl.

"I don't have any nines," he said, rooting through the drawer. "How about tens?"

"Any Ernie's?"

"Not in nines."

"I guess I'll take tens then."

Norwood shut the drawer and stood up, tossing the strings on the countertop.

"Pussies play nines, anyway," he said.

"Yeah, I know."

"You know you're overdue on that Tele payment, too."

"I haven't forgotten it," said Rolly. He'd put fifty dollars down on a flame-burst MIM Telecaster two months ago but hadn't paid a dime since.

"I need fifty more by the end of the month or it goes back on the shelf."

"How much are the strings?"

"Six bucks."

"They used to be five."

"Janis says I gotta break even this year."

"Here's a twenty. Put the rest on the Tele."

"Looks like my kid will go to college after all," Norwood said, taking the bill.

"Only if she's got her mother's brains," Rolly replied.

"Yeah," Norwood guffawed. "That and my good looks, she'll make valedictorian and homecoming queen."

"Can I show you something?" Rolly asked, as Norwood wrote up a receipt.

"As long as it ain't your dick."

Rolly pulled the CD case out of his jacket pocket and placed it on the counter.

"What about it?" Norwood said, after a cursory glance.

"You know this album?"

"Sure. Serpent. Released three albums. This was their third. They broke up afterwards."

"Anything else?"

"Title track was a minor FM hit. Had that cheesy toy piano riff? Di-di-di-dee-dee-di-di-dee-dee."

"I'm interested in the girl."

"Nice piece of ass, huh? They musta sold half the albums 'cause of that cover."

"You know her name?"

"I used to. Geez, what was it?"

"Tangerine?"

"Yeah. She was kind of famous there for a while, 'cause of this cover."

"I met a woman this morning. I think it's her."

"She still a Tingler?"

"She's older."

"You'd still do her, though, right?" Norwood said.

Rolly shrugged.

"Well, she was a Royal Tingler back then," Norwood said. "A lot of fourteen-year-old boys holding this cover up with one hand."

"Now you sound like Jimmy."

"Who?"

"Big Jimmy. Remember him? From Pelicans."

"Was he that bouncer got his dick cut off?"

"I don't know about that. He only told me somebody stabbed him."

"It's not the kind of thing you run around telling people."

"Yeah. I guess. Where'd you hear that?"

"I don't know. It was a long time ago."

"He said we were playing that night."

"Well, Moogus was probably the one who told me about it."

"So the story got Moogusized."

"Moogusized and elasticized, no doubt. Anyway, that's what

I remember hearing. Hey, I got a new one. You know the differ-ence between a drummer and a vibrator?"

Rolly shrugged.

"No. What?"

"Women aren't embarrassed to have vibrators in the house," said Norwood, laughing at his own joke. "Where'd you run into Big Jimmy?"

"He works just up the street here, at that high-rise condo. He's a security guard."

"Is that where your lady friend lives?"

"Who?"

"The girl on the cover. You said you met her, right?"

"Not there. She's in this house down by the border."

"You think you might see her again?"

"Maybe. I don't know."

"I just had a thought, if it's really her . . ."

"What's that?"

"Maybe she's got some of the original pressings. With the recalled covers."

"What are you talking about?"

"I'd give her a good deal on 'em," said Norwood. He walked out from behind the counter and over to the crates of records stacked against the wall, started flipping through them. "Tipper Gore and her bunch were all over this, 'cause of the panties thing."

"What panties thing?" asked Rolly.

"What the hell is this doing in here?" Norwood said, setting an album aside. Rolly glanced at the discarded album cover: *The Carpenters' Greatest Hits*. Norwood re-sorted his album collection on a regular basis, on various whims. Alphabetizing wasn't one of them.

"What panties thing?" Rolly asked again. Norwood continued his search.

"Hang on. I'll show you. Here we go," he said, pulling another album out of the stack. He flipped it over, perused the back cover.

"Tangerine Swimmer, that's her name. It's here in the credits. I think she wrote that song, too."

"What song?"

"'Jungle Love.'"

Norwood handed the album to Rolly, pointing to the song listings on the back cover.

"You see? Osmond/Swimmer. Cliff Osmond, he was the guitar player. I bet this chick was his girlfriend or something."

Rolly looked at the names, then flipped the album over to look at the photo on the cover. The larger picture looked even more like Tangerine, standing among the lush tropical fruits and plants. The picture was different, though. The snake looked even more frightening as it slithered over her shoulder, between her breasts and down her belly. It covered her hips with its hood and faced out toward the viewer, its fanged mouth open, hissing, daring the viewer to get anywhere near it.

"Xtabay," said Rolly.

"What?"

"This cover's different than the CD."

"Like I said, they had to change it, after Tipper complained."

"Who?"

"Tipper Gore."

"Oh."

"You see the hole here?" Norwood said, indicating a perfect round hole inside the snake's mouth, about half an inch in diameter. "That's where the panties went."

Rolly pulled the panties out of his pocket.

"Like these?" he asked.

"Holy cowbell!" said Norwood, snatching the panties from Rolly's hand. He checked the tag in the back, studying it closely. "Where'd you get these?"

"From this Mexican cowboy. I was down at the border this morning, at the bird sanctuary. I started talking to him. It's a long story."

"I'll give you twenty bucks for 'em."

"Uh . . ."

"It's the right label. The lot number's in the right range."

"What?"

"Man, guitar players are stupid. These are the originals."

"You're saying these panties went with the album?"

"Yeah, that's what I'm trying to tell you."

Norwood opened the side of the album cover, shoved the panties in on top of the record platter and pressed them out flat. He held up the album for Rolly's approval.

"You see?" he said. "They went on the inside. Inside the serpent's mouth."

"So to speak."

"Tipper Gore and the PMRC got wind of it, made a big deal. Some stores wouldn't carry the album. The record company caved, recalled the albums and made a new cover, airbrushed the photo, got rid of the panties. That's what makes the original pressing so valuable."

"How valuable?"

"I'll throw in a three-pack of strings, on top of the twenty."

"How valuable is the album?"

"I'll give you thirty bucks for 'em, plus the strings. Last offer."

"I can't. They're evidence."

"What're you trying to prove?"

"It's a long story."

"Is this that detective stuff you do?"

"Yes." Rolly nodded. "How much is the album worth with the panties?"

"Well," said Norwood, "not that I'd ever do this, but shrink-wrap the whole thing like it's new, some collectors'll pay a hundred, up to one-fifty, maybe even two bills."

"And without the panties?"

"Without 'em the record's worth twenty bucks, like I said."

"That's a big difference."

"Nothing like *Yesterday and Today* with the butcher cover, but pretty collectible."

"I could almost pay for the Tele with that."

"Don't tempt me," said Norwood. He held the front cover of the album out toward Rolly. "Here. Take 'em back."

Rolly pinched the patch of fabric between two fingers and gave a tug. The panties popped out of the cover like a Kleenex tissue. Norwood laughed.

"I just thought of something," he said.

"What?"

"Maybe we could do an autograph party. With your girlfriend. If she's got some copies, I mean. I'll split the take."

"She's not my girlfriend."

"On the album, I mean. I could advertise it like that. It'd double the price, I bet."

"You really think so?"

"It might. If it's really her."

Norwood looked at cover of the album.

"How old do you think she was, then?" he asked.

"Just old enough," said Rolly.

"Shit, I just realized something."

"What's that?"

"This hip-hop record my daughter plays all the time. They sampled that freakin' riff."

"Hmm?"

"'Jungle Love.' That piano riff. They sampled it."

"Oh."

"I wish somebody'd sample one of my riffs. I went to an Al Kooper concert about a year ago, just him in this little church up in Normal Heights. He told this story about checking his bank account, finding an extra two hundred thousand in there. He calls his manager to see what's going on. Manager tells him some rapper's using a sample from one of Al's old albums. Can you imagine that? Two hundred thousand 'cause some hip-hopper lifted four bars from one of your records."

"What album was it?"

"Hell, I don't know. I don't listen to that rap stuff."

"I mean which Al Kooper album?"

"I don't remember."

"I'll bet it was *Rekooperation*. There's a lot of funky instrumental stuff on there."

"Who cares? That's not the point. I'm just saying, you know, maybe I should send these rapper guys some of my albums. To help them get acquainted with my fine riffage."

"Couldn't hurt."

"We almost got there, huh, Rol?"

"What do you mean?"

"Fame. Money. Girls. The big stuff. All you want."

"You got a record contract. I didn't."

"You got the best girl."

"Hmm?"

"Leslie, wasn't that your girlfriend's name?"

"Yeah. Leslie."

"Finest ass I ever saw on a woman. Nice face, too. You seen her lately?"

"She married some doctor."

"The Royal Tingler," Norwood chuckled. "She's there for a second, just within reach, like the last line of coke laid out on the table in a room full of crackheads. Then she's gone."

"Yeah, I guess."

"You got me waxing nostalgic today, thinking about our glorious past."

"I don't think about that kind of stuff anymore," said Rolly. "I'm just happy if I get to play my guitar at the end of the day."

"Amen to that," Norwood said. "Amen."

9

———————

EL BATERÍA (THE DRUMMER)

At nightfall, the Santa Anas changed character. Knife-sharpening La Jolla housewives stopped studying their husband's necks long enough to kick off their shoes and sit on verandas by perfect blue swimming pools, drinking tall glasses of frozen forgiveness and reminding themselves why they'd married the overstuffed jerks in the first place. Amid the hustle of the Gaslamp Quarter, Rolly Waters collapsed into a heavy iron chair on the patio in back of Patrick's nightclub. He sipped at a club soda and lime, grateful for the cool night air, relief from the sauna-like atmosphere inside the club.

A breeze riffled through the brick-lined alley, bringing with it the smell of stale beer and discarded crab shells as it passed over the dumpsters. Rolly's phone vibrated inside his jacket pocket. He retrieved it, checked the caller name and put the phone up to his ear.

"Hey, Marley," he said.

"What's up?"

"I got a CD I want you to look at. Some computer stuff."

"What kind of stuff?"

"I don't know. That's why I need you to look at it."

"There some coil in it?"

"I can pay you the hourly."

"Where you hangin'?"

"Just finished a gig here at Patrick's. I could stop by in a few."

"I gotta eat."

"You want me to bring something?"

"I was thinking of the Cantina. Why don't you meet me there?"

"Sure. About fifteen, twenty minutes?"

"I'll bring my laptop. If it needs more forensics, we'll come back to the loft."

"Sounds good."

"See you there, bredren."

Rolly hung up the phone and slipped it back in his pocket, where he felt the cool silk of the panties Jaime had given him. He pulled the panties out of his pocket, laid them neatly on one knee and stared at them, as if hoping to divine their significance through concentrated study.

"Taking a trip down memory lane?" someone said. Rolly looked up. Moogus stood in the back doorway, drum cases packed on his cart. He eased the wheels of the cart down the steps, pulled up next to Rolly, reached down and picked up the panties.

"Looks like you got left holding the wrapper after somebody stole your candy."

"I'll take it over whatever that was you took home last night."

"Low blow. I was desperate."

"You're always desperate," Rolly said, shaking his head in mock disgust. Moogus would be hustling the nurses at his deathbed.

"Playing with some little girl's panties looks pretty desperate to me," said Moogus, tossing them back to Rolly.

"They're evidence."

"Evidence of your pitiful sex life?"

"This cowboy gave 'em to me this morning."

"He sweet on you or something?"

"No, no," Rolly said. He slid his hand into the pocket on the other side of his jacket, pulled out the CD and pointed at the girl on the cover. "He told me they were hers. He asked me to give them to her."

Moogus took the CD.

"I haven't seen this in a while," he said. "Tangerine Swimmer."

"Wait. What? You know her name?"

"Sure. Tangie Swimmer."

"How'd you know that?"

"Are you kidding? This chick's in the groupie hall of fame."

"Really?"

"Oh yeah. Ferocious. Total sex machine."

"How do you know that?"

"*Creem* magazine. They did a whole series on rock stars' favorite groupies."

"When was this?"

"Shit. I don't know. A long time ago. I was a randy young skin beater anticipating the rewards of my future rock-god status."

"How'd that work out for you?"

"I'm still a rock god to some."

"Like that psycho you took home last night?"

"They can't all be Royal Tinglers," Moogus said, handing the CD back to Rolly. "I doubt this chick looks that good anymore, either. That album's twenty years old. Some of those old groupies get pretty hagged out."

"I saw her. I talked to her."

"No shit. Where was this?"

"She lives in a house, near the cowboy, the one who gave me the panties."

"They're getting it on?"

"He thinks they are. He thinks she's some jungle goddess

that's going to kill him because he had sex with her. That's why he gave me the panties."

"Well?"

"Well what?"

"What happened?"

"She said the panties weren't hers. She said the cowboy's been spying on her. Out by her pool. It got kind of weird after that."

"Weird how?"

"She said she likes it. Having guys spy on her."

"An exhibitionist, huh? She still got something worth seeing?"

"Definitely. She's had some work, though."

"Well, that could go in your favor."

"She said I was a snake."

"Uh-huh."

"She said she likes snakes."

"What'd you do?"

"Nothing."

"Nothing?"

"I asked her some more questions, about my case."

"You are a sad little man."

"It was work. I can't be messing around."

"Utter lack of respect is what I'd call it."

"What?"

"C'mon, think about it. She's getting older. The boys in the band don't call anymore. The woman's a legend. And you won't even give her a little sympathy shtup."

"The cowboy freaked me out, I guess. It was weird."

Moogus laughed.

"Yeah, well, I should talk. I had my shot. That's really the reason I remember her."

"What do you mean?"

"I picked her up outside of Pelicans one night. Back in the day. Gave her a ride to the bus station. A year later she's on the cover of that album, getting it on with every hotshot guitar player in LA."

"You're sure it was her?"

"Dead sure. It was the same night that guy stabbed Big Jimmy."

"I don't remember that."

"I do. Clear as if it was yesterday. The police were gone. Everybody's gone. I'm packing the last of my gear when she comes sidling up, barefoot, got on a bikini top and one of those swishy cotton skirts. Asks if I can give her a ride, acting all soft and lonely like. You know me, I'm a sucker for a little belly showing."

"That's a long time ago. You're sure it was her?"

"It was the album. That's why she stuck in my head, 'cause the album came out about a year after. I recognized her."

"You took her home?"

"I took her to the bus station and gave her some money."

"Yeah. Right."

"No. Really."

"Doesn't sound like the Moogus I remember."

"Yeah. I know. Hard to believe I didn't take advantage of the situation. She was kinda strange, though. Something just wasn't right. That whole thing with Jimmy might've freaked me out, I guess. I wasn't on my game."

"Did Big Jimmy really get his dick cut off?"

"Where'd you hear that?"

"Norwood says you told him."

"Wasn't me. I don't know where he heard that."

"It's not true, then?"

"Hell, I don't know."

"You remember anything else, about the girl?"

"She had this little guitar with her. Carrying it on her back. That's when things got weird."

"Yeah?"

"I asked her about it. She said it belonged to her husband."

"What's so weird about that?"

"Nothing. I said something about her being kind of young to be married. She told me she married the serpent."

"The serpent?"

"Yeah, she started going on with this whole story, kind of biblical like, dominion and damnation, weird kind of stuff. I couldn't make head or tail of it. Freaked me out, especially after Jimmy got cut up like that. Must've been a full moon that night."

"Did she say anything else?"

"She asked about the lost angels. She said that's where her husband was. With the lost angels."

"You think she meant Los Angeles?"

"That's what I decided. Believe me, I was ready to unload this chick. She was too weird, even for me."

"So, you drove her to the bus station?"

"Gave her ten bucks for a ticket and booted her out the door. That's the last I saw of her until she showed up on that album cover."

"Serpent's the name of the band."

"Yeah, I made the connection. Maybe that's why it stuck in my mind. Anyway, that's my story. Did you get the money from Gina yet?"

"Not yet."

"I'm gonna put this stuff in my car. I'll be back," Moogus said. "Looked like there was some sweet stuff sitting by the front window."

"I'll get the money," said Rolly. "You'll need it for penicillin."

Moogus laughed, then set off down the alley, dragging the handcart and drum cases behind him. Twenty years ago, he brought two bass drums to gigs, a rack of six tom-toms and as many cymbals. There was an old joke about the inverse relationship between the size of a drummer's kit and his manhood. Rolly had no information on the truth of that, but there was a connection between a drummer's age and how much equipment he brought to a gig. Starting around thirty-five, guys started whittling it down, making do with the basics, unless they were rock stars, of course, with roadies for portage. Moogus wasn't a rock star. Moogus was just a working stiff, like Rolly and everyone else in the club.

Rolly stood up, walked inside and found Gina. She counted out the night's wages in tens and twenties, plus mixed change from the tip hat. He grabbed another club soda and walked back to the patio. There was someone in his chair.

"Jimmy. What're you doing here?"

"A friend of yours came by the building."

"Who?"

"This lady cop. Blond, all buffed out, kind of dykey?"

"Bonnie?"

"She told me she knew you."

"Was it Bonnie Hammond?"

"Yeah. I think that was her name. She wouldn't be half bad-looking if she let her hair grow or something, maybe cut back on the steroids."

"What'd Bonnie want?"

"I think the cops have that car you were looking for. They found it down near the border last night. It belongs to a guy that lives in the building."

"I thought you said nobody lived there."

"Yeah. I did. There is this one guy, though. I forgot about him. The guy that lives in unit thirteen thirteen. He's not very sociable."

"Not very superstitious either."

Jimmy chuckled.

"Yeah, I guess. Anyway, your cop friend came by to talk to him. He says his car was stolen from the building last night. I didn't hear nothing 'bout it, but your cop friend started shooting me questions, asking if I'd seen anything. That's when I made the connection. I told her about you coming by earlier, showed her your card. She got real interested then."

"What do you mean?"

"She said she'd be giving you a call. I wanted to let you know."

"Thanks for the heads-up. What's this guy's name? The one who lives in the building?"

"Burdon."

"Not Paul Barrere?"

"This guy's name is Burdon. He's really weird."

"How so?"

"Looks like a vampire. Black clothes and makeup. Lotta piercings."

"A Goth look, that kinda thing?"

"I guess. Anyway, he lives in that condo."

"Thirteen-thirteen."

"Yeah. Real estate agent who came through told me about him. This kid coulda got out of the deal, after the developer went bankrupt. Everybody else did, but Mr. Burdon wanted that number, insisted that he wanted to keep the place, even after everybody else bailed out of the deal."

"What kind of car is it?"

"A hearse."

"You mean like, for funerals?"

"Yeah. Like I said, he's pretty weird. You carry heat?"

"What? You mean a gun?"

"Yeah."

"No."

"You might wanna consider it."

"What do you mean?"

"Your lady friend, the cop, I got the feeling there was something more serious going on."

"Like what?"

"I'm just saying, there's a lot of bad stuff happens down at the border. They got some dangerous people floating around down there, both sides of the fence. You mighta stuck your nose in some nasty shit. I wouldn't be surprised if this Burdon guy's selling dope or something and that's why his car got stolen. Those Mexican gangsters he's dealing with, they'll just as soon kill you as look at you. They don't care about any damn birds."

"You think this is about drugs?"

"I think it's more than you wanna mess around with. Those drug fuckers'll cut off your balls and stuff 'em down your throat, kill you afterwards."

Rolly closed his eyes. He felt tired. Jimmy stood up, slapped him on the back.

"Your police lady friend looks tough enough," he said. "Let her handle these guys."

"Yeah," said Rolly, rubbing his temples. "I might do that."

His stomach hurt. He needed to eat.

10

LA CENA (THE DINNER)

Marley Scratch wiped his mouth with a large floral-print napkin, dipped his fingers in his water glass, then dried them with the clean side of the napkin.

"Okay," he said. "Lemme see it."

Rolly passed the CD across the table. Marley inspected it, scratched at one side with his thumbnail, then inserted the disc into his laptop.

"You know what's on here?" he asked.

"No," Rolly said. "This is the first time I've looked at it."

The two men sat in a back-corner booth at the Villa Cantina, as far away as they could get from the front entrance. When Rolly arrived, there was a line out the door, but Vera directed him to the back corner as soon as he described the large black man with graying dreadlocks. Rolly navigated his way through the boisterous crowd to find Marley sitting alone in a dark red booth, noshing on chips and salsa and drinking a pink margarita.

"Where'd you get this?" asked Marley.

"There's this state park near the border. I think it fell out of someone's car."

"Anything in particular you're looking for?"

"Just tryin' to find out what's on there."

"Something wrong with your computer?"

"I haven't been home since this morning," Rolly said. He had a clunky old HP at home that his mother had given him, but Marley knew how to find information he couldn't—invisible files, hidden user names, password protections. Marley understood digitalia at a far deeper level than he ever would. Rolly just clicked on things.

"What's your pleasure?" asked Marley, adjusting the laptop screen so they could both see it.

"Let's try the photos first," Rolly said, pointing at a folder labeled the same.

"*Dos Hermanas Bonitas,*" said Marley, reading the caption on the first photo that opened. It was a picture of two teenaged girls, perhaps fifteen or sixteen, with olive-brown skin and long black hair. The girls smiled at the camera, displaying youthful white teeth.

"What's that mean?" Rolly asked.

"Two pretty girls?"

"Sisters," someone said. "Two pretty sisters."

A short man wearing a large sombrero and sporting a bushy fake mustache stood at the end of their table. It was Hector.

"Who're you supposed to be?" asked Rolly.

"Take a guess."

"Yosemite Sam?"

"Ayy, no, guess again."

"The Frito Bandito?" said Marley.

"He's my great, great uncle."

"Who?"

"Pancho Villa."

"Oh," said Rolly.

"I'm wearing this outfit at the demonstration on Monday."

"You mean that MENCIA thing?"

"Yeah. How do I look?"

"I think you need gun belts or something," said Marley. "Make you look bad-ass."

"Yeah, I'm trying to figure out how to work it so the Border Patrol doesn't freak out. What're you guys up to?"

"Marley's helping with my case."

"This is that Border Field Park thing?"

"Yeah."

"So, who are the *chicas*?"

"I don't know. We're looking at this CD I found there this morning."

"You still think it's the AFA guys?" Hector asked, seating himself next to Rolly.

"I don't know."

"Sure be righteous if we could nail those bastards."

"Who's the AFA?" asked Marley.

"Border trash vigilantes," said Hector. "Rolly's gonna nail their asses."

"Cool beans," said Marley. "I like working for the good guys."

"I don't know that it's them," Rolly said. "I'm still looking into things."

"Let's see some more pictures," said Hector.

Rolly nodded his head at Marley, indicating he should continue. Marley clicked through more pictures of the girls, unsmiling head shots, the kind you'd get at the DMV for your driver's license.

"Hold it," said Rolly. Marley paused.

The picture on screen looked different than the previous ones. It was the same type of photo, but the girl in the picture had a cleft lip. It wasn't a large deformity, but it was noticeable.

"Go back one," said Rolly. Marley returned to the previous picture.

"Now forward."

"Looks like the same girl," Hector said. "She must've had surgery or something."

"The eyelids are different, too," Rolly said.

"Oh, yeah," said Hector. "They're more Asian-like."

"Digital surgery maybe," said Marley. "Might've been Photoshopped."

"Is there some way you can tell?"

Marley brought up both pictures, put them next to each other and zoomed in on the pixels.

"I'm not sure," he said. "It's a pretty good job if they did it."

"Let's see the rest," said Rolly.

Marley clicked to the next picture. Rolly wished he hadn't. It was a close-up of the girl's pudendal cleft, surrounded by light pubic hair.

"Hector!" cried a voice.

The three men cringed, turning to find Vera walking up to their table. She looked steamed.

"What are you looking at?" she asked. Marley reached back toward the keyboard with one hand and closed the picture without looking.

"It's Rolly's," said Hector.

Vera glared at Hector for a split second, then turned her attention to Rolly. She raised one eyebrow and twisted her mouth, glaring at him. Rolly felt like a shamed thirteen-year-old.

"I'm sorry, Vera," he said. "I didn't know that was on there. It's part of my case."

Vera crossed her arms and turned back to Hector.

"They need you back in the kitchen," she said. "Not out here playing dress-up."

"What's going on?" he asked.

"I don't know. Marco says they're out of masa, or something."

"There should be some in the freezer."

"You need to talk to him. I never understand what he's saying."

Hector took off his sombrero and mustache.

"Sorry, guys. Let me know what you find out," he said. He scurried out of the booth and back to the kitchen.

The arrival of Marley's dinner prevented any further opprobrium from Vera. She glared at the two men, then stomped off to deal with the restaurant's more respectable clientele. Rolly ordered Huevos Rancheros and a soda water as Marley tucked into a steaming plate of dark red enchiladas.

"Mind if I go through some stuff?" Rolly asked, indicating the laptop.

"Help yourself," said Marley. "Child porn ain't my thing."

"I'll think I'll skip the photos for now," Rolly said. "I wanna see what else is on here."

He pulled the computer onto his placemat and clicked to open a folder labeled "Papers." There were three files inside it. The first was a passport from the People's Republic of China. It had a photograph of one of the girls. The name on the passport was Lei Dizi. Eighteen years old. The second file provided a list of common Spanish words, with what looked like matching Chinese translations. The last file was an entry form.

"You know a TV show called *Family Act*?" Rolly asked.

"Never heard of it," said Marley.

"There's an audition form for it on here."

"Any names on the form?"

"No. It's blank."

"Sounds like one of those reality things—*America's Super Talent, You've Got Balls*, whatever. Zamora loves that shit."

"Who's Zamora?"

"My crib mate."

"What happened to Reggie?"

"She got stuck on the marriage bag. Had to part ways."

"When was this?"

"Almost a year ago. You ain't been keepin' up."

"I guess not."

Rolly returned to the computer, opening another folder entitled "BFB." There were several folders inside it. He clicked on a folder named "Maps." From there he selected a file labeled "set-up.ini." The file opened, revealing a long list of numbers.

"This stuff mean anything to you?" he asked, turning the screen toward Marley. "It's in a folder called Maps."

Marley nodded.

"Looks like coordinates," he said, appraising the numbers on screen. "Read some other file names to me."

Rolly read through the file names.

"Sounds like a mod," Marley said. "Somebody's setting up their own scenario."

"For what?"

"A video game. A lot of games these days, they let you build your own scenarios, create your own maps and characters, import them into the game."

"Sounds kind of geeky."

"It's not that hard, once you know the basics. Takes some time, though, to do it right. Guys that are into it post their files on the net, so you can download 'em. Kind of an ego thing, getting a lot of downloads."

"Can you figure out what game this is?"

"That might take some poking around. Try opening one of the files in the Characters folder."

Rolly double-clicked on another file. A picture opened on screen.

"It's some kind of person, I guess," he said. "But they're all flattened out."

"Lemme see."

Rolly swiveled the computer around so Marley could see it.

"That's the mesh for the character mapping. It gets wrapped around a wireframe so it's three-dimensional."

"Oh."

"I don't recognize the character. Try some more."

Rolly opened more files.

"This looks kind of like one of those girls," he said, turning the screen back to Marley.

"Hey, yeah. It does. That's why the photos are there. The modder used them."

"You can do that?"

"Sure. Probably explains why they've got so many."

"You think they used the naked stuff?"

"I wouldn't be surprised. A modder can do whatever he wants. It's not an official release. Could be an Easter egg."

"There's a Chinese passport here, too."

Marley scrutinized the passport.

"Well, this ain't really my line, but I'd bet that's fake. Might be used in the game. As a token or something. You can probably check that number somewhere."

"Where's the number?"

"On the side there—it's vertical, by the photo."

"Oh, yeah."

"What's this all about, anyway?" asked Marley.

Rolly ran through the day's events for Marley's edification. As he finished his story, the waiter arrived with his dinner. He pushed the computer away to allow room for the plate.

"That's quite a puzzle you're piecing together, Sir Roland," said Marley. "You think all this stuff is connected?"

"I have no idea," said Rolly.

"Mind if I see what else is on there?"

"Help yourself," Rolly said, blowing air across the top of the steaming fried eggs to cool them.

Marley reached over, pulled the computer next to him and tapped at the keyboard.

"There's some music," he said. "You wanna hear it?"

"Sure."

Marley tapped once on the keypad. Music played over the computer's thin speakers.

"Hey, I know that riff," Marley said.

"What's that?"

"That piano part. I've heard it before. Somebody sampled it."

The singer's voice came in over the rhythm track.

"I like touching you baby,

all night long,

Anaconda baby,

our love so strong."

"Yeah, that guitar and piano thing. They processed it some, but it's the same riff."

"What's the song called?"

"It's, uh . . . I'm trying to remember."

"No, no. The song that's playing now. The file. What's it called?"

"'Jungle Love,'" Marley said.

Rolly dropped his fork. It clattered against the ceramic plate, bounced off the table and fell to the floor. The band modulated into the chorus as the lead singer screamed.

"I am lost, in your jungle love.

I am lost, in your jungle love.

I am lost, in your jungle love.

Lost, in your jungle of love."

11

LA MADRE (THE MOTHER)

Rolly sat at one end of his living room sofa playing a nylon-stringed Córdoba guitar, serenading the pair of pink satin panties that lay on the cushion in front of him. He ran through scales on the fret board as he ran through the events of the day in his head, rearranging his thoughts with each pass—the panties, the take-out order from Villa Cantina, the contents of the CD. He thought about Jaime the cowboy and the infamous groupie, Tangerine Swimmer. He thought about Nuge and the Goth kid Jimmy had told him about, the one whose hearse had been stolen. He figured at least one of them would be able to tell him how those tire tracks appeared in the least tern preserve at Border Field Park.

He heard a creaking sound from outside, near the front door. There was someone on the porch. Three gentle taps sounded on the door, percussive accents to his guitar rhythm. He put the Córdoba down and glanced at his watch. Ten thirty. Only one person tapped on his door like that. He shoved the panties into the gap between the sofa arm and the cushion, walked to the front door and opened it. His mother stood on the porch, sporting a white gardenia in her hair, a red and black shawl draped over her shoulders. She looked like a chorus member in *Carmen*.

"*Buenas noches, Señorita,*" Rolly said.

"*Buenas noches,*" his mother giggled, "I saw your light. And I've had such an interesting evening."

"*Mi casa es su casa,*" Rolly replied, which was the literal truth of his housing situation. His mother owned the property. They were neighbors—landlord and tenant. She lived in the large Victorian at the front of the lot. He paid rent on the granny flat in the back. He swung the door open, sweeping his arm back with a flourish.

"*Entre, por favor,*" he said.

"*Muchas gracias,*" she said, stepping into the room.

"*De nada.*" Between them, they'd used up half the Spanish they knew.

"You left rather early this morning," his mother remarked, taking a seat at the kitchen table. "Your car was gone all day."

Rolly sat down at the table across from her. He crossed his arms, contemplating the flecks of green in the Formica tabletop. His mother bought the dining set for him when he moved in. She'd found it at the Salvation Army in the East Village, a table and four padded chairs, which she'd purchased as a home-coming present for her new tenant.

"I had some work this morning," he explained, "and then we had a gig at Patrick's."

"How was your musical engagement?"

"Fine."

He hated answering questions about his performances. What was there to say—that he'd tried to play a whole set's worth of solos from one fret position, just to amuse himself? That he'd told the band he would never, ever, play "Mustang Sally" again? She wouldn't understand, or really care. He changed the subject. He knew that look on his mother's face. She had some grand adventure to regale him with.

"You're all dressed up," he said.

"Well, I passed by El Puente this morning on the way to my

yoga class and I saw they were having a performance of mariachi music this evening, some special group from Mexico. So, I decided to go see it. Have you ever heard real mariachi music before?"

"Yes," Rolly replied. "Well, I think so, anyway." His mother's enthusiasm for any newfound art form made it sound like she'd been the first to discover it.

"Well, I must say it was quite a recital," she continued. "I mean, I've heard some of these fellows at the tourist restaurants before, like in Old Town, but this was quite different. There were five guitar players, which I thought might interest you. One of the guitars was quite large."

"A *guittarón*," said Rolly.

"Oh, is that what they call it," she said, surveying the stringed instruments strewn about the room. "You don't have one of those, do you?"

"No."

"Well," she continued, "I thought you might be interested because of the guitar playing. It's quite vigorous, you know, very exciting. And the singer would stomp his boots now and then. It just gave you a feel for the real Mexican traditions, the Gypsy culture or whatever they are. I could see the ranchos, the town squares and taverns, in my mind's eye."

Rolly wasn't sure mariachis had any connection to Gypsies, musical or geographic, but decided not to challenge his mother on her cultural misappropriation. All musicians were gypsies, of a sort. He let her continue. All it took was a nod of his head now and then, a skill he'd developed in childhood, one that proved valuable later, at bars and nightclubs, where he'd search out chatty drunks, the ones with money who'd buy you a drink, sometimes two, in return for your ears. As a private investigator, the skill had proved useful all over again, talking to witnesses who weren't sure what had happened and were trying to remember what they'd seen. He knew how to listen. He knew how to keep people talking until something useful popped out.

"Oh, I forgot," his mother said, interrupting her Old Mexico reverie, "you had a visitor stop by this evening—a doctor, I think."

"Did you get his name?"

"No. He was a rather handsome Latin type, very trim and neat, with a mustache."

"Did he leave a number or anything?"

"Actually, he reminded me of your father. Except for the mustache, of course. And those little round scars on his cheek."

"What did he want?"

"Of course, your father is Irish. And taller. It's his birthday next weekend, you know."

"Alicia asked me to play at his party."

"Oh. Well. I'm sure that'll be nice for you."

"Did he say what he wanted?"

"What's that, dear?"

"The man who came by. Did he say anything?"

"I told him you might not be back until late. He excused himself, said he'd come back another time. He had one of your business cards."

"When was this?"

"Around six, I guess. He seemed very gracious. I saw him standing outside on your porch."

"Did he say anything else?"

"No. He had one of those green outfits you see the hospital people walking around in."

"Scrubs?"

"Yes, I think that's what they call them. He's a doctor, I imagine."

There were two major hospitals located in Hillcrest, and any number of private clinics and medical offices in the area. It wasn't unusual to see the employees, dressed in their work clothes, picking up groceries at the market or ordering lunch at the taco stands. Rolly couldn't remember giving any of them a business card recently.

"There were two other people, too, an hour or so later. Just when I was leaving to go out. A man and a woman."

"What did they look like?"

"Well, I'd say they were both of the Mexican persuasion. She was a pretty young thing, quite exotic, dark lips, lovely eyes."

"And the man?" Rolly asked.

"He was quite a bit older, closer to my age. He must have been her grandfather or something. They had an old truck."

"A green pickup?"

"I don't remember the color. It was getting dark."

"Did he look like a cowboy?"

"Well, yes, now that you mention it. I think he had a cowboy hat on, and boots."

"What was she wearing?"

"I'm afraid I don't remember. I didn't speak to them for very long."

"How about her hair? Was it orange, reddish-orange?"

"No. I don't think so. I think it was dark."

Rolly furrowed his eyebrows. He stared at a divot in the Formica tabletop.

"Is this one of those cases you get?" his mother asked, making it sound like he'd come down with the flu.

He looked back at her.

"Max asked me to look into something."

"Oh."

Many years ago, Max and Rolly's mother had been close, best of friends, maybe more. Rolly wasn't sure how far it had gone. His mother trusted Max. He'd helped them both out, after the accident. Whatever Rolly was up to, his mother could count on Max to take care of him.

"Well, dear, you look tired. I'll let you get some sleep," she said, rising from the table. "Don't stay up too late."

"I won't."

His mother walked to the door and opened it. She paused and looked back.

"Oh, yes, something else. The man with the girl. They said something about music. Some records or something? Does that help?"

"Yes. It might."

"Good night, dear."

"Good night."

His mother closed the door. Rolly's thoughts traveled back to the sofa, the panties stashed between the cushions. He thought of the times he'd hidden panties from Leslie, his ex, back when they'd tried living together. He thought of the soft-shouldered sirens who left those panties behind, the ones who staked out a spot every night at the edge of the bandstand, dressed in short skirts and high heels, little rich girls with nothing to do, desperate, bored, the ones who gave themselves up to him, free, with no strings attached. That was a long time ago, before he'd crashed on the rocks of his reckless life, before the Royal Tingle became an all-consuming vibration, an uncontrollable shimmy that ended in broken glass, bent metal, and blood.

He scanned the instruments scattered around his living room. Three guitars lined the wall across from him—a dark-cherry Gibson SG, flame-burst Fender Esquire, and Martin Dreadnought perched on their stands. A weathered Gretsch arch-top hung from two pegs on the wall, next to a green Rickenbacker twelve-string and a gold Strat. Guitars were the mast he had tied himself to, his musical ships, wood and steel, trimmed out in layers of polished lacquer, abalone and mother-of-pearl.

The nylon-stringed Córdoba sat on the sofa where he'd left it. He sat down, pulled the guitar into position and finger-picked his way through a Bach fugue, one of the few classical pieces he'd memorized. The Romeros wouldn't be threatened by his tirandos, but he wasn't half bad for a rock-and-roll guy. He switched styles, vamping on a slow two-chord musical phrase he'd come up with years ago, never turned into a song. He'd made it as far as one rhymed couplet for lyrics. He sang the words as he repeated the chords:

"A wave is coming at us,
There's nothing else in sight.
On this dark, deserted ocean,
We're about to face the night."

He repeated the lyric a few more times, hoping for further inspiration, investigative or musical. Neither came, but the sound of the guitar settled the rough waves in his mind. He closed his eyes and lay on the sofa, wrapping his arms around the Córdoba like it was an old bedmate, and fell into a soft lapping of sleep.

12

———

EL VISITANTE (THE VISITOR)

Three little notes crept into Rolly's dream, like triplets tapped on a large wooden clave. He jerked awake. It was morning. The Córdoba guitar still lay in his arms. Wiping a dab of drool from the corner of his mouth, he set the guitar down and leaned it against the arm of the sofa. The three little notes came again, like a military cadence, insistent—someone knocking on the door. It wasn't his mother.

"Just a minute," he called. He rose from the sofa, clearing the soft bits of sleep from his eyes. The room was still dark, but the light outside indicated the sun would soon clear the eastern mountains. Two days in a row now he'd been awakened from half-complete slumber.

Three more taps rang out, measured and exact. Rolly opened the door. A man stood outside. He was short, in his late forties, with tar-black hair chopped in a bowl cut, a tightly clipped mustache above his thin lips. Dressed in a medical-green shirt and matching pants, the man looked like a hospital orderly. Little round divots scarred his left check. A pocket protector in the man's shirt held a mechanical pencil and some small metal implements in a plastic sheath.

"Can I help you?" asked Rolly.

"You are Señor Waters, the private investigator?" the man replied, displaying Rolly's business card.

"Yeah, that's me," Rolly said.

The man's right shoulder twitched. Rolly felt a sharp pain in his stomach. He stumbled backwards and fell on the floor. The man stepped across the threshold and closed the door. He stared down at Rolly with eyes of flat steel.

"Where is the girl?" he asked.

"Whaa . . . ffff," Rolly wheezed, clutching his stomach.

The orderly seated himself at the kitchen table. Rolly curled up on the floor, holding his stomach. It hurt like hell.

"What girl?" he gasped.

The little man smiled.

"I will find her, you know. Better you should tell me now."

"I don't know what you're talking about."

"You are a detective, yes?"

Rolly nodded his head.

"And you are looking for a girl?"

"Girl, boy, I don't know. I'm looking for someone who drove their car into Border Field Park."

"Why did you go to that house?"

"What house?"

"The house at the bottom of the canyon. Why were you there?"

"I thought they might have seen something last night."

"What happened last night?"

Rolly did a quick calculation, realized he'd added a day.

"I mean two nights ago, Friday," he corrected himself. The pain in his gut subsided to a dull throb. He sat up.

"What do you think happened at this house Friday night?" the man asked.

"I don't know. I was just checking around, asking questions. That's what I do."

"Did you speak to anyone?"

"A woman wearing a robe. She said her name was Tangerine."

"No one else?"

"I'm looking for someone who ran their car through the park. That's all."

"What is this park?"

"Border Field Park. Down at the end of the road, by the ocean. There's a bird sanctuary there, where the birds lay their eggs. Someone drove into it Friday night, crushed the nests and some eggs."

"You are looking for the person who broke the eggs?"

"Yes."

"You will receive compensation for this?"

"I'm getting paid, yes. Can I get up?"

"No, you must stay on the floor now."

The little orderly leaned back in the chair and laughed. The muscles in his arms tightened like knotted ropes.

"You Californios amuse me," he snickered. "*Niños con juegos.* Spoiled little children. You play with toy guns. Saving the little birds when there are so many."

Rolly made no response. The orderly stood up, pulling his chair out from under the table.

"Get below, please," he said, stubbing out his mirth like a spent cigarette.

"What?" Rolly said.

The orderly indicated the space under the table.

"On your knees, *amigo. Debajo de la mesa.*"

A cold electric surge ran down Rolly's spine, from his head to his socks. The little orderly planned to put a bullet into the back of his head, execution-style.

"What do you want?" he protested.

The orderly sighed.

"You must get low, down under the table, my friend."

"Why?"

"I will take a look around your apartment. I will not hurt you. Under the table. If you try to run, I will hear. If you try to escape, I will demonstrate the big pain on you."

Aside from his extra weight, Rolly had little to his advantage when it came to physical confrontations. He had no self-defense training. He didn't work out or exercise. He couldn't even throw a solid punch, the way Moogus could. He sighed, rolled up onto his knees and crawled under the table. Patience was his only ammunition.

The orderly pushed the chair in behind Rolly, creating a makeshift jail cell out of the chrome-legged chairs and Formica.

"You maintain this deception?" the man asked. "You do not have the girl?"

Rolly looked down at the top of the orderly's patent-leather shoes, the perfect crease of his lower pant legs. He wondered why anyone wearing scrubs would bother to press them so neatly. Perhaps they were new, just out of the box.

"I don't know about any girl," he said.

"You will not mind if I look around, then?"

"Help yourself," Rolly muttered, trying to sound jaded, but his voice revealed a notable tremolo.

"We shall see," the man said. "If she has left her little panties behind."

Rolly jolted his head toward the sofa, caught himself, looked back down at the man's feet.

"Don't try anything, *amigo*," the man said. His patent-leather shoes moved out of view.

Rolly heard the rattle of silverware, the clanging of pots and pans as the little orderly searched through his kitchen. The sound of footsteps moved toward the bedroom, followed by the muffled banging of closet doors, the plastic squeak of cheap sliding drawers. The orderly returned to the living room. He knelt down in front of Rolly. The look on his face resembled pity.

"*Gringo,* you got some serious wardrobe deficiencies," the man said, speaking softly. "*Pureza es mala.*"

"What's that?"

"You are too much unclean."

"Sorry to disappoint you."

"We negotiate. You tell me where the girl is, maybe I buy you some new underwear, a silk shirt, something nice."

"I don't know where any girl is. I don't know what you're talking about."

"Those tighty whities, they are not so white anymore. You should not wear them, you know. They are bad for your manhood. You do not get the circulation."

"I promise I'll buy some new underwear if you let me out of here."

"Take my advice, you get the boxers next time, eh?"

"Yes. I'll get boxers."

Satisfied that his fashion point had been made, the little orderly rose and walked into the living room.

"You have *muchas* guitars, *amigo*," he said. He pointed toward the Córdoba on the sofa. "I would like to play on this one."

"Be my guest."

"*Gracias.*"

"Can I get out from under here?"

"Not yet, I think."

Rolly's stomach felt sore. He twisted his shoulders, trying to find a more comfortable position. The orderly watched for a moment, making sure there was no escape attempt. Assuring himself that Rolly wasn't going anywhere, he picked up the guitar and sat down on the sofa. He strummed a few chords and started to sing. "Rio," by Duran Duran.

The orderly's guitar chords were brutal and clipped, barely musical. His singing voice sounded like strangulation, as if he had tilapia bones stuck in his throat. Rolly gritted his teeth and endured. There was no point in getting killed over a bad cover song. The orderly mauled his way through a few more choruses, then put the guitar down.

"You hear that song before, *amigo*?" he asked, as he pulled a packet of rolling papers out of his pocket, along with a zip-locked bag of dried leaves.

"Unfortunately."

"The girl I am looking for, that is her name," the man said, rolling a cigarette. "She is a whore."

"Oh," Rolly said. It gave him other notes to consider. Perhaps a prostitute named Rio danced on the sand Friday night, down at Border Field Park, with Nuge, or Jaime, or the Goth kid from the condo. Maybe they'd driven across the least tern preserve in their car. Maybe they'd left a CD behind.

The orderly finished rolling his cigarette. He pulled out a match and struck it on the fret board of the Córdoba. Rolly clutched his fists. It was one thing to force him under the table and make him listen to crappy, out-of-tune eighties synth-pop, but scratching his guitar was irredeemable.

"You smoke the weed?" the orderly asked, taking a puff.

"Not anymore."

"You should try some of this. It's my own mix, *especial*—half Indian tobacco, half weed. Like the best of both worlds, two countries, you know? You would enjoy it, I think."

"No thanks."

"Are you sure? I roll you one."

"Not for me."

"You got problems with the weed?"

"No. I just don't smoke it anymore."

"I know many *guitarristas* who smoke the weed. They say it is good for their musical skills."

"I stopped smoking a while ago."

"Why?"

"I just did."

"Maybe you got a medical problem? Is that it? You got some sort of medical problem, *amigo*?"

"Like what?"

"Some men, they smoke too much weed, they lose their machismo. They get breasts, like young girls. You know what I mean, their *cojones* shrivel up. Then you got no juice for your girlfriend. You have a girlfriend?"

"Not at the moment," Rolly said. The man studied Rolly, looking thoughtful.

"Where I come from, a guitar player, a good guitar player, he always has women," the man said. "So, I must think that you are not such a good guitar player. Or maybe you cannot satisfy a woman. That is why you don't smoke the weed anymore. You can't give the woman what she wants. You got a droopy *salchicha*."

The orderly seemed to have an inordinate interest in erectile functions, but speculative assaults on Rolly's reproductive health weren't going to accomplish much. It was the least vulnerable part of Rolly's psyche. As long as the orderly stopped beating on the Córdoba, Rolly didn't care what he said.

"You got some extra pounds on you, too, *un poco gordo*," the orderly continued. "That don't help much, gives you the man titties. You got to stay in good shape if you want to make the hard thing for your whores."

The orderly rested his hands on the sofa and stroked the cushions. He leaned down to inspect something, raising an eyebrow.

"Oh *amigo*, I think you are not telling me something," the orderly said. He pulled a metal blade from his pocket protector, inserted it between the seat cushions and extracted the panties. He dangled them at arm's length on the point of the blade, performing a clinical inspection.

"I thought you did not have a girlfriend," he said.

"I don't."

"Whose are these?"

"I don't know."

"Your whore did not leave them here?"

"No."

Rolly shrugged. The man stubbed his joint out on the Córdoba guitar and flicked the butt into the corner of the room. He stood up, walked to the table, squatted down and spread the pink panties on the floor in front of Rolly.

"You know what I think, *amigo*?" he said.

"No," said Rolly.

"I think you are one of those men who likes to wear the

panties sometimes. The whores, they tell me about men like you."

"I don't know what you're talking about," Rolly said.

The orderly smiled, inspected his fingernails, used the scalpel blade to scrape at something under the nail of his left middle finger, then inspected the nail again. Grooming complete, he slid the scalpel back under the panties, lifted them up on the point of the blade and dangled them in front of Rolly's face.

"What do you want?" Rolly asked.

The little orderly grinned in a sick kind of way.

"I want you to put on the panties," he said.

13

LA POLICÍA (THE POLICE)

Rolly stared at the panties dangling in front of his face.

"Someone gave those to me," he protested.

"You have the boyfriend, yes?" said the orderly. "I see the men who live around here, the fancy boys. Maybe your boyfriend likes you to wear these?"

Rolly sighed.

"Put them on," the orderly said, jiggling the panties on the tip of his scalpel.

"What if I don't?"

"*Muy doloroso.* Much of the pain for you."

Rolly heard a noise from outside, the sound of a car pulling into the gravel driveway. The orderly heard it too. He stood up, walked to the window and parted the drapes.

"*Gringo*, did you call the police?"

Rolly said nothing. A car door slammed. His inquisitor whistled.

"Ooh, it is a *chica*. Maybe she is your *novia*, eh?"

"No."

"Ay, she looks strong. *Muy fuerte.* You put on the little panties for her, I think?"

"No."

"I think that's why you got the problems with your *salchicha*. Your sperm gets all frighted and swims away."

The orderly made a little swimming motion with his hand and stepped away from the window.

"What are you going to do?" asked Rolly.

"You keep them," the orderly said, tossing the panties at Rolly. He slipped the scalpel back into his pocket protector. "I like your guitar. I will buy it from you."

"It's not for sale . . ."

"Do not argue with me, *amigo*. You must say I have purchased the guitar from you."

Rolly heard footsteps on the porch. There was a knock on the door.

"I will pay you the good money," the orderly said. He reached in his pants pocket and extracted a wallet. "*Comprende, amigo*? I am not a thief."

Rolly nodded his head.

"I *comprende*."

There was another knock.

"Go. Now," the orderly said.

Rolly crawled out from under the table, stood up and stashed the panties in his front pocket. He took a deep breath, smoothed his rumpled shirt, walked to the door and opened it. Police detective Bonnie Hammond stood on the porch. For the first time in his life, Rolly felt relieved to find a law enforcement representative outside his door.

"Hey, Bonnie," he said, swinging the door wide open to make sure each party could see the other. "What's up?"

"Thought you might like to go for a ride with me this morning," Bonnie replied. She spotted the little orderly and moved her arms into a more guarded position. The orderly took his cue, waved some money in the air and placed it on the table.

"Thank you, my friend," he said, picking up the Córdoba. "It is a pleasure to do business with you."

Bonnie moved to the side of the porch as the little orderly

stepped outside. Rolly resisted an urge to scream. If he didn't play along, the little orderly would slash Bonnie's throat before she could get the strap off her gun. He'd kill Rolly at his leisure.

"Good morning, Officer," said the orderly, passing Bonnie on the porch. "I hope my fine musician friend here isn't in any trouble."

"No trouble," said Bonnie, maintaining her guard. The little orderly stepped off the porch and walked out the driveway to the street. He glanced back at them, smiling in a way that was less than reassuring. Then he and the Córdoba guitar were gone.

"Friend of yours?" said Bonnie.

"I just met him. He bought a guitar."

"Yeah, so I heard. Can I come in?"

"Sure," Rolly said, turning back into the house.

"It smells like dope in here," Bonnie said, as she walked into the living room. "I thought you were done with that stuff."

"That guy lit up a joint," Rolly said. "Guess he assumed it was okay since I'm a guitar player."

He picked up the money the orderly left on the table—forty dollars, a tenth of what the Córdoba was worth.

"I didn't think musicians were up this early in the morning," said Bonnie.

"You know me. I get all the weirdos."

"That's for sure. How about that ride?"

"You mean now?"

"You got something better to do?"

"Is this about that stolen car?"

"What car would that be?"

"The one your guys towed out of Border Field Park early yesterday."

"Maybe. I got some things we need to talk about. Let's go."

"Where're we headed?"

"Just get ready. We'll talk on the way."

Rolly went into the bathroom, closed the door, sat down on the toilet and stared at his quivering hands. He didn't want to tell Bonnie what had just happened, not yet, not until he knew what she was up to, why she wanted to drag him out of the house at this ungodly hour. He got up from the toilet, slapped a stick of deodorant under his arms, knocked back a brace of antacids and ran a wet comb through his hair. Returning to the bedroom, he opened the dresser. The little orderly's assessment wasn't far off. Rolly's sartorial selection was almost monastic: black shirts and jeans, a penitent man's sackcloth and ashes. Guitars were his only study now, his spiritual guide. No drugs. No alcohol. No women. Guitars didn't make him stupid the way those things did. Still, he wished he had a bottle in front of him now, and a long-legged female around him. Guitars weren't always enough.

He changed clothes, walked back into the living room and picked up his cell phone and keys.

"Ready," he announced to Bonnie.

They walked outside. Rolly locked the door, glancing across the yard to see if his mother was awake. There were no lights on in the house, no sign of activity in her kitchen window. He walked to the passenger side of Bonnie's patrol car, relieved he wouldn't have to explain its presence in the driveway. He climbed in and fastened his seat belt. Bonnie put the car into gear and backed out of the driveway.

"Tell me about your friend Jimmy," she said, as they merged onto the freeway, headed north.

"He's not really my friend. I haven't seen him in twenty years. Until yesterday."

"He said you were working on something, at Border Field Park?"

"Yeah."

"Want to tell me about it?"

"Somebody hired me."

"What for?"

"My client was down there yesterday morning, counting birds for some census. Audubon Society, something like that.

Anyway, he spotted these tire tracks in the preserve, like somebody had gone off-roading through this protected area for the least terns."

"The what?"

"California least terns. They're some kind of endangered seabird. Lays eggs in the sand. Anyway, my friend was pissed off about it. He didn't think the rangers or Border Patrol would do anything, so he hired me to try and track down the guy that did it."

"Did your client call the police?"

"He didn't figure it was your jurisdiction."

"Uh-huh."

"Is it?"

"No. Not for something like that. What'd you find out?"

"I went into the least tern area, followed the tracks. They crushed some nests, killed at least one baby bird that I saw. It looked like he might have got stuck. There were some deep ruts. I got some pictures on my phone if you want to see them."

"This was inside the park?"

"Yeah. I guess your guys towed him out already."

"The car we picked up was outside the park, in the reeds like it went off the road."

"It's not the same one?"

"I didn't say that. What time were you down there?"

"I guess around seven thirty."

"How about your client?"

"He called me at six thirty, probably got there at dawn."

"What's his name?"

"You know I can't tell you that."

"I'm gonna need to talk to him."

"Why?"

"Have a look at that folder there."

Bonnie indicated a file folder on the seat cushion between them. Rolly picked up the folder. There was a case number written on the file tab. He opened the folder. It was a preliminary autopsy report. There were photographs inside of a young woman, a girl, perhaps fifteen or sixteen, her naked brown body and long dark hair laid out on a metal table like a dead robin in an ornithological display. Her body looked whole, unviolated by blade, bullet or blunt instrument. The coroner hadn't opened her up. Rolly felt grateful for that much. The morning's events had unsettled his stomach enough.

"Why am I looking at this?" he asked.

"Did you read it?"

"Not yet."

"Well, read it."

He turned his attention to the written report. Jane Doe. Body discovered at eight fifteen yesterday morning. Location: Border Field State Park. Estimated time of death between twelve and two that same morning. He looked back at Bonnie.

"Her body was there, wasn't it? When I was there?"

"Looks like it."

"Where'd they find her?"

"On the beach. Hung up on one of those metal pilings where the border fence goes into the ocean. You didn't see her?"

"No."

"You sure? Maybe something related?"

"I'm pretty sure," he replied, trying to recall if he'd seen anything that could have been the girl's body, a lump of flesh in the surf. "What happened to her?"

"Preliminary is drowning."

"Maybe a border crosser?"

"Maybe."

"You think this is related to my bird people?"

"I'd like to talk to your client."

"He didn't see anything. He would have told me. He would have called the police."

"You sure?"

"There's no way he's involved in this, if that's what you're trying to get at."

"Good. Then you can tell me who he is."

"I'll give him your number."

"I can get a court order if I need to."

"I'll have him call you. He's got nothing to do with it."

Rolly returned his attention to the report, hoping the discussion of his client was over. He flipped through the rest of the photographs, wondering if the little orderly would recognize the girl in the photos, if this was Rio, her last dance on the sand. The last photo was a close-up of the girl's left buttock. She had a small scar like the letter *m* with an extra loop.

"What's this?" he asked, showing the photo to Bonnie.

"Don't worry about that," she replied. "Did you finish the report yet?"

"Not yet."

"Finish it."

He read through the rest of the report, then closed the folder. One particular item disturbed him: a description of the girl's underwear.

"Who found the body?" he asked.

"A woman and her daughters. They were out on horses with a guide."

"Was his name Jaime? The guide?"

"You're referring to Mr. Velasquez?"

"I don't know his last name. He rents horses. I met him down there yesterday."

"Mr. Velasquez mentioned your name."

"What'd he say?"

"Just that you'd been down there earlier, asking questions. He showed me your card."

Rolly reached in his pocket and found the panties.

"I guess he told you about these too?" he said, pulling them out of his pocket.

"What are those?"

"Panties. Like the ones your Jane Doe was wearing."

Bonnie glanced at the panties, then looked back out at the road.

"Where'd you get those?"

"Jaime gave them to me. Didn't he tell you?"

Bonnie cocked her head an inch to one side and pursed her lips.

"No," she said.

"I hate it when you do that," said Rolly.

"What's that?"

"I made things look bad for him, didn't I?"

"We'll see. What'd he tell you?"

Rolly told Bonnie the story of Jaime's ghost, Xtapay. He told her about the red-haired woman who lived in the house on Smuggler's Canyon. Tangerine.

"That's quite a story," Bonnie said, when he'd finished. "Quite a story. I'll need you to surrender those, by the way."

"The panties?"

Bonnie nodded.

"You got a warrant?"

"Those are evidence."

"You don't know that. Besides, they've got my fingerprints all over 'em."

"I expect they do."

"Doesn't that fall under some law against self-incrimination?"

"I know the law."

"You know about the record album that goes with the panties?"

"No. I don't know about any record album."

"It's called *Jungle Love*. By Serpent. I found the CD in the park. This woman, Tangerine, she's on the front cover. When she was younger, of course."

"What the hell are you talking about?"

Rolly described the CD cover and told Bonnie about his visit to Norwood's Mostly Music, including Rob Norwood's estimate of the combined value of the original record and panties.

"A hundred bucks, huh?" Bonnie said, when he'd finished.

"Maybe two. What do you think?"

"I think it might explain some things."

"About what?"

"The car that was stolen."

"Yeah?"

"Yeah. There was a whole box of those records in back."

14

EL COCHE (THE CAR)

Rolly and Bonnie stood in front of lot space number twenty-three in the San Diego Police Department's automobile recovery yard, contemplating a distressed black hearse. It had tinted front windows and shiny silver hubcaps, but the paint job was scratched, the bumper pitted with early rust.

"You got those tire shots?" asked Bonnie.

Rolled pulled out his phone and scrolled through the photos until he found the tread marks he'd taken pictures of yesterday morning. He handed the phone to Bonnie. She crouched down in front of the right front tire, comparing the treads to the ones in Rolly's photo.

"Whattya think?" Rolly asked.

"Can't rule them out," she said.

"There's more," said Rolly. "You can scroll through 'em. Where are the albums?"

"Inside the back door," said Bonnie, making her way around the car, comparing each tire to the photographs.

"Okay if I take a look?"

"Be my guest. It's been dusted."

Rolly walked to the back of the hearse. A flaming cobra

had been airbrushed onto the rear door. He pulled the door open and found a cardboard box on the carpet inside. He opened the top flaps. The records inside were still shrink-wrapped, *Jungle Love* by Serpent. They were collector's editions, in pristine condition, just like the ones Norwood had told him about.

"I need you to email me those photos," Bonnie said, returning his phone.

"Sure. You think they're the same tires?" he asked.

"I'll have the lab take a closer look. Send me anything you took pictures of down there."

"I will."

"What about those?" Bonnie asked, nodding her head at the box of records.

Rolly pulled out the top record.

"You see this?" he said, indicating the round cutout inside the snake's mouth. "That's the panties, underneath."

"So they're valuable?"

"Rob knows his stuff. There's fifty records in here. At a hundred dollars each . . ."

"Five thousand bucks," said Bonnie.

"You think that's why somebody stole the car?"

"Can't rule it out."

"Why didn't they take the records, then?"

"Maybe they panicked," Bonnie said. "Maybe someone was after them. Have a look at this."

She closed the back door and walked around to the passenger side. Rolly followed.

"See that?" Bonnie said, indicating the passenger door. There were dried splatters of red along the side of the door and the window.

"That's paint, right?" said Rolly. His stomach gurgled.

"Well, it ain't blood, if that's what you're worried about."

"I talked to a guy down there, yesterday morning. He had a paint gun in the back of his truck."

"Oh yeah?"

"He's with this group, the AFA, some kind of vigilante group, trying to keep people from crossing."

"Yeah, I've heard about them."

"He says they all carry paint guns."

"You remember the guy's name?"

"Nuge."

"Nuge? Is that his first name or last?"

"I think it's a nickname."

"You didn't get his real name?"

"We didn't get along very well."

A man in a grease-monkey suit approached them, one of the mechanics who worked on the lot.

"Are you done with the car, Officer?" he asked. "The owner's wanting to claim it."

"The owner's here?" Bonnie said.

"Office just gave me a call. They finished the paperwork."

"It's Ray, right?" Bonnie said, extending her hand. "I'm Officer Hammond."

"Yeah, Ray," the man said, shaking hands.

"Well, Ray, we're done here, but I wonder if you could do me a little favor?"

"What's that?"

"I'd like a few minutes to talk to this guy before he gets his car back."

"Uh-huh."

"He's been avoiding me."

"Sound like he lacks proper respect for the work our law-enforcement officials are doing."

"You might say that."

Ray looked into the distance, toward the dry Poway hills.

"You know," he said, "the office doesn't always give me the right number. Sometimes they flip it around."

"They could've said thirty-two, for instance?"

"I'd better check," Ray said, giving a wink. He turned and walked away, headed toward the other end of the lot. Bonnie set off in the opposite direction, toward the office, a converted mobile home parked just inside the main gate. Rolly hustled to catch up.

"You haven't talked to the owner?" he asked.

"I set up two meetings. He didn't show. I called him three times since then. No response."

"Jimmy said the guy was kinda weird."

"How so?"

"Goth type. Heavy makeup. Lots of piercings. Did you catch his condo number?"

"Thirteen-thirteen?"

"Yeah. Jimmy told me the guy insisted on keeping the place, even after everybody else bailed."

"Fits with his choice of automobiles."

Rolly broke into a jog.

"He's not really my friend, you know," Rolly said. "I mean Jimmy."

"He talked like he was. Told me a lot about you."

"He worked at this bar where we played, a long time ago."

"Mr. Bodeans was quite a chatty fellow. He told me a few stories."

"About me?"

"You. And Moogus."

"What'd he tell you?"

"Nothing we can still prosecute."

Bonnie vaulted the stairs to the office two at a time, then waited for Rolly outside the front door.

"Let me do the talking with this guy," she said, when Rolly caught up. "I'll give you the sign if I want you to jump in."

Rolly nodded. He'd need another minute to catch his breath, anyway, let alone ask any questions. Bonnie opened the door. They walked in.

It wasn't hard to spot the hearse's owner, a young man slouched in a chair across from the service counter, hunched over some sort of handheld device.

"Mr. Burdon?" said Bonnie.

"My name is Sayer Burdon," the man said, jabbing his

thumbs at the device screen. His skin looked the same shade of gray as the hearse's interior. A grungy silver skull dangled below his nose, hung from a pin stuck through his septum. A dark eyeshade and black lipstick completed the look.

"I'm Detective Bonnie Hammond, from the San Diego Police Department. I called and talked to you earlier?"

"You called on my cell phone."

"Yes. We were supposed to meet. At your place."

"At my condominium. One-thousand, two-hundred-two Tenth Avenue. Unit number one-thousand, three-hundred and thirteen."

There was something odd about the kid's responses, flat and colorless, as if he were stoned or stupid, or both. Bonnie wouldn't get much traction riding the guy for his missed appointments.

"Can I ask you some questions?" she said. "About your car?"

"Somebody took it."

"When did you realize the car had been stolen?"

"Somebody took it."

"Yes. When did you realize it had been taken?"

"It was somebody I know."

"You're saying you know the perpetrator?"

"I forgot."

"You don't remember?"

"Someone borrowed my car."

"But you reported it stolen. You called it in."

"I forgot. Someone borrowed it."

"Detective Hammond?" said a voice from behind them. Bonnie and Rolly looked back toward the counter. A short, bald man in uniform stood at the window, waving a file folder at them.

"Yes?" said Bonnie.

"Mr. Burdon signed off. He dropped all the charges."

"Let me see," Bonnie said. She stepped over to the counter and returned with the file folder.

"You're sure you want to drop this, Mr. Burdon?" she asked. Burdon finished playing with his phone, or whatever it was.

"It's okay now," he said. "I forgot. Someone borrowed my car."

"Can you tell me who borrowed it?"

"Someone I know. A friend."

"Can you tell me your friend's name?"

"I paid for my car," said Burdon, producing a scrap of yellow paper from his pocket as evidence. "I paid that man over there for it. He gave me a receipt. I want to drive my car now."

"All right, Mr. Burdon," said Bonnie. "You can go soon. Mr. Burdon, do you have any idea why this friend of yours drove the car down to the border?"

"No."

"Did he say anything about it?"

"My friend knows a lawyer."

"He's going to need one if you don't help me out here," said Bonnie. "Did your friend explain why he abandoned your car?"

"It stopped working. My car stopped working."

"That's why he abandoned it?"

"No. I don't know why he did that. He said he knows a lawyer."

"I'm not sure this person is your friend, Mr. Burdon. We found a dead girl down there."

"What was the girl's name?"

"That's what I'm trying to find out. That's why I want to talk to your friend."

"You found a dead girl."

"Yes. I want to find out what happened to her."

"I don't know."

"I understand, Mr. Burdon. But your friend might."

"He borrowed my car."

"Mr. Burdon, if your friend was involved in this girl's death and you don't tell me what you know, you're an accessory."

"My car's got a snake-head gearshift."

"Yes, I saw that."

"It's an after-market accessory."

Bonnie looked stymied. She excused herself and returned to the man at the counter window, nodding to Rolly as she left, which Rolly took as an indication that Burdon was now his to question.

"Hello, Mr. Burdon," said Rolly. "My name's Rolly Waters. Here's my card."

The boy took the card, holding it as if it were a used Kleenex.

"Rolly Waters. The Rock 'n' Roll Dick," he said, reading out loud.

"That's me."

Burdon showed no indication he got the joke or cared. He continued reading out loud.

"CA PI License number two-hundred-and-three-thousand, five-hundred-and-twelve. Phone open parenthesis six-hundred-and-nineteen close parenthesis five-hundred-and-thirty-eight dash—"

"What's your first name?" asked Rolly.

"Sayer."

"Nice to meet you, Sayer. I like your skull."

"My skull's in my head. You can't see it."

"I meant that little silver one that's hanging from your nose."

"It's jewelry."

"Where'd you get it?"

"A friend."

"The same friend who borrowed your car?"

"No. It was my girlfriend."

"She gave you the skull?"

"She said I should get it. It's a token."

"What's your girlfriend's name?"

"She's a Mexican girl."

"You go out on dates with her?"

"Sometimes."

"Where do you go?"

"Sometimes we eat food together."

"Do you ever eat Mexican food?"

"She likes Mexican food. She's a Mexican."

"Where do you go for Mexican food?"

"I call someone."

"You order takeout, over the phone?"

"It's for when we play games."

"What kind of games do you play?"

"I like to play Border Lords."

"What's that? Some kind of video game?"

"Yes."

"Is that what you were playing there on your phone?"

"It's not a phone. It's a handheld gaming device."

"Oh. How do you play that game? Border Lords?"

"You get to shoot Mexicans."

Rolly didn't know how to respond to that last bit of information. He changed the subject.

"I noticed you have some old records in the back of your car."

"Yes. They're vinyl recordings."

"Where did you get them?"

"My dad. He gave them to me. They're tokens."

"You think I could talk to your dad?"

"No."

"Why's that?"

"He's dead."

"Oh."

"He's my ancestor."

"I'm sorry he's dead. When did he give the records to you?"

"After I was born."

Bonnie rejoined them. Rolly gave a little wave with his hand, hoping she wouldn't interrupt.

"What was your dad's name?" he said.

"He died. He gave the records to me after he died."

"You inherited them? Is that what you mean?"

"I want to drive my car now. My friend knows a lawyer. I paid for the car."

"They're bringing your car up now, Mr. Burdon," said Bonnie.

Burdon stood up and moved toward the door.

"My friend borrowed the car," he said.

"Mr. Burdon?" said Rolly.

"Yes?"

"I met a woman, yesterday. She's on the cover of those albums, the woman with red hair. Her name is Tangerine Swimmer."

"She's married to the serpent," said Burdon.

"Did you know she lives here?"

"She doesn't live here."

"She lives in a house down by the border, near the place where the police found your car. I spoke to her yesterday."

Sayer Burdon paused at the door.

"Did you have sex with her?" Burdon asked.

"No."

"My father had sex with her."

"She was his girlfriend?"

"They had sex."

"Did you know she was living there?"

A frown played across Burdon's face, a sixteenth-note pause in his expression before it returned to the dominant tone.

"Do you want to have sex with her?" he asked.

"I just want to talk to her, get some more information."

"You shouldn't have sex with her."

"Why is that?"

"My father is dead."

EL CAÑÓN (THE CANYON)

Sunday afternoon, Rolly joined Max at the ballpark, ingesting chili dogs and taking Max through the events of the last two days while Padre batters ground into double plays and stared at third strikes. The game didn't improve his mood any. Neither did Max's offer to hire someone else to take the case. Max's concern for his welfare made Rolly feel like he'd bungled things, like he'd screwed up again. It was an old pattern of thinking, a bad habit, blaming himself for events over which he had no control. Then came the phone call.

"Señor Rolly?" It was a girl's voice, low and shaded.

"Yes?"

"*Necesito el dinero,*" the voice said.

"Who's this?" he asked.

"Señor Jaime. *Él dice que usted me ayudará.*"

"I'm sorry. I don't speak Spanish."

"*Estoy aquí. Lo van. Debe ayudarme.*"

The line disconnected. He tried dialing the number back. No one answered. The girl had said something about Jaime. She wanted money. He understood that.

So instead of crashing in front of the TV with his guitar after the game, he drove back down to the border, guiding his Volvo over the uneven asphalt of Monument Road, on the way to Border Field Park, in search of Jaime Velasquez.

A car appeared in his rearview mirror, lurching into view like a pouncing cougar. The driver honked at him and pulled out to pass. He slowed, letting the other car pull in front of him.

It was the hearse from the police lot, the one with the flaming cobra painted on the rear door, Sayer Burdon's hearse. He followed it around a sharp bend in the road, then stomped the gas pedal to keep up as the hearse accelerated into the straightaway. They entered the gentle arc of road fronting the outlet of Smuggler's Canyon. The hearse's brake lights flashed. It slowed to a stop across the street from Tangerine's house. Its left turn signal blinked on like an afterthought.

"Crap," Rolly said, stomping the brakes.

The gate across the driveway creaked open. Rolly strained for a glimpse of the driver's face as the hearse turned into the driveway, but its tinted windows prevented him from seeing inside. He drove past the house, down to the end of Monument Road, spun a U-turn near the entrance to Border Field Park and braked to a stop. He idled the car for a moment, mulling his options, then put the Volvo in gear and headed back toward the house. He wanted to see who the driver was before he called Bonnie.

He pulled in behind the row of smoke trees on Smuggler's Canyon, just as he'd done the day before. The trees blocked his view of the house, but they would prevent anyone inside from seeing him as well. He cut the engine, coasted to a stop and cracked the door open. Three large boulders sat on a rise of dirt at the upper end of the smoke trees, a barrier to divert canyon runoff away from the house. He measured the distance, took a deep breath, jumped out of the car and skittered across the mouth of the canyon, then flattened himself down against the dirt rise. He crawled up behind the boulders and peeked through a space between them, down at the back of the house.

The sloping tile roof of the house appeared first, then the iron security fence. Between the fence and the house was a swimming pool, surrounded by a pockmarked concrete patio. A sliding glass door led out to the patio from the back of the house. The door opened. Tangerine stepped out on the patio, wearing the orange silk robe and high-heel sandals he'd seen her in before.

A voice came from inside the house, too muffled for Rolly to make out the words.

"I'm having a smoke," Tangerine responded. She lit up a cigarette. Exhaling her first puff, she tilted her head, looking up toward Rolly's hiding spot. He dropped back into the shadows, resisting an urge to flee. There was something unsettling in Tangerine's eyes, even this far away, as if she knew he was there. He kept his position, trusting the shadows to hide him.

Dangling the cigarette between her lips, Tangerine undid her belt, letting the robe slip from her shoulders. It fell like a whisper, leaving her naked except for her shoes. She kicked off her sandals, placed the cigarette at the edge of the pool and dove in. She paddled the length of the pool a couple of times, returned to puff on her cigarette, then began some stretching exercises at the shallow end. Her actions seemed willful, a show for Rolly's benefit. He remembered the story about the man hiding up in the hills, looking down on her, how she liked to flirt. The display was for him, whoever she thought he might be—a construction worker, a border crosser or Jaime, any man who took pleasure in her with his eyes.

Tangerine climbed out of the pool and spread herself out on a reclining chair, providing Rolly a full view of her assets.

"I'm all wet," she said, challenging anyone to deny it.

A noise came from inside the house. Rolly spotted someone sitting at the end of a sofa, just inside the open door. It was Sayer Burdon, the Goth kid, clutching a black object in both hands, his thumbs skittering across its surface as he stared intently at something farther inside the room.

"There's a snake in the rocks," said Tangerine.

Two shoes appeared on the linoleum floor inside the back

door, lit by a slash of sunlight across the stoop. A vague recognition stirred in Rolly's brain, rising to consciousness, even as he resisted the thought. The little orderly stepped onto the porch and looked up toward the rocks. He walked to the edge of the pool and picked up the half-finished cigarette.

"What kind of snake?" he asked, relighting the cigarette.

"A slippery, slidy snake," said Tangerine.

The little orderly walked behind Tangerine's chair, so that she couldn't see him.

"Sssssss," he said. "Sssssss."

Tangerine began rubbing her crotch.

The orderly undid his belt and dropped his pants.

"Snakebite," Tangerine said.

"Sssssss," said the orderly, stroking himself.

Tangerine groaned.

Rolly pulled his cell phone out of his pocket and switched to the camera setting. He moved into position, snapped a photo, adjusted the zoom setting, then took another one. The little orderly hissed again. Tangerine groaned. The two of them hissed and groaned, getting close, but never touching one another.

"Snakebite," cried Tangerine, louder this time. She pulled her hair to one side, exposing her neck. The little orderly leaned forward and increased the intensity of his self-stroking.

"Snakebite," Tangerine called again. The orderly took the cigarette from his mouth and plunged it into Tangerine's neck. She cried out in pain. The orderly spasmed, clutching the back of the chair.

"*Mi madre,*" he gasped. The muscles in his neck looked like grotesque steel springs.

And then it was over. The cigarette butt dropped from his fingers, slid down between Tangerine's breasts and came to rest on her belly. The orderly pulled up his pants and walked back into the house. Sayer Burdon continued with his video game, unaware, or in spite, of the activities that had just taken place on the patio.

Tangerine reached down and picked up the cigarette. She

blew on the ashes, took a drag, touched her neck again with the burning end and winced.

"Snakebite," she said, under her breath, then flicked the cigarette butt into the pool. She stood up, put on her robe and went into the house.

Rolly sat down in the dirt, checked his photos, then put his camera away. He stared up the canyon, feeling soiled and vaguely nauseated. He turned around and took another peek through the gap in the rocks. Inside the house, Tangerine stood behind the living room sofa, gently caressing the top of Sayer Burdon's head while he blasted away at alien monsters.

Somewhere an automobile engine cranked over and died. Rolly heard it again—a coughing engine, then silence. He knew that rhythm, those notes. It was his Volvo. He scrambled down from behind the boulders, squinting his eyes. Down at the end of the canyon, the driver's-side door of the Volvo sat open. The engine sputtered again. It caught sparks. He took two more steps toward the road.

"Hey there," he said. "That's my car."

The driver's-side door slammed shut. The Volvo jumped forward and turned up the canyon. Behind the steering wheel sat the little orderly, grinning his sick little smile. He spun the steering wheel, turning the car toward Rolly.

Rolly didn't know what the orderly had in mind, but it wasn't valet service. He turned and ran up the canyon. The fluttering in his stomach expanded, filling his chest like a flock of screaming seagulls. The sound of the Volvo grew closer behind him, its engine torqued into a high, whining note. The tires scratched across the canyon's dirt floor, digging harsh grooves like a pissed-off club DJ.

He spotted a crumbling section of canyon wall to his left, a low cliff where hundred-year-old rivulets had opened cracks in the slope, tight grooves leading up to a ledge where the car couldn't go. The roar of the engine grew louder. He swerved to his left, leapt over a downed tree trunk and heard a dull thump of crumpled steel from behind. He ducked into one of the fissures and scrambled up onto the ledge. The Volvo's horn blared, protesting his getaway. He turned to look back down the hill. The car had come to a stop against the downed tree, its front grill snubbed underneath. The wheels spun against loose dirt. From inside the cab the little orderly glared at him, his smile transformed into a scowl. Otherwise, he appeared unscathed.

Rolly continued up the hill, anxious to put more distance between himself and the orderly. He climbed onto a wider ledge where the hill flattened out, paused and turned to look back again. The Volvo looked smaller now, a safe distance away. The horn had gone silent. The little orderly leaned against the side of the car, smoking one of his special cigarettes. He spotted Rolly staring down at him, raised his hand as if to wave goodbye and dangled the key from one finger. Taunting complete, he stamped out his cigarette, climbed back in the car and drove back down to Monument Road, disappearing from view.

Rolly leaned over, resting his hands on his knees as he inhaled great gouts of air. The seagulls inside him had talons now. They felt like hawks clawing at his lungs, stabbing at his sternum with sharp beaks. He coughed, cleared his throat and spit out a hunk of phlegm.

After a few minutes, the pain in his chest subsided, diffusing into his shoulders. A cold ache spread into his legs. His breathing settled. It became slower, less labored. He lifted his head and looked around to get his bearings. Without realizing it, he'd managed to climb all the way to the border. A rusty fence stood twenty feet away, on the other side of the dusty ridge road.

They hadn't replaced this section of fence yet. Down the line you could see where the new one ended, two lines running parallel out to the bullring, painted an almost painful white. Curls of barbed wire ran along the top of the new fence. The wire was painted white, too. The fence across from him, the old one, looked like a piece of junk in comparison, flimsy sheets of corrugated metal, ten feet tall, bolted together and rusted to the point of translucence, like the discarded skin of a monstrous rattlesnake. He walked across the road and inspected it, pressing his hand against the rough skin. He wondered how much force it would take to break through.

A bolt popped. The metal skin groaned and the rusted sheet fell away. Rolly tumbled down into the empty space.

16

LA FRONTERA (THE BORDER)

Rolly crashed into Mexico, blundering into the land on the other side of the fence, which, when he managed to raise himself up and take in the scenery, didn't look all that different from the side on which he'd started. Four men sat around a fire pit fashioned from a discarded tire. The men stared at him, frozen in place like cautious naturalists assessing the appearance of a new species: the Black-Shirted American Idiot, native to dark urban bars, not often found in the chaparral hills of Northern Baja. Rolly smiled at the men, hoping they weren't dangerous.

"*Buenos días,*" he said.

"*Buenos días,*" they replied.

The oldest-looking man walked over to him, offered his hand and helped Rolly up. As an overall genus, Americans might be hard to classify, but the black-shirted idiot wasn't predacious.

"*Gracias,*" Rolly said, dusting himself off.

"*De nada.*" The man nodded.

Rolly checked for injuries. Finding a long scratch of blood on his left forearm, he tried to remember when he'd had his last tetanus shot. The older man inspected the damaged fence, wiggled the loose piece of rusted metal, then grabbed it with both hands and gave it a yank, ripping the entire sheet off its rivets, creating a space you could drive a Jeep through. The man poked his head across the invisible line, testing the air on the other side of the equation. The other men watched him.

"¿*Los ve?*" one of them asked.

"*No los veo,*" replied the man at the fence. He turned back to Rolly.

"*La Migra? Ha visto?*" he said, waving his hand to indicate the area on the other side of the fence.

"*No. No La Migra,*" said Rolly, shaking his head. He hadn't seen any sign of the Border Patrol. He wondered if he'd broken any laws by telling the men.

"*Vayamos,*" said the older man, waving his hands at the group. They followed him through the gap in the fence. Rolly brought up the rear.

"*Aquí, pronto, pronto, aquí,*" urged the group's leader, pointing into the shadows of Smuggler's Canyon. The men hurried down the trail, slipping and sliding along the narrow dirt path, away from the sunlit crest of the hill.

"*Adios, amigos,*" Rolly said, seating himself on a flat-topped boulder near the top of the trail. The last of the border crossers disappeared into the shade of the canyon. For all he knew, *La Migra* had tracked the men already, using some sort of high-tech spy gear, triangulating data so they could trap the men when they reached the bottom. He didn't want to be picked up along with them. The Border Patrol would assume he was a coyote, paid by the men to bring them across. They wouldn't need more than that to arrest him.

His phone rang. He took the phone out of his pocket and checked the caller name. It was his father's home number, probably Alicia wondering when he would stop by. He didn't have an answer for her. If it was his father, he was probably drunk. That was a conversation Rolly didn't need at the moment. He let the call ring through to his voice mail.

He scrolled through his contact list, wondered how much the

roaming charges would be if he connected to a Mexican tower, found Bonnie's number, punched the keypad and waited. Calling 911 seemed excessive. He wasn't in any immediate danger. The phone line transferred to Bonnie's voice mail. He left a message telling her where he was. He told her about the hearse and the house, about Burdon and Tangerine and the little orderly who'd tried to kill him.

He put the phone back in his pocket and surveyed the scenery. Autumn, such as it was, had come to the border. Along the edge of the dirt road, dried-up stands of wild daisies had shriveled to rope in the September heat, their flowers depleted, petals dropped and ground into the dirt. The sun on the horizon cast its dying warmth against the side of his face. A pair of vultures drifted along on the ridge, looking for carrion, their dark profiles outlined against the darkening blue canopy. He wondered if the vultures had followed him, if they could smell hints of death in his sweat-covered body and dry, labored breathing. Were they watching, waiting for him to falter?

Someone yelled. He heard a thump of footsteps from the trail below. A man appeared, one of the border crossers. He ran up the trail, toward Rolly's lookout.

"*¡Ayúdame! ¡Ayúdame!*" the man yelled in warning. He pointed back down the trail. "*La Migra.*"

Rolly stood up and looked back down the trail. Two men appeared from out of the shadows. They wore camouflage suits and protective visors. The men raised their guns. Rolly's companion turned to run. Rolly hit the dirt, covering his head. He heard the pop of the guns from below, the whizzing sound of projectiles passing over him, a yelp of pain. Someone laughed.

"Did you see that?" the voice said from below. "I nailed him right in the ear."

"That's one well-painted beaner."

"He'll think twice before coming through here again."

Footsteps moved toward him, then stopped. Rolly looked up. The two shooters stood over him, with their guns at the ready. They didn't look like *La Migra.*

"Who the hell're you?" one of them asked.

"I'm an American," Rolly said.

"What're you doing up here?"

"I'm an American," Rolly said. "I live here in this country."

"He don't look like a beaner," said the other man. "Some of those Mexicans look kinda regular-like, though."

"You got some ID?" asked the first man.

Rolly rolled up onto his knees, reached into the back pocket of his jeans and pulled out his wallet.

"Well, Mr. Rock'n'Roll Dick," said the first man, reading the license. "I thought that was you. What're you doing up here?"

"Hiking."

"Funny place for a hike."

"I started down at Border Field Park."

"You got a serious problem with reading signs."

"What's that?"

"You're not supposed to be up here."

"I got lost."

The second man walked over to the gap in the fence and gestured with his gun toward Tijuana.

"You seen that beaner before?" he asked.

"No," Rolly lied.

"Sounded to me like he was talking to you, *en Español*."

"I don't know what he said."

The man walked over to Rolly, waving his gun.

"You know what I hate more than Mexicans?" he said. "It's fag-ass bleeding hearts who come down here to aid and abet 'em. You one of those?"

"No," Rolly said. "I'm not helping anyone."

"Just out for a hike, huh?"

"Yes."

"I think you're a coyote. Whattya think, Nuge?"

The other man took off his helmet.

"You remember me?" he asked, dropping the gun to his side.

"You're the guy in the truck," Rolly replied. "From yesterday."

"I suppose you got an explanation for this?"

"Sure. It's part of my case."

"You mean that thing with the birds?"

"Yes."

"You got a bad habit of showing up places you're not supposed to be."

"Someone tried to kill me."

"Who?"

"He's a doctor or something. You might have seen him down in the canyon."

"You seen any doctors down there?" Nuge asked his friend.

"Can't say as I have."

"I think you better come back with us," Nuge said, returning to Rolly. "We got a nice little roundup of illegals down by the road. We'll see what they have to say about you."

"Let's go, amigo," the other man said.

"You can't arrest me."

"Why not?"

"You don't have the authority."

"We got a right to defend our country. You're breaking the law just by being here."

"I'm a US citizen, out for a hike in the country air."

"Yeah, I know. It's nature's paradise out here."

It was a waste of time arguing with the men. What had Hector called them—Asshole Fucking Anglos? An image of his camouflaged captors sodomizing each other flashed through Rolly's head. He grinned.

"Something funny to you?" said Nuge.

"Nothing."

"Well, consider yourself under arrest. Citizen's arrest."

"Why?"

"I knew you were bad news. I shoulda capped your ass yesterday."

"I'm a private detective."

"Anybody can get a card made."

"I'm working with the police now."

"Like hell," said the other man. "Whattya think, Nuge?"

Nuge scratched his late-afternoon stubble.

"Maybe we should call in BP," he said.

"There's one on the way now," said the other man, looking past Rolly's shoulder. Rolly turned. A Border Patrol truck popped over the hill, headed along the road toward them. It pulled to a stop thirty feet away. A border patrolman climbed out and approached them on foot. He paused ten feet away from them, putting his hands on his hips.

"What's up, fellas?" he asked.

"We caught some illegals down in the canyon."

"You're not allowed on the road."

"This guy was with 'em."

"You know the rules. Step off."

"He's a coyote. Look at that hole in the fence."

"Step off or I'll arrest all of you."

Nuge and his partner took a couple of steps back down the trail, away from the road.

"Okay?" said Nuge.

The patrolman nodded. He looked over at Rolly.

"All right, sir, what's your story?"

"I'm a private detective, helping with a police case."

"You have approval to be up here?"

"I guess not. Not officially."

"He's a coyote, I'm telling ya'," said Nuge. "Or maybe a drug dealer."

"It's a stolen car case," Rolly continued. "San Diego Police. I can put you in touch with the case officer."

"We grabbed three illegals just now, in the canyon," said Nuge. "Chased another one back up here. Caught him talking to this guy."

"Is that true?" the patrolman asked Rolly.

"The guy yelled at me as he ran by," said Rolly. "He tried to warn me, I guess. These guys were shooting at him."

"What about this?" the patrolman asked, indicating the hole in the fence.

"It's been like that since I got here," said Rolly, hoping the patrolman wouldn't press him for details.

"How'd you get up here?"

"I walked up," Rolly said, pointing down Smuggler's Canyon. "From down there."

"He's lying," said Nuge. "You told us you hiked over from the park."

"Is that what you told them?" asked the patrolman.

"I did say that. Yes. I . . . Somebody down there tried to kill me. I ran away from him."

"Who tried to kill you?"

"This doctor, a little Mexican guy. He ran my car into a tree."

"He's making shit up now," said Nuge.

"It's an old Volvo wagon. White."

"I didn't see any cars down there," said Nuge.

"He stole it."

"Officer," said Nuge. "We got these illegals tied up down there by the road. Why don't we bring him down, see what they have to say."

"How about it?" the patrolman asked Rolly.

"I'm not going with these guys."

"You'll have to go with me, then. In the back."

The patrolman pulled a pair of handcuffs off his belt. Rolly nodded, extending his hands. The patrolman cuffed him, walked him back to the truck and opened the back door. Rolly slid in behind the wire cage that separated him from the front seat. He sighed. At least he'd disappointed the vultures.

17

EL CAMINO (THE ROAD)

Rolly watched in the truck's rearview mirror as another Border Patrol truck arrived on the scene, followed soon after by two patrolmen on motorcycles. They inspected the hole in the fence. After some discussion, the man in the second truck parked it next to the fence, temporarily spanning the gap. The men on the dirt bikes sped off. Nuge and his buddy headed back down the trail the way they'd come up. Rolly's captor returned to his truck and put it in gear. They drove along the edge of the fence toward the bullring.

"You really a PI?" the patrolman asked, glancing back at Rolly in the rearview mirror.

"Yeah."

"How long you been doing that?"

"Ten years."

"You like it?"

"Not at the moment."

"We'll get this taken care of. You got somebody who can vouch for you at SDPD?"

"Bonnie Hammond. She's the case officer."

The patrolman turned down a steep dirt road, clearly marked with a "No Trespassing—Federal Government" sign.

"Did you work there? SDPD, I mean, before?"

"No. I was a musician."

"A musician?"

"Yeah."

"Whattya play?"

"Guitar."

"How'd you wind up being a PI?"

"It's a long story."

"I looked into it a couple of times."

"What's that?"

"Getting a PI license."

"You don't like working for the Border Patrol?"

"I'm thinking maybe when I retire, you know, to keep my hand in, supplement my pension."

"How long you been doing this?"

"Ten years. You can start collecting when you turn forty-five."

"Sounds pretty good."

"Yeah. Nine more years and I'm in."

Rolly had no retirement plan. Nothing would happen when he reached forty-five. Or fifty. His Social Security estimates had only recently edged into three figures. His mother might leave him the house when she died, assuming she checked out before he did. That was his only retirement plan. His father's US Navy pension, and the house in Coronado, would go to Alicia.

"Have you always worked here?" he asked the patrolman.

"Two years now. Started in Arizona. Then El Centro. They like to move us around."

"You know anything about that house, the one at the mouth of Smuggler's Canyon?"

"The Honey Trap?"

"What's that?"

"You mean the place with the swimming pool?"

"Yeah. That's what you call it? The Honey Trap?"

"Some of the guys call it that."

"Border Patrol guys?"

"Yeah."

"Why?"

"I don't know. That's just what they call it."

"Must be a reason."

The patrolman glanced out the side window, then back at the road.

"It's a good spot to find UDAs," he said. "There's a place out back where they like to hide sometimes."

"You mean those boulders above the pool?"

"That's the spot."

"I saw a woman today, by the pool."

"Uh-huh."

"And that doctor guy, the one who stole my car. He was there too."

"I don't know about him."

"You've seen her before, though?"

"I guess I've seen somebody down there, a couple of times."

Rolly decided not to press the patrolman any further on the topic. A Border Patrol officer wouldn't admit voyeurism to a civilian, even accidental voyeurism.

"You know anything about the stolen car they found yesterday at the park?" Rolly asked.

"That's what you're working on? With the police?"

"I think it's related to my case."

"What's your case?"

Rolly told the patrolman his story. By the time he finished, they'd reached the bottom of the hill and turned onto Monument Road.

"When did this stuff all happen?" the patrolman asked. "The stolen car, I mean, the hearse."

"Friday night, maybe early Saturday."

"There was some weird stuff going on Friday night."

"You were on duty?"

"Distress call came in," the patrolman said. "Man down. Shots fired. Sounded like all hell broke loose."

"When was this?"

"Just after midnight."

"What happened?"

"Turned out to be fake. Somebody screwing with us. A call like that comes on, we're all in, full-force response. Helicopters and all. This guy took everybody offline for at least twenty minutes, had us chasing shadows over by the water plant."

"Where's that?"

"You know that new bridge across the river, where you enter the estuary?"

"Yeah. I think so."

"It's right at the bend in the road after you cross the bridge coming in."

Rolly remembered seeing a large gray building with blue and yellow pipes.

"What's that, about a mile from here?"

"Mile and a half," said the patrolman.

"Any idea who did it?"

"Some jerk got the codes, I guess."

"What's that?"

"We use digital radios now. The signal's encrypted."

"Oh."

"You can't break in unless you have the scramble codes."

"How do you get those?"

"They're listed in our duty call. They're assigned daily."

"You think it was one of your guys?"

"Better not be. That's a suspension for sure, without pay. He'd probably get fired, maybe even criminal charges."

"So everyone on duty that night would have gone over there, to the water plant?"

"Yeah. All in. That's what we're supposed to do."

"They didn't find anything?"

"Nope."

"You think it was a trick, then? Somebody trying to draw you away?"

"Looks like it. Maybe it's got something to do with your birds. What'd your cop friend say?"

"I think she was waiting to hear back from you guys."

They arrived at the entrance to Smuggler's Canyon. A half-dozen men dressed in fatigues milled about in front of their pickups, brandishing paint guns in Rambo-style poses. The patrolman turned in and parked the truck. Rolly's Mexican friends sat in the back of one of the pickups, their hands tied behind them.

"I'm not a coyote," said Rolly.

"I don't figure you are," said the patrolman, "but I'm going to talk to these UDAs first, just to make sure."

The patrolman climbed out, took Rolly's arm and helped him climb down from the backseat. He unlocked the handcuffs. They walked over to the prisoners. The row of trucks reminded Rolly of a country-western bar the band played twenty years ago. Framed by an oversized Confederate flag as a backdrop, The Creatures thrashed away at Elvis Costello tunes, The Jam, The Clash, some power-pop originals. The look in the eyes of the audience that night was a lot like the look the AFA men gave him now—sour peanuts, stale Budweiser and loathing. The patrolman directed Rolly to the detainees in the back of the truck. Their leader looked down at him. A fresh scratch of blood ran across the old man's forehead. Drying splatters of red, white and blue covered his shirt.

"*Este hombre allí*," said the patrolman, indicating Rolly. "*¿Usted lo ha visto antes?*"

The old man looked at Rolly, then back to the patrolman. His eyes looked tired.

"*Sí.*"

"*¿Usted le conoce?*"

"*No le conozco.*" The man shook his head.

"*¿Es él un coyote?*"

"*No.*"

"*¿Es seguro?*" The patrolman pressed the man.

"*Sí, estoy seguro. No estaba con nosotros. Nunca lo he visto antes.*"

"What'd he say?" asked Nuge.

"He says this guy wasn't with them," replied the patrolman. "He says he's not a coyote."

"You're gonna take the word of some wetback over me?"

Ritchie Blackmore's guitar riff from "Lazy" played inside Rolly's left pocket.

"Okay if I answer that?" he asked the patrolman. "It might be my police contact."

The patrolman nodded. Rolly took the phone out of his pocket and checked the name. It was Bonnie. He put the phone up to his ear.

"Hey," he said.

"What's going on?" Bonnie asked. "You didn't sound too good."

"It's that guy. From yesterday. He took my car. The Mexican doctor guy. And that Burdon guy, too. He was driving the hearse. He went into the house with that woman on the album cover."

"Hang on. Slow down. Are you okay?"

"I got arrested by the Border Patrol."

"What for?"

"I ran into some illegals, crossing the border. Some of the AFA guys stopped me. They think I'm a smuggler."

"Where are you?"

"Monument Road, at the entrance to Smuggler's Canyon."

"Is the Border Patrol there with you?"

"Yeah."

"Let me talk to them."

"Umm . . . okay."

Rolly held out his phone for the border patrolman.

"She wants to talk to you."

The patrolman furrowed his brow but took the phone from Rolly.

"Hello," he said. "Who's this?"

The patrolman took a few steps away from the group, keeping an eye on both Rolly and Nuge as he continued the phone conversation. Bonnie seemed to be doing most of the talking. Nuge stared at Rolly. Rolly averted his eyes, then brought them back.

"You still got that short-wave radio in your truck?" he asked.

"Yeah," said Nuge. "Why wouldn't I?"

"The patrolman told me somebody called in a fake emergency on Friday night."

"So?"

"Did you hear the call?"

"I wasn't on duty that night, remember?"

"Call said there was an officer down. Over by the water plant."

"So?"

"He said only someone with the scramble codes would be able to make a call like that."

"I expect he's right."

"Don't I remember you telling me something about having the codes?"

"You remember wrong."

"I think you know something about Friday night."

"Yeah? I think you're an asshole."

The patrolman returned with the phone and handed it to Rolly.

"Looks like you're off the hook," he said.

"You're gonna let him go?" said Nuge.

"His story checks out. He's not a coyote."

"We saw one of the illegals talking to him."

"Maybe you did. That's not a crime."

"I caught him yesterday, at the park, breaking into the bird sanctuary."

"That's for the rangers to deal with. File a report with the parks."

"This is such bullshit," said Nuge, taking a step toward the patrolman. "The guy's an asshole."

The patrolman glared at Nuge.

"Step away, sir, or I'll arrest you for interfering with a federal officer."

Nuge stopped in his tracks and glared at Rolly.

"Whatever," he said, retreating to his truck. "Let's process these fuckers so I can go home."

The patrolman reached into his belt and pulled out a small pad of paper.

"I have to write you a citation, Mr. Waters."

"What for?"

"Trespassing on restricted federal land."

"You mean up by the fence?"

"That's right."

"What about the guy who stole my car?"

"You say your car was down here?"

"Yes."

"That's not my jurisdiction. Sorry. Talk to Officer Hammond when she gets here."

"She's coming down here?"

"That's what she said. Can I see your license again?"

Rolly handed the patrolman his license and walked out to the edge of Monument Road. He looked across it, over the rough field that led to a run-down shack and corral. Jaime's green pickup sat in front of the shack. Four horses stood inside the corral.

"Mr. Waters?"

Rolly turned back to the patrolman.

"Need your signature."

Rolly signed the citation. The patrolman tore off a copy and handed it to him.

"Talk to your friend about that," he said.

"You think I can get out of it?"

"There's channels sometimes. Check with your friend."

"I will," Rolly said. "Can I go now?"

"Officer Hammond asked me to keep you here."

"I'm not going far," Rolly said. "I don't have a car." He

pointed toward Jaime's house. "I want to talk to the guy that lives over there."

A second Border Patrol truck appeared from around the bend of the road and pulled up next to Nuge's truck.

"You do what you want," the patrolman said. "I gotta process these UDAs."

The patrolman turned and walked back to the group. Rolly trudged down to the road, stopped by the entry gate to Tangerine's house and looked up the driveway. The hearse was gone. He rang the bell. No one answered. No one was home at The Honeytrap. He walked across Monument Road, then down the dirt track that led to Jaime's house. He hoped the old cowboy was home. He hoped the old cowboy was sober.

18

EL RÍO (THE RIVER)

As Rolly hiked past Jaime's corral, the palomino perked up its ears and stared at him. It whinnied once, then went back to whatever horses do to kill time. The other horses paid him no mind. He walked past Jaime's truck, stepped onto the porch and knocked on the front door. No one answered. Even in the fading light, you could see the house needed repair. Patches of bare wood showed through flaking paint. He knocked again. He looked through the windows for signs of life, but didn't see any. He grabbed the doorknob and gave it a twist. The door latch clicked. He pushed on the door and watched it swing open.

"Hello," he called, squinting into the dark interior. "Anyone home?"

No one answered. Rolly turned away. He surveyed the fields for anyone working them. He looked back toward Smuggler's Canyon, checking to see if any AFA goons or border patrolmen were watching him. The lights of Tijuana began to blink on above the border hills, floating on a shadow horizon. The sky had turned violet. He turned back to the open doorway. It was a black hole.

"Jaime?" he called through the doorway. "Señor Velasquez?"

A horse whinnied. Rolly looked back at the corral. The palomino raised its head again and looked toward the river, its ears pricked as if someone might be approaching from that direction. Rolly walked to the edge of the porch and peeked around the corner. He didn't see anyone. He looked back at the horse corral. The palomino stood alert, sniffing the air, staring down toward the river. Rolly stepped off the porch and crept down toward the back of the house. A light wind blew through the valley, whiffling through the dry grasses. Clouds of willows rustled along the river's edge thirty yards away. The faint smell of stale water, perhaps sewage, tingled his nose. The land was empty. His mouth itched.

Night would be falling soon, a darker shade than he was accustomed to. It never got dark in the city. The light sources just changed. He'd spent his life in the forlorn illumination of dive bars and clubs, the neon glare of twenty-four-hour diners and taco stands, the gnawing fluorescence of empty streets after closing time. That was his darkness. He owned it. Not this. The darkness was different down here.

He turned the corner of the house and examined Jaime's backyard. It was filled with junk, a repository for wooden boxes and old tools, large metal shapes of indeterminate function, some hard to identify in the fading light. The screen door on the back of the house clattered, unlatched in the wind. Two wooden steps led up to the door. He walked to the edge of the steps and called into the house again.

"Hello," he said. "Is anyone home?"

A fluttering sound, like bird's wings or a skittering rodent, came from inside the house. There had to be all sorts of vermin out here—rats and mice, maybe opossums or raccoons. He paused at the doorway, waiting for some wild creature to snarl at him.

"Hello," he called. "Is anyone here?"

No one answered, not even the rodents. As his eyes adjusted to the darkness, he could make out more of the room—a kitchen table and chairs, the sink and a countertop running out to the edge of the doorway. An irregular patch on the floor looked like motor oil. He reached a hand inside the door jamb, felt along the wall, found a pair of switches and flicked on the closest one. The porch light above his head enrobed him in bug-safe yellow. He flicked the second switch. A naked light bulb glared from below the ceiling fan. He looked down at the floor.

It glimmered because it was covered in blood, a deep wet red congealing to brittle purple at the margins. It flowed down toward the doorway, smeared with footprints along the edges, where it had dried. The smell flowed along with it. He covered his nose and mouth with his left hand, reached back inside the door and flipped off the lights. He pulled out his cell phone and stepped down into the yard. He punched in Bonnie's number and lifted the phone to his ear. He couldn't go into the house, not until the police and paramedics had checked it out first. As he waited for Bonnie, he considered the possibility that Jaime had butchered some animal, that a man of the backcountry might kill and dress his own meat.

A red light blinked, down by the river. It blinked again. He watched the light blink on and off in a steady pulse. A dark winged fear cut through him, blacker than the primeval night. He shut the phone, put it away and listened to the sounds of the river valley. His straining ears could make out the faint tink-tink of a car turn signal that came from the riverbank.

There were other sounds, too, ones he couldn't identify, scratches and whispers. Wild animals came out of hiding at night, coyotes and whatever coyotes ate. Wild humans, too, desperate, running away from their old life in search of a new one, nocturnal creatures moving in darkness where the world would not see them. Trying hard not to think about coyotes, or any large predators, he crept down to the river, toward the blinking red light.

He arrived at a shallow embankment leading down to the riverbed and heard water trickling through it in delicate streams. At the bottom of the embankment sat his Volvo. The driver's-side door leaned halfway open, caught on the bent support of a willow's branches. As the wind caught the door, it swung wider, as if someone were trying to get out, only to be pushed back by the branches as each gust of wind died. A creaking sound accompanied each push and pull.

Rolly sighed, shifting his weight. He was dirty already from the dried sweat and dust he'd collected in Smuggler's Canyon. A little extra mud was fair exchange for getting his car back, assuming he could drive it out of the river. He slid down the embankment, placing a hand on the roof of the Volvo to steady himself. The ground under his feet felt slick and slippery. Grabbing the back-door handle for support, he inched his way down to the driver's-side door in small, careful steps. The river mud slurped at his feet as if he had suction cups attached to his shoes.

The willow resisted as he pulled the door open. The branches crackled as they bent, complaining against the intrusion. He looked inside. A squirrel ran across the front seat, scampered up his arm and past his right cheek. He screamed, then steadied himself, and peered into the cabin. There was a dark shape inside—a man in a cowboy hat.

"Jaime," he whispered. "Is that you?"

There was no movement, no answer. He raised his voice.

"Jaime? Are you hurt? Jaime? Can you hear me? Jaime?"

The only answer he got was the whisper of willow leaves overhead, the murmur of water trickling through the riverbed. He closed his eyes and focused his listening, tuning his ears to any sound that would indicate the man was alive, a breath or a gurgle. There was none. He pushed his fingers against the cowboy's pant leg, prodding for some sign of life. The pants slid a couple of inches along the man's leg, but he didn't respond. A faint whiff of excrement settled into Rolly's nose, a singular note that stood out from the brackish chords laid down by the river. There was another smell, too, like the one in the house, the smell of blood.

As he pulled his hand back, it brushed against something soft on the car seat, a pair of women's satin panties. He jerked away from the cabin and slipped in the mud, grabbing the door handle to prop himself up. He leaned against the side of the Volvo and closed his eyes, waiting for his stomach to settle. His legs felt weak.

To steady himself, he ran through a set of minor pentatonic scales in his head, visualizing each note on the fret board until he'd played through each minor key, taking a deep breath between each fret position. It was a diversion he used to ward off the desire for alcohol, a way to keep his head above water, to take his mind off a bottle or bimbo. He worked his way through three sets of scales before feeling settled enough to try his legs again. Making his way to the back of the Volvo, he scrambled up the embankment, then stumbled back to the house. He paused in the yard to collect himself and sat down on the back doorstep. He pulled out his cell phone, took a deep breath and punched 9-1-1. It was time to call the police, any police, not just Bonnie.

He would have done it, too, except something hit him in the back of the head. He fell, face first, to the ground. Tiny footsteps cantered away from him. Through the inky clouds filling his brain, he heard a sound. It was an engine starting, a car pulling away. He pushed himself up but fell back on his face. As consciousness faded, he noticed a smell. It was earthy, like dirt. Or maybe horse manure.

19

EL RESCATE (THE RESCUE)

The voice split his head like a chainsaw.

"Rolly Waters!"

He opened his eyes, stared at the pockmarked surface above him, recognized it as acoustical tiles in the ceiling. Soft noises surrounded him, a hum of activity. He turned his head on the pillow and saw light creeping in from beneath drawn curtains. Shoes padded by on a linoleum floor.

"Welcome back," the chainsaw voice said, spinning down.

He lifted his head. There was someone perched on a stool in the corner of the room.

"Bonnie," he said, dropping his head back on the pillow. "Where am I?"

"Mercy. Chula Vista. Emergency."

"What happened?"

"I was hoping you could tell me."

"Somebody hit me," he said.

"Yeah. We managed to figure that part out. What else?"

"I don't know."

"You don't remember?"

"No. What time is it?"

"Nine thirty."

"At night?"

"Yeah. At night. Jaime Velasquez, you remember him?"

"The old cowboy, with the horses?"

"Yeah. We found him in your car."

"He's dead, isn't he?"

"Yeah. You kill him?"

"What? No. Of course not."

"Have you had any alcohol?"

"No."

"There was an empty tequila bottle on the front seat."

Rolly closed his eyes. Bonnie knew his history, the drinking, the accident.

"I'll take a test, if you want."

"I already had 'em give you one."

He looked over at Bonnie.

"You're clean," she said. "I just wanted to hear it from you."

A doctor burst in through the curtains.

"Well, it looks like you're doing better," he said, stepping between Bonnie and Rolly. "Let's take a look."

The doctor pulled a flashlight from his shirt pocket. He reached over, lifted Rolly's left eyelid, flicked on the flashlight and pointed it into Rolly's left eye, then repeated the procedure on the right.

"Everything looks normal in there," he said, placing the flashlight back in his pocket. "How are you feeling?"

"My head hurts."

"Well, that's to be expected. You've got a hairline fracture of your temporal bone, behind your right ear. We sewed up the skin there. Seven stitches."

The doctor stepped back and turned on the flashlight again. He moved the light to different positions, asking Rolly to trace its path with his finger. Then he asked some questions to test Rolly's memory—home address and mother's name. Appearing satisfied, the doctor pulled out a small notepad, scribbled something on it, then tore off the top sheet and handed it to Rolly.

"I'm giving you a prescription for Perkushen. It's a painkiller," the doctor said. "I wouldn't do any driving for a couple of days. Other than that, you should be okay."

"I can go?"

"We can check you in overnight for observation, if you want, but that's up to you."

Rolly rubbed his head.

"I want to go home."

The doctor went over the recommended dosage for the prescribed pills and advised Rolly to contact a physician if he experienced any blackouts or dizziness. Rolly nodded in acknowledgment. The doctor said good night, then left them alone again. Bonnie put her notes away and stood up.

"You ready?" she said.

"Where's my car?" Rolly asked.

"Impound lot," Bonnie said. "It's evidence. I'll drive you home. You're gonna need alternate transportation for a few days."

Rolly sat up, swung his legs over the side of the bed and waited for equilibrium to return.

"You okay?" Bonnie asked.

"I think so," Rolly said. He stood up.

"I got your phone," Bonnie said, handing it to him. "And your jacket."

Rolly put on the jacket and slipped the phone into his pocket. Bonnie ushered him out of the room and down the hall, through a door to the purser's office. He signed his checkout papers and handed the clerk a credit card, hoping it was good. The clerk handed him back a receipt. Max would be spending a lot of money on this case. Almost none of it would go into Rolly's bank account. Business completed, they walked out to Bonnie's car. She popped the locks and climbed in. Rolly opened the passenger door and sat down in the front seat.

"Buckle up," Bonnie said, starting the car. Rolly reached around, pulled the shoulder belt across his chest and inserted the buckle. They drove out of the parking lot, down three blocks to the freeway entrance, and merged into the late-night traffic, headed north.

"You told Officer Belmont that your car was stolen?" said Bonnie.

"Who's Officer Belmont?"

"The border patrolman who arrested you."

"He gave me a ticket. He said you could fix it."

"I don't know where he got that idea. Tell me about this guy who stole your car."

"It was that guy from yesterday, the one who bought my guitar."

"The little stoner in scrubs?"

"Yeah."

"Why'd he steal your car?"

"I don't know."

"You ever seen him before yesterday?"

"Not that I remember. He tried to run me over. In the canyon."

"What'd you do to this guy?"

"I didn't do anything. He came after me."

"You don't know why he tried to kill you?"

"I think he killed Jaime."

"What makes you say that?"

"He took my car. Jaime was in it, dead, the next time I saw it."

"What about yesterday morning?"

"Hmm?"

"At your house, before I came by? Did this guy act suspicious or threaten you in any way?"

"Well," Rolly said, trying to think of a non-incriminating way to provide Bonnie with the pertinent facts. "He started talking about whores, like maybe he thought I could find one for him. He sang this song, 'Rio,' talked about this hooker he knew. That was her name, I guess. Rio. He kept hinting around, like he thought I knew her, or how to contact her."

"Rio?"

"He said that was her name. Seemed to think I'd know where she was."

"You didn't think that was weird?"

"Sure, it was weird. A guy lights up a spleef and starts asking me about hookers, sure, but, you know . . ."

"No, I don't."

"I mean, the guy's a guitar player, after all."

"What's that mean?"

"We're all weird."

"You get his name?"

"I think he's a doctor."

"That's not a lot of help."

"Wait. I remember now. The hearse. The one at the impound lot. I forgot. I saw that Burdon kid driving it. He went to that house. Where the woman lives."

"You're sure you saw Mr. Burdon there?"

"Yes. He knows her. He knows Tangerine. The doctor was there, too, the orderly."

"The guy behind her? I thought he looked familiar."

"What do you mean?"

"I checked your phone. While you were out at the hospital."

"I think that's illegal."

"When'd you take those pictures?"

"This afternoon. Just before the doctor guy stole my car."

"Burdon was there too?"

"Yeah. Inside. He was playing a video game."

"Hmm," Bonnie said, furrowing her brow.

"What?"

"Maybe this doctor guy's the friend Mr. Burdon told us about, the one who borrowed his car Friday night?"

"The Border Patrol calls it The Honey Trap."

"What's that?"

"The house. Where she lives. Tangerine. The Border Patrol guys call it The Honey Trap."

"Sounds like you're not the only one who's seen a show."

"She told me yesterday she had an exhibitionist streak."

"This doctor guy said he was looking for whores?"

"Yeah."

"You think she's one of them?"

"He said her name was Rio."

"He's probably got more than one. Sounds to me like he might be running 'em out of that house."

"She was kind of a famous groupie, Tangerine I mean. Moogus told me about her."

"Moogus keeps up on those kinds of things, I suppose."

"Did you hear anything from the Border Patrol yet? He said there was a fake emergency call that came in."

"You mean Officer Belmont?"

"Yeah, him. Friday night. He said someone broke into their radio frequencies, called in an officer down, over by the water plant. But it was a fake. There was nobody there. All of their guys headed inland. Away from the beach."

"Away from the car. And our Jane Doe."

"Yeah."

"That's why they're not calling me. They want to get their story straight first."

"Maybe your Jane Doe is Rio."

"Our Jane Doe wasn't a prostitute."

"How do you know?"

"The coroner. He always checks for signs of sexual entry. Standard procedure. There weren't any."

"How far back can they check on that kind of thing?"

"What do you mean?"

"Maybe she hadn't been working for a couple of days."

"Our Jane Doe has something you don't find in prostitutes."

"What's that?"

"A hymen."

"She's a virgin?"

"Yep. Still intact."

"So much for my theory."

"Yeah. You remember that mark on her butt that you asked about, in the coroner's photographs?"

"Uh-huh."

"It's Virgo, the astrology sign. It's the virgin. She's the fourth one in six months."

"Why didn't you tell me?"

"I'm working with the Sheriff's Department on this. The murder investigations are theirs. It's their jurisdiction. Information only on an as-needed basis. I got involved because of the auto theft."

"I thought you said she drowned."

"She did, but the other three didn't. They've been dumped all over the area. Roofies in their system. Otherwise they're the same, similar anyway. Thirteen to fifteen years of age. Latinas. All with their hymens intact. All virgins. They all had that mark."

"You think it's some kind of serial killer?"

"I think you should stick to rousting deadbeat dads for a living and maybe step back from this one."

"I'll talk to my client."

"Don't tell him anything until I've spoken with him."

"I'll make sure he calls you tomorrow."

"Tell me more about your friend Jimmy."

"What do you want me to tell you? He's not really my friend."

"You know he's one of those AFA guys?"

"He is?"

"I saw him down there."

"You did?"

"Yeah. When I went down to get you. I saw him standing around with the other dopes."

"Did you talk to him?"

"Didn't get a chance. Your nine-one-one came in about two minutes after I got there."

"I didn't see him."

"How about Velasquez's truck?"

"What about it?"

"Officer Belmont saw someone driving out of Jaime's place,

in a truck."

"When was this?"

"About three minutes earlier."

"Did he see who was driving it?"

"He said it was a female. We got an APB out."

They sat in silence for a minute before Bonnie flipped on her turn signal, crossed to the far-right lane and took the Cesar E. Chavez Parkway exit off the freeway.

"I thought you were taking me home," said Rolly.

"I want to talk to this guy first. Rico Chacon."

"Who's he?"

"You never heard of Ricardo Chacon?"

"No. Should I?"

"He's only the most famous ex-cop in this town."

"He lives around here?"

"He runs a bar. Retired. You never heard of him?"

"No. What'd he do?"

"Chacon and his guys worked a special detail on the border. It was a while ago. Undercover. Tracking down bad guys that preyed on illegals."

"Coyotes?"

"Some of them pretended to be coyotes. They'd offer to take people across, then rob 'em. Most were just thugs, lying in wait. Assault, murder, rape. There was a lot of bad stuff going on in those canyons back then."

"When was this?"

"Twenty, twenty-five years ago. They made a movie about it."

"What's the name of the movie?"

"I don't remember. It's not important."

"So why are you talking to him?"

"I ran the address of that house, the one on Smuggler's Canyon, where your lady friend lives. There's a file. Cold case. Twenty years old. Chacon's listed as one of the investigators."

"What happened?"

"Somebody killed the owner."

20

EL SALÓN (THE BAR)

"Who was he? The guy that was killed?"

"Name was Lewis Spencer. Had a teenage daughter living in the house with him. She disappeared."

"They never found her?"

"If they did, it's not in the report. That's why I want to talk to Chacon."

"They never arrested anyone?"

"There were three possible suspects listed. One of them was an unknown UDA."

"A border crosser?"

"Yeah. A José Doe."

"Who were the other ones?"

"The missing daughter. And Jaime Velasquez. He's the only one they actually interviewed."

"Why'd they suspect Jaime?"

"Apparently Mr. Velasquez had some kind of sexual relationship with the girl. The father found out. They had an argument."

"Jaime was robbing the cradle, huh?"

"They dropped all the charges, including the statutory."

"But they never found her?"

"Not that I could tell. There's something you'll find interest-ing, about the girl."

"What's that?"

"She had red hair."

"You think . . .?"

"I think red hair is uncommon."

"What was her name?"

"It's not listed. Anyway, Chacon's the only person who was around then, other than Mr. Velasquez."

"And now Jaime's dead."

"Mr. Velasquez had a few drunk and disorderlies over the years. First one was about a year after the murder. Chacon was the arresting officer."

"Hmmn."

"Yeah, that's what I said. Hmmn."

Bonnie pulled into a parking lot next to a small Quonset hut. A fluorescent sign out front flashed "Rico's Roundup" in neon blue. They were about ten blocks from police headquarters, close enough to be handy, far enough out of the way that Chief Preston could avoid passing through and spotting San Diego's Finest stumbling out of the place.

"Cop bars make me nervous," said Rolly.

"You ever been to one?" Bonnie asked.

"No," he responded, envisioning a new level of hell, one that combined cheap liquor and his local constabulary. "But I'm not fond of the general idea."

"They're not in uniform. You won't know they're cops."

"I can always tell cops."

"Don't be a jerk."

"You been here before?"

"A couple of times. To be honest, it's not my kind of place, either."

They climbed out of the car and walked in. Three men sat together at the bar, chatting up the middle-aged matron who poured their drinks. At the pool table a hungry-looking woman leaned over the felt surface, lining up a shot while her male opponent leaned on his cue, watching her twitch. In the back corner of the room a bald man sat in a wheelchair. A snifter and a bottle of Courvoisier sat on the table in front of him. Bonnie walked over to the man in the wheelchair. Rolly followed her.

"Captain Chacon?" Bonnie said. The bald man nodded.

"I'm Detective Hammond. I called earlier."

A drop of Courvoisier hung off one end of Chacon's bushy mustache like amber sweat. Chacon licked his chops, wiped the amber away.

"Who's your friend?" he asked, raising one unkempt eyebrow.

"Rolly Waters," said Rolly, extending his hand. "An honor to meet you."

Chacon didn't move.

"You a cop?" he asked.

"No. I'm a private detective."

"I didn't think you were a cop," Chacon said, ignoring Rolly's outstretched hand. Rolly dropped it.

"You want a drink?" Chacon said.

"I'm on duty," said Bonnie, taking the chair next to Chacon.

Rolly contemplated the bottle of Courvoisier with the glazed look of a baby eyeing its mother's breasts.

"Just a club soda for me," he said, averting his gaze. "With a lime."

"Annie," Chacon called toward the bar, "Bring me a soda, with fruit."

The three men at the bar looked over at Chacon's table, then returned to their drinks. Rolly sat down next to Bonnie, using her as a buffer between himself and Chacon. He wanted to go home, crawl into bed, let his mother ply him with green tea and Kashi for a couple of days. He needed a detox. Chacon turned back to Bonnie.

"Nice delts, Officer Hammond," he said. "How much you press?"

"I've done two hundred," Bonnie replied.

Chacon whistled.

"You *chicas* are tough these days."

Bonnie blew past the compliment, if that's what it was.

"I wanted to ask you about a case file. It's from a long time ago."

"Lay it on me."

"About twenty years ago. Down at the border. Someone was killed near Smuggler's Canyon."

"A lot of folks got killed down there. Robbed, assaulted, raped. It was like the freakin' Wild West in those days."

"There's a house at the mouth of the canyon, big security fence and a swimming pool."

"Sure. I remember it. Guy who owned it thought the world was gonna end. It did, for him."

"You're referring to Mr. Spencer, the murder victim?"

"Yep."

Annie arrived with a glass of club soda and placed it down in front of Rolly. He stared at the bubbles clinging to the slice of lime.

"Jaime Velasquez?" said Bonnie. "Do you remember him?"

"Sounds familiar."

"You arrested him on a drunk and disorderly, about a year after the murder. A Mexican cowboy? Lived across the road, near the river."

"Oh yeah, Velasquez. What about him?"

"Do you know why Mr. Velasquez was a suspect in Mr. Spencer's death?"

"It should be there in the file."

"I thought you could provide some more details."

Chacon rubbed the top of his head and drank a shot.

"You know, I wasn't the primary on this. Just the originator. You should talk to the primary."

"The primary's deceased."

"Who was it?"

"Daniel Walters."

"Danny Walters is dead?"

Bonnie nodded her head.

"When'd he die?"

"Two years ago, according to his wife."

"Shit. Danny retired the same year as me. What'd he die of?"

"She didn't say."

"Christ, I never hear anything anymore. I mean I woulda liked to have gone to his funeral, sent flowers or something."

"I've got his number, his wife's, if you want to call her."

"Why would I call that bitch? She's the one probably killed him, gave him a heart attack."

Bonnie gave Chacon a moment to ruminate on his departed work mate, then steered the conversation back to the case.

"Was there any connection between Mr. Velasquez and the minor female that you know of?"

"We thought there was. It didn't pan out. Velasquez was just a horny little *campesino*. Why're you asking about him?"

"Somebody murdered Mr. Velasquez this evening. In his house. Someone slit his throat."

"No shit," said Chacon. He took a slug of Courvoisier.

"And Mr. Velasquez's truck is missing."

"Probably a border crosser. Those UDAs ain't all happy strawberry pickers, you know. Did they take anything else?"

"Not that we know of. Whoever killed Mr. Velasquez dumped his body in the river, along with Mr. Waters's automobile."

"My car was stolen," Rolly said, responding to Chacon's puzzled look.

"There was a pair of panties on the seat next to him," said Bonnie.

"What kind of panties?"

"Pink ones, with the words 'serpent' and 'jungle love' on them."

"Any blood on them?"

"Yes, there was. We assume it's Mr. Velasquez's blood."

"Make sure the lab doesn't fuck it up."

"Captain Chacon, this minor female in the report, the missing girl?"

"Yeah. What about her?"

"It says Mr. Velasquez had some sort of sexual relationship with her?"

"He wanted to. I remember that much."

"Meaning?"

Chacon swirled his Courvoisier around the side of his glass, set it down and stared at the oily liquid as it slid down into the bowl.

"The Chief put us down there, you know. In the canyons. Undercover. We dressed up like UDAs so no one could tell we were cops."

"I've read about it," said Bonnie.

"We worked the big canyon a lot. We'd start around dusk, down near that house, work our way up the canyon, see what we could find. It was a nice place, that house, had a swimming pool. Sometimes this girl would be out there, by the pool. She'd go swimming sometimes, take off her clothes. Nice-looking chick, young, in her teens, but her body was all there, if you know what I mean."

Bonnie nodded. Chacon continued.

"I won't say me and the boys were above taking a look now and then, but I mostly kept 'em on the straight and narrow. We had work to do. Anyway, there were these big rocks, boulders, on a little hill behind the house."

"That's where I was today," Rolly said to Bonnie. "When I took the pictures."

"I was on lookout one night," Chacon said. "Farther up the hill. It's just about dark and I see this shadow moving down in the canyon, somebody sneaking in behind those rocks. It just didn't look right, so me and Eddie went down there, snuck up on the guy. Caught the guy with his pants down, watching this girl and stroking his pud."

"It was Jaime?" said Rolly.

Chacon leaned forward, took a sip from his snifter and leaned back again.

"Gold star for the college boy," he said.

"Did you arrest him?" said Bonnie.

"Nah. The guy looked so embarrassed when we put the light on him, kind of pitiful, really. I didn't have the heart. He wasn't bothering the girl or nothing. She didn't even know he was there. I sent him home, made him promise to stay out of the area, never do it again."

"That wasn't the drunk and disorderly?"

"No. That came later. I felt sorry for the guy, living in that shack by himself, musta been kinda lonely. It was later they found the panties."

Bonnie's phone rang.

"I gotta take this," she said, glancing at the screen. She turned to Rolly.

"Tell him about your case, everything you told me." She stood up and stepped away from the table to speak on her phone.

Rolly turned to Chacon and ran through the events of his last thirty-six hours. He told Chacon about Jaime's ghost and the panties, the red-haired woman who lived in the house. The woman named Tangerine. He told him about the CD he'd found, the record albums in the back of the hearse.

"You ever seen my movie?" Chacon asked.

"I don't think so. What's it called?"

"*Border Lords*, that was the name of the movie. It had that Estrada guy in it, the one from TV. They told me they were gonna get Pacino, you know, to play me. They fucked up that movie. I mean the gun he carries around, it was huge, a Magnum, you know, like I was Dirty Harry or something. I couldn't a' run around in those canyons with something like that strapped to my leg."

"They like to exaggerate."

"No shit. They exaggerated about all the money I was gonna see, too."

Chacon poured himself another drink.

"You got that CD you were talking about?" he asked.

Rolly extracted the CD from his pocket and handed it to

Chacon.

"I ain't seen this in a long time," said Chacon. "It must've been Eddie that showed it to me. The record, I mean. Something looks different, though. They covered her up a little more."

"Eddie was one of your crew?"

"Yeah. Good kid. Had a serious hard-on for that chick."

"The minor female?" Rolly asked.

"Yeah," said Chacon. "Just between you and me, I think she knew we were up there."

"What makes you say that?"

"Just the way she acted sometimes. She knew what she had. Liked to show off."

"I've been up in those rocks you were talking about," Rolly said. "I was up there today. I saw the woman I told you about, out by the pool."

"It sure sounds like her," said Chacon, staring at the CD cover. "I'll give you that."

"She's about the right age, I think," Rolly said. "And Jaime— Mr. Velasquez, he seemed to think it was her."

"And Velasquez is dead," said Bonnie, returning to the table.

"The guy deserved it," said Chacon.

"He didn't seem like a bad guy to me," Rolly said.

"Not Velasquez. I mean the guy who lived in the house."

"What'd he do?" Bonnie said.

"You should ask Eddie about this," said Chacon, sliding the CD across the table to Rolly. "He followed the case, after we turned it over. Eddie was there when we found the guy. Eddie barfed. I remember that."

Rolly downed the last of his club soda. His stomach felt queasy.

"You want another drink?" asked Chacon.

"I'm fine."

"Do you remember anything else?" asked Bonnie.

Chacon poured himself another shot of Courvoisier.

"This might take a while," he said. "Sure you don't want a drink?"

21

LA HISTORIA (THE STORY)

"It starts with the guy in that house," Chacon continued. "The one that was killed."

"Mr. Spencer," said Bonnie.

"Yeah. He was this born-again type, bought the house down there for cheap, did some work on it. This is a few years before we were out doing patrols. Anyway, this Spencer guy moved in with his wife and daughter, fixed up the place. Did all the work himself, added a safe room, stocked it with supplies. He was really into this book that came out back then, *Earth's Final Hour* I think it was called. It was a big deal back then. End-of-times stuff, only the pure and righteous will survive, blah, blah, blah. This Spencer guy was into it big. He moved his family to the country so they could prepare for the end times, because the heathen cities would burn up in flames."

"Doesn't seem like they moved very far," Rolly said.

"That area was a lot more rural back then. Tijuana was nowhere near as big. San Ysidro was nothing, dairy farms and stuff. Guys like that are a couple shells shy of a full clip, anyway, if you ask me. Only God knows when the end times will come. That's what it says in the Bible. I guess he figured the Almighty would slice Baja off right at the border line, drag a line across it with heaven's razor, drown all those brown heathens and Catholics in the ocean, and he'd be rewarded with some nice waterfront property for his penitence."

"Must have been disappointed," said Bonnie.

"Yeah, but not half as bad as his wife. About a year after the big event doesn't happen, she decides she's had enough of the guy, takes off one night, never comes back. She's done with this shit. Leaves him, and their daughter, to fend for themselves."

"How old was the girl?" Bonnie asked.

"Fifteen, I think."

"Tough age."

"Yeah. They hadn't been sending her to school or nothing, either, just homeschooling, Bible studies stuff. That part of the county was really off the grid back then."

"Still is in some ways. Go on."

"Well, anyway, this guy, Mr. Spencer, he runs out of money. He's only saved enough to get him through the end times. I guess he thought he wasn't gonna need any after that. He'd already planted a few tangerine trees, so he marks out more groves, decides he'll go into business. He trades out part of his land to this Mexican cowboy that comes through, lets him live on the property."

"Jaime?" said Rolly.

"Yeah, Velasquez. Anyway, the cowboy lends a hand with the fruit trees, but that doesn't work out. Neither of them's really a farmer. A lot of trees die. Mr. Spencer and the cowboy don't really see eye to eye. Meanwhile there's more UDAs coming through every day, crossing the border, eating his tangerines, stealing whatever else they can find. This is back when they had those signs on the freeway, the yellow warning signs with the silhouette of the families crossing."

"I remember," said Rolly.

"Anyway, a lot of the UDAs were coming through Smuggler's Canyon, down past Mr. Spencer's place. He starts blaming them for all his troubles, his tangerines not growing and that.

He's out of money, so he decides he's gonna take something back, starts robbing the immigrants. We didn't know about that until later, after he was dead."

"Nobody reported him to the police?" Rolly said.

"Nah. These UDAs are afraid they're gonna get sent back across the border if they talk to the police. After Mr. Spencer took their money, put the fear of God in 'em, they were happy just to be alive and still in the USA. He wasn't the only bad guy down there, remember. A lot of the UDAs got hit by gangs before they made it that far. That's why the chief put us down there. The gangs'd leave 'em in worse condition than Spencer did."

"How long did this go on?" asked Bonnie.

"A few months, I guess."

"The report says his daughter may have been involved?"

"I don't remember anything about that. Danny might have been speculating there."

"What do you mean?"

"You remember that story I told you about the girl, hanging out by the pool, how we found Velasquez sitting up there in the rocks, peeping on her?"

"Yes."

"That's where we found the guy. That's where he got killed."

"I'm not sure I understand."

"He used that spot for a hideout. There were always some young bucks passing through, guys who couldn't help stopping for a peek at the Promised Land. They step in behind those rocks, take a break, get a look at the girl. Then suddenly there's a guy with a sawed-off, got 'em trapped, forces 'em to hand over their money and valuables."

"The Honey Trap," Rolly said.

"What's that?" said Chacon.

"That's what the Border Patrol calls the house. The Honey Trap."

"That's mine," Chacon chuckled. "I came up with that name. Guess it stuck."

"The report says he was stabbed to death," Bonnie said.

"Yeah. Me and Eddie found him. We were walking back down the canyon. It was sunrise, after our shift. Saw his body, out by those boulders. There was blood everywhere. I remember that. They musta got his carotid. The coyotes had been at him a little bit. It smelled bad. Eddie threw up. I remember that too."

Rolly felt queasy. He fished the lime out of his soda and bit down on it, fighting acid with acid. Chacon poured himself another shot and leaned back in his chair, swirling the liquor in his glass.

"I thought we should wait for support before going into the house, but Eddie started worrying about the girl, talking about how she might have been raped or kidnapped, might be dying in there. He took a look inside, while I waited down by the road."

"She wasn't there, I take it?" said Bonnie.

"No. A couple of sheriffs showed up, and an ambulance. Eddie came out, let us in through the front gate. The girl was gone."

Chacon pointed at the CD.

"Eddie picked up that album somewhere, showed it to me. It was later, maybe a year or so after the incident. We were on different details then. The patrol thing was over. It got all political."

"There's no mention of the album in the report."

"Eddie said he was gonna show it to Walters."

"It's not in the report."

"I guess it didn't pan out. Maybe it wasn't her."

"What about Mr. Velasquez? Why was he a suspect?"

"That day, when we found the dead guy, I knew whoever picked up the case would wanna talk to us, so we waited around at the scene. Danny came down, I guess. I told him about the cowboy, how we'd scared Velasquez outta his hiding place a few weeks earlier, how he'd been looking at the girl. Next thing I knew, they arrested him."

"It also says his truck was stolen."

"Yeah. They recovered it a couple days later. In the parking lot of that nightclub in IB."

"Pelicans?" Rolly blurted.

"Yeah. Pelicans. How'd you know that?"

"Yeah? How'd you know that?" said Bonnie, turning to Rolly.

"Something Moogus told me," said Rolly. "I showed him the CD cover. He remembered giving this girl a ride one night. We used to play down there. It was the same night Big Jimmy got stabbed."

"This is the same club where Mr. Bodeans worked?"

Rolly nodded.

"You played at Pelicans?" said Chacon.

"Yeah. A long time ago."

"That place was crazy. We used to hang out there sometimes after our shift. What was the name of your band?"

"The Creatures."

"No shit. What's your name again?"

"Rolly Waters."

"I remember them. You were the guitar player, right?"

Rolly nodded.

"Well, shit," Chacon said. "I thought you seemed familiar." He raised his glass to Rolly. "You survived Pelicans, you must be tougher than you look, college boy."

"Thanks," said Rolly, grateful for whatever respect Chacon granted him.

"Anyway, Danny found some panties in the cowboy's truck, had some blood on 'em. Combine that with my story, I guess Danny figured Velasquez for some kind of sex killer."

"But they dropped all the charges," said Bonnie.

Chacon shrugged.

"I don't know what happened," he said. "It wasn't my case. The last thing I remember about it was Eddie showing me that album. That's when I found out he'd been keeping up with the case. Actually, it was Eddie who told me a lot of that stuff I been telling you. You oughta talk to him."

"Would that be the Officer Sanchez who's listed in the

report?" Bonnie asked.

"Yeah. Eduardo Sanchez."

"You know if he's still on the force?"

"Nah. Eddie's a preacher, now. He got religion."

"You know how we can contact him?"

"He's got a storefront place, over on Island and Seventeenth."

"That's his church?"

"Yeah. Reverend Eddie. He got fired, you know. He was crazy about that chick."

"Did his firing have something to do with the case?"

"Eddie lost himself a little bit. You should talk to him."

"Thanks for your help, Captain," said Bonnie, rising from the table. Rolly stood up. Bonnie and Chacon shook hands.

"Hey college boy," said Chacon, turning to Rolly and extending his hand. "You're okay. We had some good times there at Pelicans. You're okay by me."

"Thanks," Rolly said, shaking hands, trying not to wince under Chacon's crushing grip.

"Oh, I almost forgot," said Bonnie. "That drunk and disorderly, when you picked up Velasquez. That was about a year later, right?"

"I guess, if that's what it says."

"You remember anything about it?"

"Not much. We ran into Velasquez walking up the canyon, singing like a fool, carrying a tequila bottle."

"You remember anything else? Something he might have said?"

"Nah. Wait. That's weird."

"What?"

"That song he was singing. I think it's on that record, the one Eddie showed me."

"'Jungle Love'?" Rolly said. "Was that the song?"

"How's it go?"

Rolly sang the chorus from the song Marley had played for him at the Cantina last night.

"Yeah, that's it," said Chacon. "That's the song."

22

LA IGLESIA (THE CHURCH)

As Bonnie pulled into the yellow zone near the corner of 17th Street and Island Avenue, church had just let out. Ragged old men and plump middle-aged women milled about on the sidewalk, sharing farewell amens as they headed home or back to the streets. It was not the best part of town—an empty, uncomfortable triangle of city blocks crammed in between the historic barrio to the south, the shipping district on the bay and the newly developed East Village and ballpark. A dim yellow light from inside the storefront spilled out on the sidewalk, a pallid beacon of heavenly grace.

"You awake?" said Bonnie.

Rolly jerked to attention. He'd slumped down in his seat, drifted off somewhere that wasn't quite sleep. He sat up and looked around.

"Yeth," he said. "I'm fine."

"This must be the place," Bonnie said. She opened the door and climbed out, walked around the front of the car to the sidewalk. Rolly opened the door, stepped out on the sidewalk and stumbled into Bonnie. She caught him by the arm, supporting his weight.

"Take it easy," she said.

"Tha' wath weird."

"You sure you're okay?"

"Give me a thecond . . ." He shook his head, trying to clear out the pile of cotton someone had stuffed inside it.

"You feel faint?"

"I think ith the drugth kicking in."

"You're talking kinda funny."

"I am?"

"Maybe you should wait in the car."

"Nah. I wanna talk to thith guy," Rolly said, shaking his head again. "I'm okay, juth a little high."

"Perfect," said Bonnie. She studied Rolly's eyes for a moment, then shrugged and set off for the front door. Rolly followed, on his vigilance. They walked through the crowd and stepped into the light of the storefront. The folks outside probably thought he was one of them, a drunken bum, brought in by the police for salvation.

A few devotees still lingered inside, gathered around a small man dressed in navy-blue trousers, with a loose blue tie dangling from the collar of his sweat-stained white dress shirt. There were four rows of folding chairs inside the room, a raised platform in back. Above the platform, along the back wall, hung two crosses on either side of a sign reading "Iglesia del Perdido." The man in the trousers glanced up as they approached.

"Welcome to God's place, my friends," he said, extending both hands.

"Thank you," said Bonnie. She reached into her pocket and pulled out a badge. "I'm Detective Bonnie Hammond from the San Diego Police Department. This is Rolly Waters. He's a private detective."

"I am Pastor Eduardo Sanchez," said the man. "How can I be of service?"

"You used to be on the force, I understand?"

"Yes. Many years ago."

"We've just been talking to Ricardo Chacon. He said you might be able to help us."

"I have not spoken to Captain Chacon in many years."

"It's about a murder case, back when you were both working the border. A cold case involving a young girl and her father."

The pastor's eyes turned to black holes for a moment.

"That was a long time ago," he said. "In a different life."

"I'd still like to ask you some things, if you don't mind?"

"Certainly, certainly. Let me finish here with my flock. I won't be long."

Bonnie nodded her head. Pastor Sanchez guided the remaining parishioners to the front doorway, then cast verbal loaves to those still lingering on the sidewalk before closing the door and returning.

"Please have a seat," he said, indicating the plastic folding chairs. He grabbed a chair, swung it around and sat down, facing across the back of it, an informal pose, and a defensive one. Bonnie and Rolly did as instructed, pulling up seats in front of him, the three of them forming points on a perfect isosceles.

"What did Captain Chacon tell you about me?" Sanchez asked.

"He said you took a special interest in the case. He thought you might have some more information for us."

"Is that what he said? That I had a special interest?"

"He said you followed the case more closely than he did, after Detective Walters took over."

"That is what he said? Exactly?"

"He said," Bonnie replied, making air quotes with her fingers, "'Eddie was crazy about that chick.'"

Sanchez smiled and looked down at the floor.

"It is true," he said. "I was crazy. *Loco.* Out of control. Why do you ask about the girl?"

"Jaime Velasquez was killed tonight. Murdered."

"I'm sorry to hear that. He was a decent man. He carried a large burden."

"You mean his drinking?"

"That was an escape from his burden. I prayed he would find God as I did."

"Was this burden in any way related to the girl, or her father?"

"What did Captain Chacon tell you?"

Bonnie related the story Chacon had told them.

"That is all true," Sanchez said, nodding his head when Bonnie had finished.

"Can you tell us any more?" she asked.

"You think this is connected to Señor Velasquez's death?"

"Two nights ago, a stolen car was recovered at Border Field Park. Inside the car was a case of old records. *Jungle Love* by Serpent."

Sanchez furrowed his eyebrows.

"This is strange," he said.

"Mr. Waters here thinks they're worth a lot of money."

"How much?"

"Five thouthand dollarth," said Rolly. "Thrink-wrapped with the orithinal panties."

"*¡Mi dios!*" said Sanchez, crossing his heart.

"You remember showing Chacon the record?" said Bonnie.

"Yes. Captain Chacon is correct. I was the one who showed it to him. I pray Señor Velasquez was not killed for these records."

"What makes you say that?"

"I do not know. I fear it is possible. What more can you tell me?"

"Before he died, Mr. Velasquez told Mr. Waters there was a woman, a 'ghost,' living in that house, the one on Smuggler's Canyon. He gave Mr. Waters a pair of panties like those that were packaged with this album. He claimed that he and this woman had engaged in carnal relations the night before."

"His mind was gone, from the liquor. He was repeating the old story."

"Mr. Waters went to the house. He met the woman. He says she bears a strong resemblance to the girl on the cover of the album."

"You spoke to her?" Sanchez asked Rolly.

"Yeth. Thee told me her name. Tantherine."

"What else did she say to you?"

"Thee thaid I was a thnake."

"Show him the pictures," said Bonnie. Rolly pulled his cell phone out of his pocket and scrolled to the pictures he'd taken of Tangerine by the pool. He passed the phone over to Sanchez. The pastor shifted in his chair as he looked at the photograph.

"Who is this man in the picture?"

"Have you seen him before?" said Bonnie.

"No. I do not know him."

"He threatened Mr. Waters earlier today, tried to kill him."

"I am sorry to hear that."

"What about the woman?"

"It's not a very good picture," said Sanchez, checking again.

"Here," Rolly said, taking the phone back. He scrolled to the second picture, the zoomed-in one. He handed the phone to Sanchez.

"You must understand," Sanchez said. "I do not enjoy looking at these kind of pictures."

"I understand, sir, but this is important to our case."

"There is someone else here, inside the house."

"His name's Sayer Burdon. His car was stolen two nights ago, ended up down at Border Field Park. Have you seen him before?"

"There was a man like this, here, several nights ago."

"Did you speak with him?"

"No. He left before the service had ended. Only now have I realized the purpose of his visit."

"What was that?"

Pastor Sanchez stood up, handing the phone back to Rolly.

"I will show you. Wait here."

Sanchez walked behind the stage, out of view, and returned a moment later, carrying a familiar cardboard box. He placed the box on the floor between them and opened the flaps. Rolly reached in the box and pulled out a shrink-wrapped copy of one of the records inside.

"Where'd you get these?" Bonnie asked.

"The man left them, under his chair. One of my parishioners discovered them and brought them to me."

"When was this?"

"Wednesday night. I was disconcerted at first. I did not understand. There was a note on the box: *To the priest. From the pallbearer.* It was a postcard. Of Border Field Park."

"You still have the card?"

"I thought it was a cruel joke. To put this woman in front of me. To bring up my past. I thought the man came to haunt me, that he was an agent of the devil."

"What makes you say that?"

"I do not think so now. I believe he intended these as a donation, a gift to my house of worship. To pay the rent. To keep our light shining. So that the sins of the past might be turned to God's glory. That is what I believe now. I only hope they were not purchased with Señor Velasquez's life."

"Mr. Velasquez was alive yesterday," said Bonnie. "Do you have the postcard?"

"It disturbed me very much. I threw it away."

"But the man in the photograph, you're sure he's the one who gave these to you."

"Let me see it again."

Rolly passed his phone over to Sanchez.

"I believe it is him," said the pastor, looking at the picture. "I am not sure."

"And the woman? Do you think she could be the girl from the album cover?"

"I cannot deny it."

"Captain Chacon said you were fired from the police force."

"That is true."

"Did it have something to do with this case?"

Pastor Sanchez rubbed his forehead. He looked out the window, into the night.

"I have renounced the serpent," he said. "I am saved."

"What about the girl?"

"She was married to him."

Rolly and Bonnie glanced at each other. Neither of them was much for religion. They preferred facts.

23

LA SERPIENTE (THE SERPENT)

"Pastor Sanchez," said Bonnie, "do you know what happened to this girl?"

"The serpent's fire was in me," said Sanchez, still staring into the darkness outside. "The Prince of Darkness used me as his agent."

"Could you maybe be more specific?"

Eddie turned back to them. His eyes had gone black again, looking inside. A trace of moisture covered them.

"Captain Chacon has told you of my interest in the girl."

"You were crazy about her."

"Yes."

"He indicated that she was often out by the pool."

"That is how it began. I was young then, full of my masculinity. I was anxious for glory, for adulation in the eyes of women. I joined the police force, but it was not the life I expected. It was drudgery—the rules and the forms. The criminals we arrested were mostly drunks and drug addicts. Sad, depleted men. That is who we put in jail."

"Yeah." Bonnie nodded. "That's the life sometimes."

"That's why I signed up with Captain Chacon. He was going

to get the real bad guys. And we did. Some of them. Rapists and murderers. There were gunfights some nights. I shot two men. I killed one of them."

"I've read the book," said Bonnie. "It sounds pretty crazy."

"Many nights, though, nothing happened. We would wait. All night. Eight hours alone in the hills. I think that is when I first lost myself. I did not know why I had chosen this path, my place in this world. Until the girl appeared. I would watch her, many nights, through my binoculars. She became my reason for continuance, for doing my job. It was not, for me, a sexual thing. Not then. I was married. She seemed like a child of Eden to me then, living in an innocent, pure world, a golden angel in blue water. My job was to protect her, to keep her safe. I could manage my travails so long as I could keep her there, safe. She lived on an island of bliss in this dark world. That is what I thought, anyway."

"Captain Chacon indicated you were very concerned about her, when you found her father dead."

"I had seen women, in the canyon, who had been raped by gangs of men. Raped and killed. I feared the same, that somehow I had failed to protect her. There was blood in the house."

"Captain Chacon suggested you might have lost your job because of this case."

Sanchez flattened his hands against each other for a moment, as if in prayer, then reached into the box and pulled out an album.

"I have wished often never to have seen this," he said. "I went to a concert, where the band was playing."

"When was this?"

"After the album came out, not quite a year later. I went backstage, to talk to them, to ask about the girl. They were reluctant, at first. I used my badge to threaten them with statutory rape, contributing to the delinquency of a minor, whatever I could think of. They directed me to their lawyers. From the music company. In Los Angeles. The lawyers took me to the girl."

"You found her?"

"Yes."

"Why isn't that in the report?"

"I was not on official police business. No one knew of my quest. I was a serpent in service to the Devil."

"Where was the girl?"

"She was in rehab, one of those expensive movie-star places out by the ocean, in Malibu. The music company lawyers put her up there. She had become addicted to cocaine. To sex. They were protecting the band members."

"Because she was underage?"

"Yes. And because of the child."

"Some guy in the band got her pregnant?"

"She had carnal relations with all of them. The lawyers took care of everything. They kept it a secret. The child was placed in a foster home."

"Cleaned up nice and tidy," said Bonnie.

"Yes. They set up a trust fund for the child, using royalties from the song."

"'Jungle Love'?" Rolly asked.

"Yes."

"Why didn't you report any of this?"

"I began to visit her, you see," Sanchez continued. "No one else knew. Every weekend, I would drive up to Malibu. I lied to my wife. I convinced myself that I was doing police work, for the case. I wanted to help this girl. I told her about my old job, on the border, how I used to watch her from above, in the hills, how I had failed to protect her. She began to accept me. She told me of her father, how he had tried to protect her, after the serpent had married her. How he lay in wait and struggled with the serpent each night. Until he was killed."

"Captain Chacon said something about her father robbing the UDAs."

"He used her as bait, you see. As I heard more of her story, I began to understand. It was a deception he put upon her, a punishment."

"What did she do?"

"It was he who made her go out there, by the pool, without clothing, while he waited, hidden in the rocks above. She would hear him nightly, up in the canyon, battling with the serpent."

"So, he was up there robbing these guys all the time, anybody who stopped by to take a look?"

"Yes. He would preach to them. '*¡Renuncie al diablo! ¡Renuncie la serpiente!*' she would hear him say."

"What about this 'marrying the serpent' stuff?"

"Thath the name of the band," Rolly said.

"Yeah, but that was afterwards, right?" Bonnie asked Sanchez.

"Yes," he replied. "I believe she was drawn to the band because of their name. That is how she understood the words of her father. The girl was an innocent. She knew so little of the outside, the real world."

"Captain Chacon said you caught Velasquez looking at her one night."

"Yes, but that was not the whole story. It began when she went to Señor Velasquez's house. I believe, in her mind, that is when it began. And her father's. It created the rift between them —Señor Velasquez and her father."

"What happened?"

"One day she went to visit Señor Velasquez. I do not know why. He had been friendly to her, I believe, not as stern as her father. Her mother had left them, you see. The girl had no other friends. Velasquez was not at home this day. She went into his bedroom, found magazines that he had, of naked women and men. She returned to her house, ashamed, but she could not stop thinking of the things she had seen. Each morning she waited until her father and Velasquez would go to work in the trees. She would go down to Velasquez's house and look at the magazines. She began to imagine herself as those women. She imagined herself with Señor Velasquez. She became flirtatious with him, less concealed."

"How so?"

"She began to be less careful, at first, moving things, leaving pages of the magazines open. She was a phantom to him, a ghost. She would climb in his bed, leave her scent and strands of hair, and more intimate things."

"Her panteeth?" said Rolly.

Sanchez nodded.

"Yes."

"She told you all this?" Bonnie asked.

"Yes. I confirmed much with Velasquez."

"You spoke to him too?"

"Yes. I told him of the child."

"You thought it was his?"

"I thought it was possible."

"He must have figured out she'd been in his house."

"He knew from the very first time. It was a great torment for him. He began to desire her. He did not wish to cross with her father. He consorted with harlots, but he could not stop thinking of the girl."

"Her father found out then?"

"Yes. It began with the pool, you see. One night she awakened. She felt restless. She went outside, in back of the house, by the pool. Her father was asleep. She felt someone watching her. She thought of Señor Velasquez, and his magazines. She took off her clothes. She posed as they do in the magazines. Again, the next night, and several more nights. One night, a man came to her. He took her in carnal embrace."

"Velasquez?"

"She could not describe the man, except that he spoke a strange language."

"Spanish?"

"I believe so. The next night her father discovered her. Out by the pool. He became greatly agitated. She told him everything that had happened. He told her she had sinned, that she had been with the Serpent, Satan's agent, that the Serpent would return for her soul. That she would only be saved if they captured and exorcised him."

"That's when he started these stakeouts?"

"Yes."

"How long did this go on?"

"Several weeks. She heard the shotgun go off one night."

"When her father was killed?"

"Yes. The serpent came to her, out of the rocks."

"She saw him? The killer?"

"She accepted him into her life. He was a pitiful creature. Wounded. She brought him into the house and dressed his wounds. He had the head of a snake, a mark upon his mouth, and great teeth. That is how she described him."

"You never told Detective Walters about this?" said Bonnie.

"It had been more than a year since her father's death. Señor Velasquez had been released. They would not find the man, anyway. It seemed to me that the man who killed her father had done so in self-defense."

"So, you agree with the report, that the killer was an unknown UDA?"

"It would do nothing for the girl to have the police in her life."

"Is that why you lost your job?"

"The girl's story touched me. Her mother was gone. Her father was dead. The more I spoke to her, the more I began to feel a deepening relationship between us. She trusted me. I cannot say what it was then, but I began to love her, in some way. Perhaps I am denying myself, but I did not feel it as sexual. Not then. I was the only man who could protect her. That is how I felt. I knew also that I wanted to keep her close to me. I could not lose her. That is when the serpent came. The voice of Satan spoke to me."

Sanchez paused, then cleared his throat.

"My wife and I, we tried to have children. We had been married three years then, but the Lord had not blessed us. My wife had become listless, forlorn. We no longer had a physical relationship. I do not know when it started, but I began to think of the child of this girl, that my wife and I could take care of it, that somehow it was a gift to us. I spoke to the lawyers. We made an arrangement."

"You adopted the baby?"

"Yes."

"Did your wife know about the girl?"

"I said it was temporary, at first, that this baby needed some-one, that his mother was injured, in the hospital. She believed me. She was happy."

"What happened to the girl?"

"I continued to visit her. Every weekend. I would bring her small gifts, even cigarettes. I should not have done that. I saw the marks later. She would burn herself with the cigarettes."

"On her neck?" said Rolly.

"Yes."

"Her father had done it to her. As a warning, to remind her of the fires of hell, how it would be if she remained married to The Serpent, if he did not save her. How do you know of this?"

"The woman I saw today. The man did it to her."

"The one in the picture?"

"Yes."

"It is the same. It must be her."

"You're sure?" said Bonnie.

"Yes. It can be no other. It is what she desires. I have seen it myself. I have done this thing."

"So, you're saying . . ."

"Yes, Officer Hammond. I broke the bonds of my marriage. That is why my wife divorced me. I broke the oath of my office. I had carnal knowledge of this girl. The serpent entered my heart. I lost my job. I lost everything."

24

———

EL FANTASMA (THE GHOST)

"Hell of a story, huh?" said Rolly, as Bonnie drove him back to his house. His head felt clearer. The drugs had faded.

"He crossed the line," Bonnie replied. "Way over the line."

"I felt kinda sorry for the guy."

"Not me."

"Not a little?"

"Not the least. Stealing babies, sleeping with minors. He took a vow to uphold the law."

"She wasn't a minor when he slept with her. They let her out on her eighteenth birthday, remember?"

"That's what he told us. Don't forget hiding evidence and obstruction of justice."

"Well, yeah, there was that."

"And abusing his authority under color of law."

"What's that?"

"That last stuff he told us, how he put the girl up in a motel after she got out of rehab. Getting that deal from the owner to give him the room for nothing. You think you'd get that kind of deal?"

"If I had something on the owner, I might."

"Exactly what I'm saying. It was a protection racket. And don't forget him thinking about murdering his wife."

"He didn't go through with it."

"Only because she found out about the girl first."

"That's why he got fired, huh?"

"Any and all of those things, probably. Take your pick."

"I thought maybe you read something about it in the book, that *Border Lords* thing."

"This stuff happened after the book ends. I'll check with Internal Affairs. They'll have his records."

They passed under the Laurel Street Bridge. Rolly looked out the side window, up toward the lights of Balboa Park.

"She was a Royal Tingler, that's for sure."

"What's that?" asked Bonnie.

"Something Moogus used to say, back in the old days. The hottest girl in the club, the one he'd get stuck on, the one he couldn't stop looking at."

"The one he couldn't stop harassing?"

Rolly chuckled.

"We used to have contests."

"I don't wanna know," Bonnie snorted.

"It changed some, the meaning," Rolly continued. "We used it to refer to anything you were jonesing about, something you just had to have, that makes you crazy until you get it. Drugs were the same way. Alcohol. Jimmy said it about his burrito the other day."

"Speaking of Mr. Bodeans . . ."

"You're sure he was with those AFA guys?"

"He's hard to miss."

"It makes sense now. His trying to scare me."

"Are you saying Mr. Bodeans threatened you?"

"He stopped by to see me at Patrick's last night, started telling me about how dangerous things could be down by the border, that I needed to be careful with all the drug gangs and stuff that were down there."

"He's right about that."

"He said he was just looking out for me, being a buddy."

"Mr. Bodeans is not your friend."

"I've been trying to tell you that. Are you going to arrest him?"

"Let's just say he's near the top of my list."

They were silent a moment, thinking separate thoughts. Then Bonnie spoke.

"I think you should throw in the towel on this one," she said.

"I need the money."

"Forget the money. This is dangerous. Tell your client it's a murder investigation now. He'll understand."

"The tire tracks are my case. I need to finish it."

"You're in over your head."

Rolly shrugged.

"Only my whole freakin' life."

Bonnie went silent, staring out the front windshield, up the road. Rolly thought for a moment, then turned back to her.

"It's just that, you know, there's something about that kid, the Burdon guy."

"What about him?"

"He kind of reminds me of me at that age."

"You were that weird?"

"I'd obsess over things like he does, playing those video games, except for me it was the guitar. I wouldn't let myself out of my room sometimes until I'd figured a part out, something I heard on a record."

"Nothing wrong with being focused."

"It was a defensive thing, though. Because of my parents."

"My dad was a drunk, you know," said Bonnie.

"Yeah, you've told me."

"You got this thing, just like he did. You get fixated on one thing and that's all you think about. Like that Royal Tickler or whatever it is."

"Royal Tingler."

"You've got an addictive personality type. I've seen it before."

"So now you're a shrink?"

"Okay, forget it. I'm just suggesting you step back and think about things, maybe take a wider view of the situation you got yourself in."

"Okay, okay. I'll think about it."

"It wouldn't hurt to take my advice now and then."

"I said I'd think about it. Is there anything else?"

"No."

"Good. I want to go home."

Bonnie exited the freeway. She pulled up at the stoplight on Robinson.

"On second thought, can you drop me at the drugstore?" said Rolly. "I want to get this prescription filled. Over on Fifth."

"I ain't your freakin' chauffeur," said Bonnie. She turned left anyway, drove down four blocks, then into the Rite Aid parking lot.

"How old do you think that kid is?" she asked, pulling to a stop in the fire lane outside the store.

"Burdon?"

"Yeah. How old?"

"I don't know—nineteen, twenty, maybe a little more?"

"Sanchez didn't say anything."

"What's that?"

"Just a thought. I'll see if I can find Sanchez's ex-wife."

"You want to get her side of the story?"

"I want to find out what happened to that baby."

Rolly nodded. His head hurt. He needed more pills.

"Can I go now?" he said.

"Nobody's stopping you."

Rolly climbed out of the car and shut the door. He felt stupid, standing there, watching her drive away. Bonnie had said something important, but he was too tired and in too much pain to hear it. He entered the store, walked to the back and handed his prescription to the pharmacist behind the counter. The pharmacist was a Latino man named Lucius. He looked about thirty years old, wore a pink blouse under his lab coat and stood about five-ten in spike heels.

"So, what's on the menu tonight?" said Lucius, reading the doctor's scrawl.

"I cracked my skull," Rolly replied.

"Oh, honey, what happened?"

"It was an accident. My car. I, uh . . . It's complicated."

"Bad day, huh? Well, give me a couple of minutes."

Lucius walked into the back to fill the prescription. Rolly leaned against the counter and closed his eyes, listened to the low buzz of the fluorescent ceiling. His thoughts drifted. Dark shapes and shadows loomed toward him.

"Mr. Waters?"

Rolly jerked awake. Lucius had returned with the prescription.

"I'm here," Rolly said.

"I need your driver's license."

Rolly passed over his driver's license and a credit card.

"You been on this train before?" the clerk asked as he slid the cards through the register.

"Hmm?"

"The Perkushen train. One dose as needed, no more than six a day."

"Okay."

"Drink plenty of water. No alcohol. You don't want to drive or operate heavy machinery."

"Uh-huh."

Lucius returned the license and credit card and pushed the credit card slip across the counter.

"You got someone to drive you home?" he asked, as Rolly signed the slip.

"No. I'm walking. It's close."

"You got any heavy machinery?" Lucius winked.

"No," Rolly said. He signed the slip and passed it back to the clerk, too tired to entertain Lucius's flirting.

"Here you go, then," said Lucius, stapling the receipt to the bag and passing it to Rolly. "Twenty boxcars on the Perkushen choo-choo."

"Thanks."

"Get some rest now, honey," said Lucius.

"Yeah," Rolly said. "Thanks."

He picked up a ham sandwich and a bottle of iced tea from the cold cases, paid for them and left the store. Pausing outside, he opened the pills, knocked one back with a slug of iced tea, placed all the items back in the bag and started toward home. His head hurt.

There had been a time, when he first started working for Max, that a private investigator's life seemed quiet, almost magically dull, an orderly sanctum far removed from the misspent evenings of his rock-and-roll youth. He put in his days on the computer in Max's office, or at the library. He chatted up clerks at the Hall of Records who could help him find the right documents. Sometimes he'd drive out to the location of a legal dispute, photograph the scene. It was easy stuff. That, and a regular paycheck, gave him the illusion of normalcy, of competence. But things had changed after Max retired, when Rolly went into business for himself. Bonnie was right. He was in over his head.

He stopped at the corner of Fifth and waited for the traffic light. The pain in his head eased. The lights of the city, the cars and pedestrians, began to converge in a dazzling harmonic hum. Three young women approached him, crossing the street. They were gorgeous, the most beautiful women he'd ever seen in his life—Royal Tinglers all.

"Good evening, ladies," he said to them.

The women giggled as they stepped around him, giving him a wide birth. For some reason Rolly's right hand appeared in front of his face, brandished in chivalric flourish. He put his arm down. No wonder the women laughed. The high had jumped him even faster this time.

The light changed. He crossed the street and continued down the block, relieved there were only two-and-a-half more blocks to go. He turned down Eighth Avenue. The city lights faded. He heard someone singing. "Sweet Baby James."

He walked past the front of his mother's house, two stories tall with gabled windows, and turned into the driveway. He walked back toward his flat. The Perkushen might bring out his inner James Taylor, but he wasn't so high he couldn't find his way home in the dark.

When he entered the backyard, he came to a halt. So did "Sweet Baby James." There was a truck parked in the gravel driveway. It looked familiar: an old Chevy, rusty and battered. He caught his breath and snuck in closer, hoping the gravel under his feet didn't sound the way it did in his head, icebergs cracking. He peeked into the bed of the truck and spotted some leather halters, a long string of rope arranged in a lariat. As if by magic, Jaime's old truck had appeared in his mother's backyard.

The light over his mother's porch steps flashed on. Rolly ducked down behind the truck cabin.

"Hello," said his mother. "Is someone there?"

Rolly lifted his head.

"It's me, Mom."

"What are you doing, dear?"

"How did this truck get here?"

"You've got a visitor."

Rolly stepped out into the light.

"Who is it?"

"A young woman. She's in here with me."

"A woman?"

"Yes, dear. Why are you acting so strangely?"

"I thought it might be someone else."

"Are you in some kind of trouble?"

"No."

Rolly walked to the bottom of the steps.

"What's that you've got there?" said his mother, indicating the plastic bag.

"Dinner."

"Come on in, dear. We're having tea. I'll make you some."

His mother turned back inside the house. Rolly climbed the steps and followed her into the warm light of the kitchen, wrinkling his nose at the onslaught of rose hips and incense. A teenaged girl sat at the kitchen table, holding a large, white mug painted with yin and yang symbols. She had long black hair and wore a dark blue Mexican blouse with bright yellow daisies stitched into the fabric. She looked like one of the girls in the pictures on Marley's computer, like the girl in the coroner's photographs. She smiled at Rolly, young white teeth beneath cabernet lips, then fixed her eyes on his with a charcoal-black stare. She wasn't the least bit deceased.

"What's your name?" Rolly asked. The girl stared at him.

"*¿Como se llama?*" said Rolly's mother.

"*Me llamo Rio,*" the girl said.

The chorus of the song blazed into Rolly's head. He saw the little doctor's face, his fierce teeth, a pair of pink panties balanced delicately on the point of a scalpel. He thought about what might happen to them if the doctor returned.

"We have to get out of here," he said. "All of us. Now."

25

LA MUCHACHA (THE GIRL)

Rolly opened the front door of the Villa Cantina and showed the girl in. A crowd stood inside, waiting for tables. He took Rio's hand and worked his way through the waiting customers to the hostess station. Vera was perched on a stool behind the stand, overseeing the late-night reservations.

"I need to thee Hector," said Rolly. His tongue had bloated up again from the Perkushen.

"What's this all about?" Vera said, as she sized up Rio, assessing the level of trouble Rolly had dragged in.

"I need thumun who thpeak Thpanish," he said. The drugs had kicked in again.

"I speak Spanish," said Vera.

"Thumplathe private."

"Hector's helping out in the kitchen. You'll have to wait."

Rolly nodded.

"You want a table?" asked Vera.

Rolly looked at Rio. He was hungry. She probably was, too. It wouldn't hurt to eat. It might do them both good. They wouldn't have much to talk about with his limited Spanish, but they'd be safer hidden away in a booth, just another mismatched couple out on a first date.

"Okay," he said.

"It'll be twenty minutes."

They took a seat in the waiting area. Rolly gave Rio what he hoped was a reassuring look.

"*Un hombre,*" he said, searching for the words. "*Un hombre que habla ethpanol aquí.*"

Rio nodded, turning her head to survey the scene. Her eyes brightened as she looked over the customers—date-night couples dressed to impress; groups of friends absorbed in chummy banter. Rolly sighed and closed his eyes. The dense chatter of the crowd grew distant and soft, as if someone had wrapped pillows around his ears.

His mother was safe, at least for now, ensconced with their neighbors, Doug and Will, the gay couple who lived next door. His mother had let them use her kitchen last summer, while theirs underwent renovation. As Rolly saw it, they owed her, but it wasn't a hard sell. The two men welcomed her without much fuss. He warned them against opening the door for anyone they didn't know, to call the police if they heard anything funny, that he'd return in the morning.

"Rolly?" a voice said, interrupting his feather-bed thoughts.

He opened his eyes. Vera stared down at him.

"Yeah?"

"Hector said to put you at the chef's table."

"Wherth that?"

"Back in the kitchen. He thought you could talk while he worked."

"Thure, fine."

Vera led them to the back of the restaurant, into the kitchen, and seated them at a tiny booth near the rear exit. The kitchen looked even more crowded than the dining room as Hector's staff, a motley bunch dressed in white aprons and hairnets, minced cilantro and onions, folded tortillas around steaming fillings, and doled out green and red sauces on brightly colored plates. They barked to each other in snippets of Spanish and English, dashing from stovetops to storage bins, too busy to give more than a cursory glance at the middle-aged man and his pretty young companion who'd appeared in their kitchen.

Vera left them with a bowl of guacamole, chips and a trio of salsas. Rolly grabbed a chip, scooped up a hunk of the chunky green dip and shoved it in his mouth. Recovering his manners, he indicated to Rio that she was welcome to partake. She took a ladylike portion, chewing it slowly as she looked around, wide-eyed, soaking up the scene like a sponge.

Hector emerged from the frenzy.

"*Hola*," he said.

"*Hola*," Rolly replied.

"For special guests," Hector continued, indicating the table. "Just like the high-class joints."

"Theemth a little cramped," Rolly said as a waiter squeezed through behind Hector.

"That's what makes it special," Hector replied. He turned to Rio. "*Buenas noches, Señorita.*"

Rio batted her eyes, tilted her head like a little girl and smiled. She hadn't spoken one word on the drive down.

"Thee dunthn't thpeak Englith," Rolly said. "I need to athk her thum quethdionth."

"Are you drunk or something?"

"No."

"You sound drunk."

"Ith painkillerth."

"What happened?"

"Thumbody hit me. Lithen, thith girlth in trouble. Sumbodeeth lookin' for her. He, heeth a killer."

"No shit?" said Hector, raising his eyebrows. "A killer?"

"Heeth looking for me, too."

"Eechi Mama, Rolly. Why don't you go to the cops?"

Rolly shook his head.

"The polith might depaart her," he said.

"Wait," said Hector. "She's one of those girls we saw on the computer, isn't she?"

"I think tho," said Rolly.

"Geez, Rolly. You got *cojones*."

"Nahh . . ."

"You're *muy loco*."

Rolly shrugged. He wasn't brave. He wasn't crazy. That left just plain stupid. He had shelves of stupid stacked up in his brain, like bottles of Kahlúa at a Tijuana tourist shop.

"*Ayúdame*," said Rio.

"What'd thee thay?" Rolly asked Hector.

"She's asking for help," said Hector.

"How about it?"

"I'm kinda busy, right now," said Hector, looking like a bug had flown down his throat. It was easy to carry a picket sign, spout politics over *café con leche*, much harder when it got down to cases, when reality showed up at your door.

"*Por favor*," Rio said again. "*Ayúdenos*."

Hector sighed, swallowed the bug and reached into his pocket. He pulled out a set of keys.

"Vera will kill me for this," he said, tossing the keys on the table. "Outside back, there's a studio apartment up the stairs. We stay there some nights when we're here late and have to open up in the morning."

Rolly grabbed the keys.

"I should call Roberto," said Hector.

"Whoth that?"

"My lawyer. He handles all the green card stuff for my employees."

"No. No lawyerth. Not now."

"Okay," Hector said. "I'll be up in a while, when things settle down here."

Hector turned and headed back into the fray. Rolly stood, signaling for Rio to follow him. He grabbed the basket of chips and guacamole and pointed toward the back door.

"Thith way," he said.

Rio frowned, then stood and followed. They walked out into a narrow alley that smelled like old grease. A rickety stairway led up the back of the building. Rolly climbed the stairs, rebalancing the chip basket on one arm as he tried different keys in the lock. He found the right key, lifted the tumbler and opened the door. He looked back down the stairs. Rio stood on the bottom step, drenched in a pool of light spilling out from the kitchen. She looked as if she might run away, out to Tenth Avenue, into the city. She had a thirty-foot head start over flat pavement. She was young. He'd never catch her.

From a rarely used corner of his brain, Rolly extricated a few more words of Spanish.

"*No peligrotho,*" he said, recalling the words he'd seen on yellow warning signs. "*No peligrotho. Eth bueno.*"

He nodded toward the open door. Rio crossed her arms.

"*¿Es verdad?*" she said.

"*Yeth. Verdad. Mi verdad. Mi no peligrotho.*"

Having told Rio he was truth itself and not danger, he flashed a smile, the last and best weapon he had in the world. It was a goofy, lopsided thing many women had trusted over their own common sense, the scruffy grin of an abandoned Labrador retriever who only needed a little care and affection to become a faithful companion.

It still worked. Rio uncrossed her arms and climbed the stairs. Rolly entered the apartment and found the light switch. A naked light bulb glared from the ceiling. Rio stepped in beside him like a tentative house cat assessing new digs.

The apartment was small, a bit forlorn, saved from grimness by the decor on the walls: large fans made from palm fronds, colorful photos of rural Mexican towns, pop-art posters of Latino revolutionaries—Cesar, Pancho and Che. A full-sized bed stood at the opposite end of the room, below a garret window. Two chairs and a table, made of tanned hides stretched over rough-cut wooden frames, stood against one of the walls. A vase of declining flowers sat on top of the table, next to a portable CD player, a bowl of fruit and a yellow notepad. An open door led into a bathroom on the opposite side of the room.

Rolly placed the guacamole and chips on the table, motioning for Rio to sit and partake with him. As they munched along in the glaring light, he found himself wondering how old she was —fifteen, sixteen, possibly older. Her skin looked as smooth as coffee ice cream. He wanted to touch it. He took another chip, stabbed it into the guacamole. That kind of thinking would only lead to new levels of hell.

He turned away, surveyed the room again and spotted something stashed under the bed that looked like a guitar case. He walked to the foot of the bed, knelt down and slid the case out, undid the brass latches and opened the lid, revealing a mahogany-topped Taylor acoustic. He lifted the guitar from the case, took a seat on the end of the bed, strummed a few chords and adjusted the tuning. The guitar was beautiful, with a silky, smooth action and resonant tone. He looked back at Rio. Her eyes remained bright and curious. The rest of her face told him nothing.

He leaned into the guitar, playing more forcefully, stretching the strings, plucking out country-blues licks, combining phrases and turnarounds from songs that he knew, testing his vocabulary with a new voice. The strings were bright, fairly new, but there was no brittleness in the sound. He'd tried Taylors before, but never quite saved up enough money to buy one. Running a restaurant paid better than detective work.

He looked back at Rio. She smiled at him. Music was the international language, after all, the one that needed no translation. He remembered the song on the record, the one on the CD. "Jungle Love." He fiddled around a bit, trying to get the guitar part, the rhythmic figure. It started on the root, then up an octave, back and forth on the fifth and the seventh. There was one other note in there, as well. He found it, the major sixth, then fiddled around a bit until the sequence sounded right. He looked back at Rio to see if she'd noticed, if he'd made an impression. If the riff sounded familiar to her, she didn't show it. She didn't smile, either.

He needed to pee, wondering if he could chance it. He stood up and walked to the bathroom, nodded at Rio to indicate he wouldn't be there long and closed the door. He waited a moment, half-expecting to hear the clip-clop of tiny heels across the floor and down the staircase. Nothing happened. He turned to the toilet and unzipped. As his flow wound down to its final drops, he heard an unexpected sound from the other side of the door—guitar and voice, the sounds he loved most dearly in life.

He flushed the toilet, washed his hands and opened the door. Rio sat on the bed, the guitar in her hands. She looked at him. He smiled. She sang in a soft voice, bright and pure as a shiny copper bell. He imagined her on a Sonoran hillside, dressed in a white cotton dress and leather sandals—a goatherd tending her flock, singing "Cielito Lindo" as she hiked through the cactus and sage, sad and lonely. It wasn't an old *canción* she crooned now, though. The words were in English, but she sang them just fine.

"I like touching you baby, all night long.
Anaconda baby, our love so strong
In the river baby, or on my knees
Vines are creeping, and I can't breathe
I am lost, in your jungle love,
I am lost, in your jungle love."

26

LA ENTREVISTA (THE INTERVIEW)

The song ended. Rio smiled at Rolly. He smiled back. He felt stupid. The front door opened. Hector walked into the room.

"*Canta bien,*" he said, nodding at Rio. She smiled again.

"Rolly?" said Hector.

"Huh?"

"You okay?"

Rolly snapped out of his enchantment.

"Yeah."

"You sure?"

"I'm fine. How long you had the Taylor?"

"What's that?"

"The guitar."

"It's not mine. Roberto, my lawyer, he leaves it here sometimes. For when we have jam sessions in the club."

"Thoth thingth are expenthive."

"He does okay for himself. You want me to talk to her? I got a few minutes."

Rolly nodded.

"Tell her I want to akth some quethionth."

Hector spoke to Rio. She put down the guitar and looked back at Rolly.

"*¿Tiene mi dinero?*" she asked. Hector laughed.

"Whath that?" Rolly asked.

"She wants her money."

"Thee wanth me to pay her?"

"Apparently."

"Why?"

"I thought maybe you'd know. You want me to ask her?"

Rolly nodded. The little doctor said Rio was a whore. Perhaps she'd misinterpreted the nature of his interest. He'd brought her up to the bedroom, after all.

"*¿Por qué debe él pagarle?*" asked Hector.

"*Señor Velasquez dijo que usted me pagaría,*" she said. Rolly understood the first part of her answer.

"Jaime?" he said, before Hector could translate. "Did thee thay thumthin about Jaime?"

"Who's that?"

"Theenor Velasquez, thath wha thee thaid, right?"

"Yeah. Señor Velasquez said you'd give her money."

"When wath thith?"

Hector asked Rio. She replied. Hector turned back to Rolly.

"When they drove up to your house. When they talked to your mother."

Rolly nodded, remembering his mother's description of the old man and young girl from the previous evening.

"Who's this Velasquez guy?" asked Hector.

"Heeth dead. Thumbody killed him."

"Oh."

"Akth her when thee thaw him lathd."

"What's that?"

"How'd thee get hith truck?"

"She has the guy's truck?"

"Yeth."

Hector turned back to Rio and questioned her.

"*Necesito el dinero,*" she said.

"She says—"

"Yeah, I underthood that one," said Rolly. He reached in his pocket, pulled out the cash he had left and counted it. Thirteen dollars and two quarters. He offered up a ten for her, hoping it was enough to get started. Rio scowled at him.

"*Ciento,*" she said. "*Él me prometió ciento.*"

"She wants a hundred," said Hector. "He promised a hundred."

"Velathqueth?"

"I guess."

"I'll give her ten now, the retht later, if she antherth my quethdionth."

Hector translated the offer.

"*Necesito el dinero,*" she repeated, shaking her head.

"I'll pay two hundred . . . tomorrow."

"*Dos ciento, mañana,*" Hector told Rio. She shook her head again. Rolly sighed.

"You got ninety dollarth?" he asked Hector.

Hector pulled out his wallet.

"I got forty," he said, extracting two twenties. "I guess I could get more from downstairs."

"You okay with that?"

"Yeah. I'll go get it."

"No. Wait."

Rolly gave his ten to Hector.

"Tell her half now, half after thee talkth."

Hector laughed.

"Cool, man. Just like in the movies."

Hector addressed Rio, displaying the cash.

"*¿Dosciento en todos?*" she replied. Hector looked back at Rolly. He laughed.

"She wants two hundred now," he said.

"Figurthe," said Rolly.

"*Esta noche,*" said Rio. "*No mañana. Ahora. Esta noche.*"

"Tonight, huh?" said Rolly. He sighed, turning to Hector. "Can you loan me that muth?"

"You got a credit card? I could charge it and give you the cash."

Rolly looked back at Rio. She didn't seem as credulous as she had five minutes ago. He nodded.

"*Sí,*" he said. "*Ethta noche.* Thee hath to anther thum quethionth firthd."

Hector translated Rolly's capitulation. Rio smiled. She put the guitar down and took the money from Hector.

"Akth her again," said Rolly. "About the truck."

Hector interrogated Rio. They conversed for a moment before Hector turned back to Rolly.

"She took the truck. She was frightened. There was blood on the floor. There was someone outside. She wanted to get away. That is why she took the truck. She is sorry."

"Who wath outhide?"

"*¿Quién estaba afuera?*" asked Hector. Rio looked at him, then over at Rolly. She pointed at him.

"*Creo que era usted.*"

"She thinks maybe it was you," said Hector.

Rolly nodded.

"*Sí,*" he said, rubbing the back of his head. Rio packed a big wallop for such a small package. "*Es verdad.*"

"*Lo siento,*" said Rio.

"She's sorry," said Hector.

"*De nada,*" said Rolly.

"What's that all about?" Hector asked.

"Thee knocked me out."

"Really?"

"Put me in the hothpital."

Hector whistled.

"Don't mess with Mexican girls, *amigo.*"

"Yeah," said Rolly. "Tell her heeth dead. Theñor Velathqueth. Thumun killed him."

"*Señor Velasquez es muerto,*" Hector said to Rio. "*Lo asesinaron.*"

Rio looked down at the ground, then back at Rolly.

"*Sí. Temí tanto.*"

"She feared as much," said Hector.

"Doth thee know who killed him?" said Rolly. Hector asked.

"*Sí, le conozco,*" she replied.

"Who wath it?"

"*El doctor.*"

The glinting blade flashed in Rolly's memory. He put his hand to his neck, stroked the loose skin and stubble under his chin.

"Doth thee know the doctorth name?"

"*¿Usted sabe su nombre?*" Hector asked Rio.

"*Llaman Ramoñes,*" said Rio.

"Ith that hith firthd or lath name?"

Hector asked. Rio said something, shook her head.

"That's all she knows," Hector said. "Ramoñes."

"Why did Ramoñeth kill Theñor Velathqueth?"

Hector asked, then translated Rio's answer.

"Velasquez tried to marry her. The doctor did not like it."

"Ith the doctor her pimp?" Rolly asked.

"*¿Es el doctor su chulo?*" said Hector.

Rio looked at Rolly like he was an idiot.

"No," said Hector. "He is the doctor."

Rolly sighed. Knowing the doctor's name didn't make him feel any safer, but it might be useful to Bonnie. He reached in his pocket and pulled out his phone.

"*¿Quién es él que llama?*" said Rio.

"She wants to know who you're calling," said Hector.

"A friend of mine," Rolly said, putting the phone up to his ear. "Poleeth."

"*No policía,*" said Rio. She stood up and glared at Rolly. "*No policía.*"

"She says—" Hector began.

"I got it," said Rolly. He hit the cancel button and looked over at Rio.

"*No policía,*" she said.

"No poleethia," said Rolly, agreeing. He tapped on the

phone, switched over to camera mode and found the pictures of Ramoñes and Tangerine on the back porch.

"Ith that the doctor? Ramoneth?" he said, passing the phone to Hector, who passed it to Rio.

"*Sí*," said Rio.

"And the woman?"

"*Señora Tangie.*"

"How doth thee know them?"

Rio didn't respond to Hector's question. She looked back and forth from Rolly to Hector.

"*Necesito el dinero,*" she said. "*Ahora.*"

Rolly didn't need Hector's translation. He reached in his pocket and pulled out a credit card.

"You better get that money," he said, handing the card to Hector.

"Definitely," said Hector. "I wanna see how this turns out."

"Tell her thee hath to tell me everything, the whole thtory, or no *dinero*. Thee can't leave anything out."

Hector nodded, then laid out the terms for Rio in Spanish. She listened and nodded.

"*Sí*," she said. "*Hablaré todo.*"

"We're good?" Rolly said, checking with Hector.

"We're good," said Hector. He turned toward the door. "I'll be back. Pronto."

Rolly and Rio listened to Hector thump down the back stairway. They looked at each other. Rolly smiled. He didn't know what else to do. She had him beat. They waited in silence until Hector returned.

"Here's the money," said Hector, brandishing the bills in a fan.

"I'll take it," said Rolly. He took the money from Hector and turned back to Rio. There was a spark in her eyes. Men would trade money for anything. She didn't even have to let these men touch her.

"Thtory firthd, money after," Rolly said, displaying the twenties Hector had given him.

"*¿Qué?*" she said.

"Tell her I want the whole enthilada. About her and Velath-queth. About Ramoneth and Tangerine. About Friday night."

Hector conveyed Rolly's demand. Rio looked back at Rolly. She began her story.

"This doctor guy, Ramoñes," Hector said, interpreting as she spoke, "and Señora Tangie. They brought her here, from Tijuana. To help her. So she could go on TV."

"What did they do?"

Hector asked. Rio looked around the room. She seemed uncomfortable, looking for an escape. Rolly waited. She turned back to face them.

"Her father. He hit her," Hector said, as Rio began speaking again. "Her father said she was a witch, that her face had been marked by the devil. Sounds like she had a scar, maybe a cleft palate, something like that."

"Like in those pictures," Rolly said. Hector nodded.

"She ran away with a man, when she was fourteen. This man hit her also. So she ran away from him too. Then she lived in a house, with other women. The women were prostitutes. Ramoñes came to the house, once a week. He gave them medicine, inspected them. He said he could fix her, make her face so that men wouldn't hate her, so they wouldn't hit her. He said he would make her like the girls on TV. Sounds like maybe he's a plastic surgeon, or something."

"He operated on her?"

"Yes. He made her face like it is now."

"*Muy bonita,*" Rolly said, indicating approval of the doctor's handiwork. Rio tilted her head and blinked her eyes, a slight, bashful flirt.

"Smooth operator," whispered Hector, singing the words from the song.

"Yeah, yeah," Rolly protested. From what Rio had told him so far, Ramoñes was an angel of mercy, not the scalpel-wielding, dope-smoking psycho who'd tried to kill him. Rio continued her story.

"One day a rich American lady came with the doctor," said Hector. "It was Señora Tangie. The doctor said Señora Tangie was looking for girls like her, to put on TV, that she would pay for her operation. Señora Tangie had beautiful clothes and jewelry, like the women on the *telenovelas*. She decided to go with them."

"Where did they go?"

"The doctor gave her some medicine. She fell asleep. When she woke up, she was in Señora Tangie's house. She had bandages. All over her body. There was much pain."

"The doctor operated on her?"

"Yes. Señora Tangie was there. She took care of them. She gave them new clothes."

"Them?"

"There was another girl. Like her. The doctor fixed them both."

"He worked on her face, too?"

"Yes. He fixed everything."

Rolly thought for a moment. Ramoñes and Tangerine weren't benevolent angels. He'd seen enough to know that.

"Hector?"

"Yeah?"

"Thee thaid thee had bandajeth all over?"

"Yeah."

"Why?"

"Huh?"

"Where elth did he operate?" said Rolly.

"Besides her face, you mean?"

"Yeth."

"You want me to ask her?"

Rolly nodded. Hector spoke to Rio. They conversed for a moment. Hector's eyes grew larger with each response she gave. His legs curled up under the chair.

"*Ay, caramba!*" he said when they'd finished. "You're not going to believe this."

"What?"

"Well, I had to ask her a couple of times, to make sure. She started telling me the doctor fixed them, made them whole, she and the other girl, like they used to be. I didn't understand at first, but, well, it sounds like he did some operation to make them, uh . . ."

"What?"

"They're virgins."

"Are you sure? "

"Yes. That's what she said. He put the mark on her."

"What kind of mark?"

"I'm not sure."

"What's it look like? Can she show it to us?"

Hector asked. Rio stood up, undid the top button of her jeans. They dropped to the floor, exposing her delicate tan legs, and a pair of pink panties with the words "Jungle Love" printed on the front. It wasn't the best time for Vera to walk into the room, but Rolly had no control over that.

27

LA DISCUSIÓN (THE DISCUSSION)

"Hector!" screamed Vera. Both men jumped, then turned to face Vera as she stood in the doorway, steaming like a basket of fresh tortillas. Rio remained unfazed, with her pants on the floor.

"It's not what you're thinking," said Hector.

"Why'd you take that money out of the cash box?" Vera said.

"It was for Rolly. For her."

"For her?"

"It's okay. I charged his credit card."

"What for?"

"He's trying to get some information from this girl. She's like a witness. She needed some money."

"How stupid do you think I am, Hector?"

"Vera, ith—" Rolly said, trying to intervene.

"I'm not talking to you, Rolly Waters," said Vera, refusing to look at him. "I thought you were a nice man, a real *caballero*."

"Hector wath helping me."

"You're drunk, too. I could tell when you came in."

"Ith the painkillerth."

"She hit Rolly over the head," said Hector, nodding at Rio.

"Yeah, well, he probably deserved it."

"She knocked him out."

"Good for her."

"The poleeth have a body," Rolly said. "Atha morgue."

"They're gonna have a couple more pretty soon," Vera said, "unless you explain why Señorita Jailbait's standing there in her undies."

Vera paused, looking around the room at each of them, including Rio.

"I'm waiting," she said, crossing her arms. "And it better be good."

"Sheeth got a mark," said Rolly. "The dead girl. On her rear end."

He walked to the table, picked up the notepad and searched for a writing utensil.

"Here," Vera said, pulling a pencil out from behind her left ear. Rolly took the pencil and drew the pattern he'd seen in the coroner's photograph, the letter *m* with a dropped loop at the end. He showed the picture to Vera.

"Ith Virgo," he said.

"Yeah, and I'm an Aries. So what?"

Rolly and Hector glanced at each other.

"She's a virgin," Hector said.

"And how do you know that?"

"She told us. This doctor, he's a plastic surgeon or something. He did some sort of operation to make her a virgin. He fixed her lips. Her mouth, I mean."

Vera rolled her eyes.

"And I suppose you guys were just checking to make sure she was telling the truth?"

"No, no," said Hector. "It's the mark. She said the doctor put a mark on her. Rolly wanted to see it."

"Yeth," Rolly nodded. "I, umm . . ."

"What is it, like a tattoo or something?" asked Vera.

"More like a thcar."

"A car?"

"No. Thscar."

"Oh. So, does she have one?"

Rolly and Hector looked at each other.

"We don't know," Hector said. "We were just getting ready to look."

Vera crossed her arms again.

"No, really," Hector pleaded. "We haven't seen it. You came in before she showed it to us. Really. You speak Spanish. Ask her yourself. Ask her about any of it."

Vera glared at them both again, lowered her arms, then took a step toward Rio.

"*Hola,*" she said to Rio. "*¿Está bien?*"

"*Sí.*" Rio nodded. "*Estoy bien.*"

Vera began a rapid-fire interrogation. Rolly couldn't understand a word either woman said, but he detected a certain protectiveness creeping into Vera's tone as they spoke. Rio smiled. Vera pointed at the two men. Rio laughed. Hector and Rolly exchanged diffident glances. Women were brutal.

Vera concluded her interview, then turned back to the men.

"Turn around," she said. "Look away."

"What?"

"She's going to show me this mark. You don't get to look. Now turn away and face the door."

Rolly and Hector did as they were told, waiting until Vera told them they could turn back.

"Did you see it? Was it there?" Hector asked.

"Yes." Vera nodded. "She told me about some other stuff, too. This cowboy who helped her."

"Jaime," said Rolly.

"Yes. And she told me your mother was very nice."

"You trust us now?" asked Hector.

"Trust, no, but I believe you."

"Did thee thay anything about the other girlth?" Rolly asked.

"What other girls?"

"The oneth I told you about, in the morgue. They had that mark too."

"You want me to ask her about them?" said Vera.

"I know what's going on," said Hector.

"What?"

"They do this operation sometimes. It's called a hymenectomy."

"What are you talking about?" said Vera.

"I read about it in *Mother Jones*. There was this article about the global sex trade, international sex slavery. They kidnap young girls, sell them in other countries. The doctor fixed them up to make them more valuable."

"There was a Chinese passport on the CD," said Rolly.

"Yeah." Hector shrugged. "In some cultures, like Arabs, some Asian countries, it's a big deal if a girl's a virgin. I mean they're jonesing on it even more than the born-again abstinence Nazis we got over here. A girl's more valuable if she's a virgin. You can sell her for a lot more. This Ramoñes guy's probably got some Chinese guys lined up already. That's what the symbol means. It's like an inspection stamp."

"Men are so fucking weird," said Vera.

"They got too many men in China, too," Hector continued. "Because of that one-child policy thing. They got a shortage of girls. Economics one-o-one, supply and demand."

Rolly looked at Rio. Her face appeared blank, almost bored. Dr. Ramoñes didn't want Rio back because he missed her, because she was his Royal Tingler. He wanted her back because he expected a return on his investment, before it was spoiled. The virgin Rio was money.

"I should call Roberto," said Hector. "She'll need a lawyer."

"You gonna let her pull up her pants first?" said Vera.

"Yeth, yeth," Rolly said, nodding. Vera spoke to Rio, who buttoned up her pants.

"*¿Puedo tener mi dinero ahora?*" Rio said, reseating herself on the end of the bed.

"She wants to know if she can have her money now," said Hector.

"I have a couple more quethdionth," said Rolly.

"Oh, just give her the damn money," said Vera. "Stop playing around."

Rolly counted out the bills and handed Rio the money. She slipped it into her pocket and smiled like victory. Rolly thought for a moment, reminded himself that Max had only hired him to find the driver of the car that ran through the terns' nests. He could hand everything else over to Bonnie.

"Friday night," he said. "Akth her what happened Friday night."

"*¿Qué sucedió en la noche del viernes?*" asked Hector.

"Everything," Rolly added.

"*Todos,*" said Hector. Rio looked at all three of them, then at the ceiling. She looked over at Rolly and began.

"They were watching TV. Friday night," said Hector, interpreting. "She and the other girl, and Señora Tangie. They watch every week. *Family Act.*"

"How long hath thee lived there? At the houthe?"

"A month, maybe a little more. The funeral car came to the house. It always comes by on Friday. The doctor is gone then."

"A hearthe? Ith that what thee meanth?"

"A hearse, yeah. I think that's what she means. El Portador comes to visit them. He gives money to Señora Tangie. He brings them food."

"El Portador? Thath hith name?"

Hector quizzed Rio, then turned back to Rolly.

"She calls him El Portador. She doesn't know his name. Like a guy at a funeral. El portador de féretro."

Rolly nodded.

"Okay," he said. "What happened after El Portador got there?"

"It wasn't El Portador. Not this time. It was another man. A *luchador.*"

"Whath that?"

"Like a wrestler, a big man, with a mask. He had a gun, too. He made them get into the car. He drove them out to a dark place."

"Where?"

"She doesn't know. It was dark. In the country. She heard the ocean."

"Wath it clothe? To the houthe?"

"It wasn't very far. The man went outside. He had to pee. A truck arrived. Another man got out of the truck. This man also wore a mask. Señora Tangie thought the men would do bad things. She tried to save them."

"What did she do?"

"She took the car. The man had forgotten the keys. She tried to escape. Señora Tangie was not a very good driver, though. She got stuck in the sand. The men came after them. Señora Tangie told them to run away. She ran away from the men. She hid in some trees near the river."

"What about Señora Tangie and the other girl? Did she see what happened to them?"

"She does not know. She runs very fast. She ran very far."

"And Jaime? How did thee meet him?"

"It was the next day. She fell asleep, near the river. A man came by on a horse. It was Jaime. He took her back to his house. He gave her clothes, and some food. He told her about the dead girl he found on the beach, that she looked like her."

"She knowth the other girlth dead?"

Rio dropped her eyes as she spoke.

"Yes. She is sorry. Señor Jaime told her about the house, and Señora Tangie, that it is an evil place, that Señora Tangie is the demon Xtapay. Señor Jaime told her he would die soon, that Xtapay had come back to claim him, that she had seduced him."

"He told me that too."

"Señor Jaime said you were strong, that you had fought off the demon who lives in the tequila, that you were strong enough for Xtapay. He showed her your card. He said you would pay money to her. Because she lived in the house with Xtapay. He said you would have magic to protect them. That is why they drove up to your house."

"Doth thee believe that?"

"She knows that you are a shaman, that you have the magic in your hands."

"How doth thee know that?"

"From the way you play the guitar," Hector said. He laughed. "Sounds like you got a groupie."

Rolly smiled. Compliments were welcome, whatever the circumstances. It wasn't sorcery, though, that gave him magical hands. It was practice.

"How doth thee know the doctor killed Jaime?"

"A car came to the house. Señor Jaime hid her under the floor. She heard them talking. She heard horrible sounds. When she came out there was blood on the floor. There was a man sitting on the back steps. She hit him with a pot. She didn't know it was you."

Rolly nodded. It all sounded plausible, even probable. Ramoñes found evidence of the girl in the house and killed Jaime. The doctor collected on Xtapay's bill.

"I think we should talk to my lawyer," said Hector. "She's gonna need one."

"Yeah," said Rolly.

"Okay if I call him?"

"Ith kinda late."

"He'll come over. Me an' Roberto are like brothers, man."

"Okay."

As Hector pulled out his cell phone, Rolly's phone buzzed. He looked at the name on the screen. It was Marley.

"Yeah?" said Rolly, putting the phone to his ear.

"Border Lords," said Marley. "That's the name of the game. You ever heard of it?"

"Sounds familiar."

"Yeah? Well, it should be. There's a mod called Border Field Blues."

"Oh yeah?"

"Yeah. And you're in it."

28

EL PORTADOR (THE PALLBEARER)

Rolly peered through the glass door of the high-rise condominium on Tenth Avenue. He waved at the security guard behind the desk. The guard wasn't Jimmy.

"Yes?" came a voice from the speaker next to the door.

"I'm here to see Sayer Burdon," Rolly said to the speaker. "He lives here."

"Is Mr. Burdon expecting you?"

"Yes," Rolly lied. Perhaps Burdon did expect him, in some weird way. Rolly was part of the game now.

"What's your name?" the guard asked.

"Rolly Waters."

"Hold on."

The guard looked down at his desk, punched a number on the phone and spoke to someone. He hung up the phone. The door buzzed. Rolly grabbed the handle, opened it and walked in.

"You got a business card?" the guard asked when Rolly got to the desk.

Rolly pulled out his wallet and handed the man a card. The guard looked at it and chuckled.

"Mr. Burdon's a funny guy," he said.

"What's that?"

"He asked me if you were 'Rolly Waters, the rock-and-roll dick.'"

"Oh."

"Missing Persons. Insurance," the guard said, reading from Rolly's card. "He recited your phone and license number, too, to the letter."

"I can go up, then?"

"Yeah, sure. You must be the guy."

"Thirteen-thirteen, right?"

"Yeah. It's crazy how he remembers that stuff."

Rolly got into the elevator and punched a button. The doors closed and the elevator began its ascent.

He'd left Rio at the restaurant, watched over by Hector and Vera while they waited for Hector's lawyer to arrive, and walked over to Marley's loft, where Marley showed him the Border Lords video game. As Marley explained it, enthusiasts could create their own scenarios—mods, they were called. The mods included new locations, characters and soundtracks.

Border Field Blues was the title of the mod Marley had downloaded. It looked like Rolly's whole case file, all the places he'd been: Border Field Park and The Honeytrap, Jaime's house and corral, Rico Chacon's bar, Pastor Eddie's sidewalk church. Each of the locations was marked on a satellite map that stretched from the police recovery lot to the border, all the ground Rolly had trod. The people were there, too. The names were different—Cowboy, Red, El Doctor and Gordo—but it had to be them. Avatars for Rico Chacon and Eddie Sanchez were there, along with various border patrolmen, AFA goons and young girls like Rio. Jaime's green truck was part of the game. So was an old hearse.

A new version of the mod had been uploaded last night. Rolly was part of the game now, although his avatar's face wasn't as clear as some. His character was named Dick.

The elevator door opened. Rolly stepped out onto the thirteenth floor, walked down the hall to number thirteen and knocked on the door. No one answered. He knocked again. There was no response. He tried the doorknob. It turned. He pushed the door open and walked in. The apartment was dark, except for a flickering glow at the end of the hall. He walked down the hall, announcing himself as he went, but no one called back to him. Turning the corner, he entered the living room. It was dark too, except for a gigantic TV hanging on the far wall. The screen's ghostly light overwhelmed the figure slouched on the floor in a beanbag chair, with a pair of large headphones clamped over his ears. The man's fingers and thumbs danced across the plastic controller he held in his hands, clicking out a soft, frenetic rhythm as the pictures on screen swerved and exploded, a battle between the shooter and some sort of militant zombies.

The man shooting zombies was Sayer Burdon. Vera had misheard the name when taking the order Friday night. It was The Pallbearer, not Paul Barrere. It was his character's name. The Pallbearer. El Portador, Rio called him. Whatever the name, Sayer Burdon knew something, perhaps everything, about what happened Friday night. Rolly just hoped it made sense.

"Mr. Burdon?" he said, raising his voice, trying to get through the kid's headphones. Burdon didn't acknowledge him. Rolly stepped in closer. Burdon glanced up at him, unsurprised, with no hint of emotion, and returned to his game. There was something queer about the kid, something damaged, but here he sat, living in his own apartment, capable enough to get by. Rolly waited a moment, thinking the game would end soon, that Burdon would speak to him once he'd killed enough zombies. It went on for a while. A lot of zombies went down, minus various body parts.

The game ended. Burdon dropped his arms, rested the controller in his lap and stared at the screen.

"Mr. Burdon?" said Rolly. The kid turned and stared at him. He didn't say anything.

"You remember me, from this morning?" Rolly continued. "I'm the detective—"

"Rolly Waters, the rock 'n' roll dick. CA PI License two-zero-three-five-one-two. Phone—"

"Yes, that's me. Can I talk to you?"

"You can talk," Burdon said.

"I need to ask you some questions."

Burdon made no response. Rolly continued.

"When you picked up your car, this morning, when the policeman talked to you, you said a friend borrowed it."

"Yes. A friend borrowed my car."

"Is he one of the security guards?"

"He is one of them."

"Is your friend Jimmy?"

"Yes. Jimmy plays games with me."

"Do you know why Jimmy borrowed your car Friday night?"

"He took the money."

"He took money from you?"

"I gave him money."

"Why?"

"It was Friday. He took the money."

"He stole it from you?"

"No."

"He didn't threaten you? He didn't steal it?"

"No. I gave him money. On Friday. He went to get the records. They're tokens."

"That's why you gave him the money?"

"Yes."

"Does Jimmy work for you?"

"He works downstairs. He's a security guard. Pantera Security. Badge number zero-four-eight-zero."

"I thought maybe he did other jobs for you, in his spare time, something like that."

"He's a security guard. That's his job."

"Why did you give him the money? Are you buying those records?"

"It's a charity. It goes to a charity."

"What kind of charity?"

"The charity is for girls. For Mexican girls. It's for a church."

"Are those the girls in your game?"

"There aren't any girls in this game. It's Zombie Apocalypse."

"Not this game. The one you told me about at the police lot. Border Lords."

"I play Border Lords."

"Yes. I know. Are the Mexican girls in that game?"

"There are Mexican girls in that game."

"So, they're in Border Field Blues?"

"Yes."

"Did you make up that game?"

"Yes."

"Did you put me in the game?"

"You're not in the game."

"That character, Dick? Did you put him in the game?"

"Yes."

"Why?"

Burdon didn't answer.

"Why did you put him in the game?"

"Everyone's in the game."

"But why me?"

Burdon looked blank. Rolly tried another angle.

"Do you know all the characters in the game?" he asked.

"I made them. I put them in there."

"What about that woman? Red? Did you put her in there?"

"Yes."

"Is she Tangerine Swimmer?"

"She's Red."

"But you know Tangerine, don't you?"

"Did you have sex with her?"

"No."

"Then you won't die."

"Why do you say that?"

"I programmed the game."

"I'm not talking about the game. I'm talking about real life."

"Tangerine sleeps with too many men. That's what my mother said."

"Your mother knows her?"

"They are sisters."

"Tangerine is your aunt, then?"

"Yes. She is Aunt Tangie. That is how I know she is my mother's sister."

"Where is your mother? Can I talk to her?"

"You can talk to her."

"How would I contact her? Does she live here?"

"No. She moved away. With her husband."

"Your father?"

"No. It is her husband."

"He's not your father?"

"My father gave me money. When he gave me the money, she moved away. My father is dead."

"I'm sorry," said Rolly. "When did he die?"

"It was a long time ago."

"What was his name?"

"He's my ancestor."

"Yes, I know. What was his name?"

"I don't want to talk anymore."

"Can you tell me your father's name?"

"I don't want to talk. I want to play the game. Do you want to play the game?"

"Some people are dead, Sayer. I need to know why."

"I want to play the game," Burdon said, shifting in his beanbag chair.

Rolly paused for a moment. He felt tired. The back of his skull started to throb again.

"What about Border Field Blues?" he said. "Can we play that?"

"Yes. I would like to play that game," Burdon said. He didn't move.

"Okay," said Rolly. "I'll play with you."

Burdon pushed some buttons on his controller, closing down

the zombie apocalypse, and switching over to Border Lords, selecting Border Field Blues from a list of titles. He paused.

"What is it?" said Rolly.

"You have to choose a character."

"You can choose it for me."

"You have to choose."

Rolly scanned the list of characters and their pictures.

"I'll be me, I guess," he said.

"You have to pick someone from the list."

"Dick, I mean."

"Dick is a private investigator," said Burdon, selecting Rolly's avatar on screen. He handed the game controller to Rolly, reached down and picked up another one lying on the floor next to his chair.

"Who are you going to be?" Rolly asked.

"The Pallbearer."

"Of course," Rolly muttered to himself, then louder, to Burdon, said, "I'm not very good at these games."

Burdon reached down, found another headset on the floor and handed it to Rolly.

"You talk into there," he said, indicating a curved tube of plastic that angled in from the right earpiece. "Dick and The Pallbearer can play as a team."

Rolly put the headphones on and adjusted the microphone.

"Can you hear me?" he said.

"This is the Pallbearer," Burdon's voice said, coming through the headphones. "Who's this?"

"It's me," Rolly said.

"Who?"

Rolly looked over at Burdon. Burdon looked at the TV screen.

"Dick," Rolly sighed.

"Are you ready?"

"Yes."

Burdon clicked his controller. The game started. From an overhead view of lower San Diego County, the game zoomed in toward downtown, then over to Burdon's condominium building. It switched to an internal shot, looking out on the city from Burdon's apartment. The picture on the TV screen divided into two halves.

"What should I do?" Rolly asked.

"Follow me," said Burdon, his voice coming through Rolly's headphones.

As Burdon spoke, a figure moved into view on Rolly's side of the screen. It was The Pallbearer. The figure walked away from him.

"Use the joystick," said Burdon. Rolly pushed the joystick forward to follow him.

"Where are we going?" he asked.

"We have to get the car."

"What for?"

"I have to look for the dead ones. That's the Pallbearer's first task. To pick up the dead ones."

29

—————

EL MÉDICO (THE DOCTOR)

R olly climbed the wooden stairs to the apartment above the Villa Cantina, opened the door and walked in. No one was there. All evidence of last night's occupants had disappeared. The bed was made. He sat down at the table and looked at his watch. Eight thirty in the morning. He'd spent all night in an elevator.

Seven hours earlier, after leaving Burdon's apartment, he walked down the hall and rang for the elevator. During his descent, somewhere around the fifth floor, the elevator came to a stop. He waited a minute, rang the alarm bell. Nothing happened. He tried the emergency phone inside the elevator. It rang and rang, but no one answered. He took out his cell phone. The battery had gone dead. He sat on the floor and waited. He fell asleep. At eight fifteen in the morning, the cables creaked. The elevator rumbled to life. It descended to the first floor and belched him out into the lobby, much to the surprise of the new guard on duty.

"Who're you?" the guard asked.

"I've been stuck in there since one thirty," said Rolly.

"Really? Did you ring the alarm?"

"More times than I can count. How long have you been here?"

"Just got in. I saw number three stopped, so I reset it."

"You have the controls there?"

"Yeah, like I said."

"Was the other guard here when you arrived?"

"Who are you, anyway?"

"Rolly Waters. I'm a friend of Mr. Burdon's. Thirteen-thirteen."

"Oh. You want to talk to him?"

"Who was on duty before you?"

"I don't know."

"Wasn't he here when you arrived?"

"No. I can look it up, if you want."

"Please."

The guard checked his computer, then turned back to Rolly.

"It was that fat guy," he said. "Bodeans."

And now Rio had disappeared from Hector's apartment. She was probably perched in the kitchen with Hector and his crew, bright-eyed and better rested than Rolly, eating chilaquiles and eggs. He wondered if Hector's lawyer had talked to her yet.

Rolly rubbed the stitches behind his right ear. He'd taken another pill in the elevator, but the effects had worn off. His head throbbed. He went into the bathroom, washed his face and pulled the bottle of pills out of his pocket, then thought about their effect on his speech. A cup of Hector's coffee might be a better choice. He slipped the pills back into his pocket, walked out of the bathroom and opened the door leading back down the stairs. A man stood on the stoop. It was Ramoñes, the little doctor, dressed in green scrubs and sporting his pocket protector filled with sharp steel.

"*Buenos días,* my friend," said Ramoñes, blocking the door with his foot.

"*Buenos días,*" said Rolly, backing away. Ramoñes entered the room and closed the door.

"Please, have a seat," he said, indicating the table against the wall. Rolly sat.

"Is this where you fornicate on your whores?" the doctor asked, surveying the room.

"No," said Rolly.

"Where is the girl?"

"I told you I don't know about any girl."

"Then why did you come here?"

"I wanted to get out of the house."

"*Sin su madre.*"

"Don't bring my mother into this."

"She does not approve of your whoremongering?"

"No. I mean, that's not why I came here."

"I have seen a truck, on the street nearby. A green truck."

"I see green trucks all the time."

"What becomes of your car?"

"The police have it. No thanks to you."

"Ah, your *novia,* the one with the muscles, she takes your car?"

"Yes. No. Kind of."

"You have seen this green truck before, I think."

"Why don't you show it to me?"

"You are not helpful to me with these answers."

"I figure you already know the answers."

The doctor nodded.

"That is true. I know many things. It is the girl whore who took the *vaquero*'s truck. That is clear to me now. And now you have the truck. Therefore, I think that you have the girl."

"You killed him, didn't you?"

"Who?"

"Jaime. The *vaquero*. It's his truck."

"The *vaquero* was a whoremonger. He fornicated on whores."

"That's why you killed him?"

"He made his own death."

"But you helped," muttered Rolly.

"What is that you say?"

"Nothing."

Ramoñes clasped his hands together.

"You were a surprise to me, my friend, very agile for a portly man. I am glad to see you alive, though. I became angry. I do not want to kill you. That is no good. Then I would never find the girl."

"I took Jaime's truck," Rolly said. "I figured he wouldn't miss it."

"I am done with these bothersome lies," said the doctor. "Let us make an exchange."

"What do I get out of the deal?"

"You own your life, my friend. It is in your hands."

"Every single day," Rolly said.

"We will not bandy words any longer," said the doctor. "I think you have the girl here."

"You see her anywhere?" Rolly said, throwing his arms wide to encompass the empty room.

"Did you fornicate on her?"

"I did not fornicate on her or anywhere near her."

"Perhaps you fornicate on her and throw her away. When you have paid her the money."

"The flower of her womanhood remains intact."

The doctor furrowed his brow.

"What do you mean by this?" he asked.

"No girl. No fornication. The seal is still good."

"What is this seal you speak of?"

"You know what I mean."

"She is intact, then?"

"The police have a girl, at the morgue. She's dead. She has

the mark. They showed me a photograph. I know all about your little racket. So do the police."

The doctor looked thoughtful. He walked to the table, looked at Rolly for a moment, then sat down in the opposite chair. He pulled out his plastic baggie of smoking supplies and rolled a joint. It didn't make Rolly feel any better, but at least it bought him some time. The doctor licked the edges of the rolling paper, added a measure of his herbal mixture and rolled it between his fingers.

"You still do not smoke?" Ramoñes asked, twisting the ends of the joint.

"No," Rolly said. The doctor leaned back against the wall and pulled out a silver Zippo.

"You know what a whore is, my friend?" he said.

Rolly shrugged.

"I will tell you," the doctor said. "She is nothing. A bag of flesh. She is grease, like the animal fat you consume so much of. She is blood and urine and shit."

Ramoñes lit the joint, took a hit, held it in for a moment and exhaled.

"That is what men like you turn them into," he continued. "I have made it my life, to save the young girls from whoremongers like you."

"I didn't touch her," said Rolly.

"Who?"

"Whoever she is."

Rolly had never paid for a woman. There'd been so many free ones. The doctor's definition of whoremongers might not be so finely tuned, though. Groupies might count. He hadn't violated Rio. That was the point he needed to make.

"I didn't touch her," he repeated.

The doctor stared into Rolly's eyes.

"You will swear on your mother's grave," said the doctor. "*¿El sepulcro de su madre?*"

"Leave my mother out of this," Rolly replied.

"You must swear on your mother's grave."

"Are you threatening my mother?"

"No." The doctor smiled. "I will not harm *su madre*. But you must be willing to swear."

"All right, all right," Rolly said. "I swear."

"*¿En el sepulcro de su madre?*"

"Yes, yes. On my mother's grave. Just leave her alone."

The doctor nodded his head.

"I believe you, my friend. Your *madre* is safe."

The doctor grabbed a tangerine from the fruit bowl and began peeling it.

"My name is Ramoñes," said the doctor. "Dr. Zildjian Ramoñes. My mother was a whore. Does this surprise you?"

"Should it?" said Rolly. He glanced at the door, considering what would happen if someone walked in. Rio, Hector, anyone.

"You think someone will come?" said the doctor, noting Rolly's glance.

"I doubt it," said Rolly.

"We will wait here a while," said the doctor. "There is no hurry."

Rolly looked away. The doctor finished peeling his tangerine and left it on the table.

"You have heard this name before?" he said. "Zildjian, I mean? You are a musician."

"You mean the cymbals?"

"Yes. Like the cymbals. They are pretty to look at, no?"

Rolly shrugged.

"My drummer uses them."

"*Instrumentos hermosos, sí.* The Zildjians are shiny and beautiful, but they have sharp edges. My mother, you see, she knew many musicians. This is how I came by my name. I spent much time with them, the musicians, as a boy. In the whoremonger's house. I was drawn to the cymbals, these Zildjians. I liked to touch them, to play with them. 'Zildjian, Zildjian,' I would say. Soon, that is what the men call me, the guitar players and mariachis. They would say, 'There goes Zildjian, come here, Zildjian.' They never know my real name."

"What is your real name?"

"I have always been Zildjian."

Ramoñes took another toke, then offered it to Rolly. Rolly considered it. If he was going to die, he might as well be high when it happened. He shook his head. He needed to be clear. The doctor shrugged, took another toke.

"The Zildjians are beautiful, yes, but they are also dangerous," he continued. He held up his left hand, revealing a long scar across his palm. "You see this?"

Rolly nodded.

"That is from one of the Zildjians. The cymbals. I gave it a great spin. On the stand. I tried to grab it. It cut me there, much blood. That is when I first learn. There is danger in beautiful things. The things that attract us. Like women."

Rolly didn't argue the point. Royal Tinglers often had a sharp edge. The doctor separated the tangerine into two halves. He ate one of them.

"My mother was a beautiful woman," he said. "Men gave her money. To fornicate on her. I would see them, sometimes, rooting in her body, grunting like pigs. They leave their ugliness in her, like rot. She became ugly with the disease. No man would touch her then. We were put out of the whoremonger's house, onto the streets. Soon after, she died."

"Why are you telling me this?" Rolly said.

"So you will know. When you die."

"I told you. I'm not like those men. I didn't do anything to any girl."

"We shall see. When she returns."

"She's not coming back."

"Then you will help me find her."

"Did you sell her to someone? Is that it?"

"I do not understand."

"The operations. You fix up the girls and sell them."

"Who would I sell them to?"

"Rich Arabs, somebody like that. Maybe Chinese?"

"For what reason?"

"They pay a lot for virgins."

"I too would be a whoremonger, then, would I not?"

Rolly shrugged.

"That woman, with the red hair, at the house on the border, is she a prostitute?"

"The Señora is my benefactor."

"She gives you money?"

"She has provided for me. She has made a place for my work."

"What's she get out of the deal?"

"I offer my services."

"A little nip and tuck?"

"The Señora gave her soul to the devil many years ago. We are joined together in sin."

"I saw you out on the patio, the two of you."

"You think she is my whore?"

"Something like that."

"I do not touch a woman with my *pito*. I am not a whoremonger."

"What about the other girls?"

"I marry them to God," said the doctor.

"What?"

"They are whores. I make them as nuns. They leave the world without sin. Immaculate."

"I don't understand."

Doctor Ramoñes leaned forward in his chair.

"After my mother died, I was sent to a home for those without parents, un *orfelinato*, how do you say it?"

"An orphanage."

"Yes. The women there, they are married to God. They do not sin as my mother did. They do not fornicate with men. Only God."

"I'm not sure that's exactly—"

"A holy man. He joined me with God. His blood is within me. That is why I became a doctor. I am his body."

There was a noise from outside, on the stairwell. Both men

looked up as the door to the apartment opened. Vera stepped into the room. She was dressed in blue-jean cutoffs, strappy sandals and a loosely buttoned shirt with the ends tied in a knot just above her navel. She stopped when she saw the two men, put her hands on her hips.

"Is this your new whore?" asked Ramoñes.

30

LA PISTOLA (THE GUN)

"Hello, Vera," said Rolly.

"Where'd you run off to last night?" she asked. "And who's this jerk?"

"I am Dr. Zildjian Ramoñes," said the doctor, answering for himself.

"Well, ziljun on this, doc," said Vera, flipping a middle finger at him.

"She is a lively one, my friend," said the doctor, winking at Rolly.

"I thought you'd gone with Hector," said Vera.

"Where is he?" asked Rolly.

"They went down to that protest thing. At the border park. He and Roberto. And that girl you came in with last night."

Ramoñes raised an eyebrow and looked over at Rolly.

"This is not good, my friend," he said. "You have not told me the truth."

"When did they leave?" Rolly asked.

"About a half-hour ago, I guess," said Vera. "What's the story on that chick, anyway? Hector was bouncing off the walls all morning."

"I do not like this bouncing," said Ramoñes, stubbing out his joint in the discarded tangerine skin. "Who is Hector?"

"He and Roberto must've spent a couple hours up here talking to her," continued Vera.

"What about?" said Rolly.

"Getting her a green card, I expect. That's what Roberto does."

"They are whoremongers," said the doctor, shaking his head.

"Fuck you, asshole," said Vera, flaring her nostrils like an angry gazelle.

Ramoñes smiled and reached for his pocket protector. He withdrew a scalpel and inspected his fingernails, scraping the dirt under them. Rolly recognized the move. It was the doctor's signature riff. Vera reached for something inside her purse. Rolly slipped his left hand under the table.

"You will please to take off your panties," said Ramoñes, scraping his cuticles.

Rolly didn't wait to hear Vera's response. He lifted the table as he sprang from his chair, slamming it into the doctor as hard as he could. There was a split second of resistance. The table rebounded, bouncing Rolly backwards and into the wall. He heard a loud bang. Bits of pressed wood exploded around him. Someone screamed. Rolly stumbled and fell to the floor. The table flipped over and fell down on top of him. Then something fell on the table, rolled across him and crashed onto the floor. Then silence.

"Shit," someone said.

Rolly crawled out from under the table and looked around the room. The front door stood open, a shaft of sunlight streaming in across the floor from the alley.

"Vera?"

"Over here."

The voice came from behind him. He turned around and saw Vera sprawled on the floor between the wall and the bed, one bare leg draped over the mattress, a sandal dangling from her big toe.

"Did I get him?" she asked.

"He's gone."

Vera pulled her leg down off the bed. Rolly reached down and helped her up.

"What happened?" he asked.

"I almost shot you, you dumb-ass. That's what happened," she said, waving a petite pearl-handled pistol in her right hand.

"Where'd you get that?"

"From my purse. Didn't you see me?"

"I guess not."

"That was the guy, wasn't it? The guy you were hiding from?"

"Yeah, that was him."

"I knew something was funny when I came in. You looked white as a ghost. Then he started in with that whore shit . . . Did you hear what he said to me?"

"Yeah, I heard."

"Fuckin' pimp. I hope I shot his balls off."

"You think you got him?"

"I don't know. I had my shot all lined up. Then you had to go and play hero."

"I thought he would cut you."

"There's his knife," Vera said, pointing at a silver blade on the floor. Rolly knelt down to pick it up, then stopped. The police would want the scalpel for prints. He surveyed the room for other evidence.

"Did I get him? You see any blood?" Vera said, sounding hopeful.

"None that I can see."

Vera sat down on the bed, placed the gun next to her and began rubbing her wrist.

"You okay?" asked Rolly.

"That little fucker's strong," she said. "I saw the table up in the air and heard my gun go off, then he came at me. Next thing I knew I was lying over there in the corner."

"At least you held onto the gun."

"Yeah."

Rolly heard footsteps outside, someone climbing the stairs. Vera heard it too. She picked up the gun and pointed it toward the door. A small, round woman stepped into the doorway. Rolly recognized her from the kitchen last night. Vera lowered her gun.

"*¿Jefe?*" said the woman. "*¿Se duele?*"

"*Estoy bien,*" Vera said. "*Estoy bien. No se preocupe.*"

The woman lingered at the door, looking back and forth from Vera to Rolly.

"*Estoy bien,*" said Vera. "*Estaré abajo pronto.*"

The woman left, chided by her boss's reassurances. God only knew what she thought, seeing Vera disheveled on the bed, gun in hand, with a strange man in the room.

"You think we should call the cops?" Vera asked.

Rolly nodded, reached in his pocket, then stopped.

"My phone's dead," he said, recalling his elevator adventure.

"There's one in my purse," Vera replied. "Over there."

Vera pointed behind Rolly. He turned, spotted the purse, retrieved it from the floor near the bathroom and handed it to Vera. She rummaged around inside.

"I forgot about your gun," Rolly said.

"I get out of here pretty late some nights."

"Hector told me he bought you one."

"Romantic, huh?"

She pulled her cell phone out of the purse and flipped it open.

"Wait," said Rolly.

Vera looked up at him.

"Is it registered? The gun?"

"Yes."

Rolly nodded.

"Okay," he said. "No, wait."

Vera gave him an exasperated look.

"Let's call Hector first. I want to talk to him."

Vera punched a button and put the phone up to her ear.

"Hey babe," she said. "It's me. Rolly's here. He wants to talk to you. I think I shot a guy. Call me."

She flipped the phone shut, then offered it to Rolly.

"That should get his attention," she said. "You wanna call the police?"

"I want to know about Hector and Roberto first. And the girl."

"They went to that rally."

"At Border Field Park?"

"Yeah. Hector had his Pancho Villa outfit on. He's been working on it for weeks."

"They took Rio with them?"

"That's your little girlfriend's name?"

"Yes. She was supposed to stay here until I came back."

"Where'd you go, anyway? Hector was worried."

"It's a long story."

"She went with 'em. They got her all dressed up too."

"Why?"

"Everybody's going as something. That's the idea. Roberto's wearing a baseball uniform. I don't know who he's supposed to be."

"You said Hector got all worked up this morning. What'd he say?"

"I don't know. Lots of stuff. He kept going on about 'those assholes.'"

"Did he mention any names?"

"It was some kinda group."

"Was it the AFA? Is that what he said?"

"He said he was gonna nail those fascist assholes."

"Anything else?"

"He's always going on about fascists. Roberto came over early this morning. He brought some papers for your girlfriend to sign."

"What kind of papers?"

"I don't know. Green card stuff, I assume. They were all sitting around at the table. I brought 'em some coffee and *conchas*, up here. They were all speaking in Spanish. She was signing some things. I couldn't follow most of what they were saying, except, I remember Roberto saying something kinda grand-like. After she signed the papers, he took the pen from her, held it up like it was a religious object or something."

"What'd he say?"

"I don't remember, it sounded all dramatic-like. You know Roberto?"

"No. I don't."

"He likes being a lawyer. Everything's a big drama. Wait, I remember now, what it was that he said."

"Yes?"

"'Con esta pluma' . . . wait . . . It was '*Con esta pluma, una niña destruye a fascistas.*'"

"What's that mean?"

"With this pen, a little girl destroys fascists."

Vera's phone rang. She glanced down at the display.

"It's Hector," she said. She flipped the phone open and put it up to her ear.

"Some guy just tried to fucking kill me," she said to Hector. Then she burst into tears.

31

EL CIRCO (THE CIRCUS)

Driving toward Border Field Park, Rolly hoped Jaime's old truck would survive one more traverse of the cracked asphalt and potholes of Monument Road. It had to. He had to. He drove past Jaime's house and The Honey Trap, through the narrow part of the road where the brambles and thickets closed in. The road opened out again near the entry to Border Field State Park, the lower parking lot where he'd talked to Jaime two days ago. The gate to the park was open. There were cars parked at the top of Friendship Hill, human figures moving across the backdrop of blue sky and white border fence, the faded old bullring. He drove through the gate and turned onto the road that led up the hill.

He didn't know what kind of story Rio had told Hector's lawyer, but he knew it wasn't the whole story. Whatever confrontation they'd planned with the AFA could backfire on them. Hector and Roberto didn't know about the video game, the one Sayer Burdon had built for himself, a shadow puzzle of his own existence, a ghost world to the real one. The game had its own logic, Burdon's logic. Burdon adjusted the power of each character, gave them new powers if he wanted. He made up the rules. The kid was smart, a genius. He could program the game in a thousand different ways, but he couldn't deal with real people. His emotional register just didn't work right. Every word that came out of Burdon's mouth had the same weird flatness. Except in the game. In the game, Sayer Burdon could be anybody—the Pallbearer, Red, The Cowboy, El Doctor. He took on the traits of whatever character he played. He spoke with their tongues. When the game ended, he went back to his normal voice—flat, unemotional. It was creepy.

Psychiatrists probably had a name for Burdon's condition, but Rolly didn't care what it was called. He just wanted Rio to confirm a few things, to tell him which parts of the game were real. She was the only person available and, Rolly hoped, willing to confirm what he'd learned. She knew who The Pallbearer was. She'd seen the game. She might even have played it.

There was one character from the game Rolly couldn't match in real life, an amorphous figure in a swirling black cape called The Ancestor. The Ancestor was omnipotent. Other characters could hide from him for a while; they could run, but they couldn't destroy him. That was how Sayer Burdon set up the game. In the Border Field Blues game, The Ancestor always got you. You couldn't win.

Jaime's truck sputtered as it climbed the hill, huffing and puffing like the little engine that could. The hill leveled off as it entered the upper parking lot. Rolly glanced over the scene, searching for Hector and his retinue. He spotted Nuge's black pickup, along with other trucks of the same general model and style. A squad of paramilitary types, AFA members, milled about near the trucks, dressed in camouflage gear, brandishing paint guns and flags. They'd unrolled a sign near the fence that proclaimed "Americans First" in large type. Rolly turned and drove to the other end of lot, where the automobiles varied more widely—compacts and a few beaters, a couple of nicely appointed low-riders and one shiny silver Mercedes.

He pulled into a parking spot and climbed out of the truck. People at this end of the lot varied more widely as well, dressed in what looked like costume-party attire. Three men in bandito outfits stood under a tree. One of them walked over to Rolly.

"Hey amigo," said Hector. "Vera said you were coming down."

"I need to talk to the girl."

"Sure."

"What's she doing down here, anyway?"

"We're gonna nail these bastards."

"The AFA, you mean?"

"Yeah."

"How?"

"I tried to call you last night, to tell you."

"What did she tell you?"

"It was them, the AFA guys. They assaulted her, killed the other girl."

"She told you that?"

"In so many words. Roberto thinks she can collect on it."

"You're going to sue them?"

"Damn right. We're going after the whole organization."

"That's why you brought her down here?"

"She's gonna try to ID some of them."

"Where is she?"

"I tried to call you last night to explain things."

"I need to talk to her. Just for a minute."

Hector stared at Rolly a moment, then nodded his head.

"C'mon," he said.

Hector led Rolly back along the sidewalk and walked up to driver's side of the silver Mercedes. Two people sat in the front seat, a large man in a powder-blue Dodger uniform and a woman in vestments, with a long scarf draped over her head. The man in the Dodger uniform lowered the window.

"Roberto, this is Rolly," said Hector. "The detective guy I told you about. Rolly, this is Roberto Torres, my lawyer."

"*Hola*," said Roberto, extending a large hand.

"That's Fernando's old number, right?" said Rolly, shaking hands.

"El Toro. You got it," said Roberto, looking pleased. He bore a puffy-faced resemblance to his Chicano hero.

"Who's she supposed to be?" Rolly said.

"The Virgin of Guadalupe," said Hector. "Whattya think?"

"Cute."

Hector turned back to Roberto.

"Rolly wants to ask her some questions," he said. "I told him it was okay."

"Feel free to ask," said Roberto. "But as her lawyer, all questions will have to go through me first. I may advise her on how to answer."

"I brought her to you guys, you know."

"That doesn't mean you own her."

"Well, whatever you're planning here, you may want to reconsider."

"What's that mean?"

"You'll see. Ask her if she speaks English."

"You know she doesn't speak English," said Hector.

"We'll see. Ask her."

Roberto gave Rolly a confrontational look, then turned to Rio.

"*¿Habla inglés?*" he asked.

Rio's head scarf swished back and forth.

"No," she said.

"Tell her I think she's lying," said Rolly. "I think she speaks English."

"*¿No habla inglés?*" Roberto asked her. "*¿Es verdad?*"

"*Sí. No hablo.*"

"*Este hombre dice que usted habla inglés,*" Roberto told her.

Rio's eyes fixed on Rolly.

"*No hablo inglés,*" she said, daring him to take on the virgin patroness of Mexico.

"Tell her I've met him, The Pallbearer."

"Who?"

"The Pallbearer. El Portador. I've talked to him. I've played the game with him."

"What the hell are you talking about?" said Roberto.

"She'll know," said Rolly. "She already knows."

He'd seen Rio's eyes flash when he mentioned the name. She knew Sayer Burdon. They were in this together. She'd seen the game.

"What's this about?" Hector asked.

"It's an act. That's what it's about."

"What do you mean?"

"It's all a game."

"What about that doctor guy who came after you? And those dead girls you told me about? They're not a game."

"They're real enough, but she's not telling us everything."

"What about the AFA guys?"

"What about them?"

"They paid for her."

"She told you that?"

"You remember what I told you, about the sex slave trade, those rich Arabs who'll pay for virgins?"

"Yeah."

"She told us it was the men in the masks."

"They were Arabs?"

"No. The man in the mask, who came to the house. Don't you see?"

"No."

"It's the AFA, man. They're the buyers."

"How do you know?"

"She described 'em more. She said the men had camouflage suits. That they had paint guns."

"She told you that?"

"Yeah. I'm telling you. This is huge. We're gonna expose them."

"We're going to sue their asses off," said Roberto. "That's what we're going to do."

Rolly looked at Rio. She stared back at him. Her eyes were dark and impassable.

"That's why you brought her down here?" said Rolly.

"Yeah," Hector said. "Roberto suggested it."

"It'll strengthen our case if she can ID some of the guys specifically," said Roberto.

"How much will you make from this?" Rolly asked Roberto.

"I'll take my cut. She'll make a fortune."

"If she wins."

"If she identifies any one of these guys, we can win."

"It didn't take much to convince her, Rolly," said Hector.

"I'm not surprised."

Rolly wasn't sure how much of this Rio had planned, if any, but she was one of the best improvisers he'd ever met. She followed the changes without missing a note. Perhaps she'd run into the AFA Friday night. Perhaps they'd killed the other girl. But he wasn't ready to believe it yet.

"I want to know about the records," he said to Roberto.

"What?"

"The record albums. Did The Pallbearer give her any record albums?"

"Who's this pallbearer guy?"

"El Portador. Did he give her any record albums?"

Robert spoke to Rio. She shook her head.

"*No entiendo*," she said.

"She knows about the game," Rolly said. "She's seen the tokens. They look just like the records."

"What're you talking about?" Hector asked.

"You remember that CD we looked at with Marley?"

"With the girls' pictures?"

"Yes. It's all part of a video game. She's in it. So am I. So is the doctor and everyone else I've talked to in the last two days."

"Am I in it?"

"The restaurant is."

"No shit?"

"No shit. Listen, there's these records, collector's editions. The night she came by the house, with the cowboy, when they talked to my mother, they said something about the records. I think that's what she wanted the money for."

"You want your money back?"

"No, that's not the point. These records keep showing up everywhere. In that car that was stolen. Somebody left a whole box of them at this church in the barrio. I want to know why. I want to know why they're all in this game."

"You think she knows?"

"You remember when we got the money for her last night?"

"Yeah."

"How much did she ask for, at first?"

"A hundred bucks."

"And how much did I end up paying her?"

"Two hundred."

"I talked to a friend of mine. The going price on the record is between one and two hundred dollars."

"I see where you're going, I guess. What's it got to do with this video game?"

"The records are in the video game, too. It's what the characters use for money. They're tokens."

"This is some crazy shit, Rolly," said Hector.

"Crazy bullshit. That's what it is," said Roberto. "She told you she doesn't know anything."

"Ask her if she knows who The Ancestor is."

"The Ancestor?"

"Please. Just ask her."

Roberto asked. Rio shook her head again, then looked Rolly in the eyes. She'd recovered from whatever small dent he'd made in her story. To be truthful, he didn't know if she was from Guadalupe, Tijuana, or National City. She wasn't going to tell him, either. Not now. Not with the money Roberto and Hector had promised her.

One of the other Pancho Villas walked up to the car and tapped Hector on the shoulder.

"Hey Hector," he said, pointing to a white van that had pulled in on the other side of the parking lot. "The TV people are here."

32

LA BATALLA (THE BATTLE)

"Time to go," said Roberto. He climbed out of the car, walked around to the passenger side and opened the door for Rio.

"All right, folks," called Hector to the protestors milling around behind him. "Let's keep to the plan, like we talked about. No calling names. Signs to the front. Heroes in back. Roberto and I will take the middle with Our Lady."

The sign-bearers scuffled past Rolly, arranging themselves in the middle of the parking lot, while those dressed in costumes hung back on the sidewalk. Hector moved to the point position. Rolly grabbed Rio's arm as she passed.

"Are you sure you want to do this?" he said.

"*Deseo mi dinero*," said Rio.

"Tell me who The Ancestor is."

"Let her go," said Roberto, stepping between them.

Rolly let go. Roberto was too big for him. The whole situation was too big for him.

"Let's go!" shouted Hector.

The group began to move, making its way toward the AFA line.

"*¡Para la Raza!*" Hector called.

"*¡Que viva la Raza!*" the crowd echoed back.

"*¡Para el Chicano!*"

"*¡Que viva el Chicano!*"

Rolly stopped, letting the group pass. The protestors paraded across the parking lot. They halted on Hector's command, forming a line about ten feet from the AFA group. The TV cameras moved in. Hector moved out in front of the line and raised his hands. The chanting stopped. Someone handed him a megaphone.

"Good afternoon," Hector said, addressing the AFA and the TV cameras. "My name is Hector Villa. I am the great-great-grand-nephew of Pancho Villa, the liberator of Mexico. Today I am proud to present to you a cavalcade of Chicano heroes."

He dropped the megaphone to his side. No one said anything. No one on either side moved. Hector returned to his megaphone.

"First on our list is the NASA astronaut and first Hispanic woman in space—Ellen Ochoa."

Hector's crowd cheered as a woman in an astronaut suit stepped out from behind the line and took up a position to the left and behind Hector. Hector continued his roll call, introducing each hero in costume. Rolly knew some of the names, musicians like Carlos Santana and Sheila E., but there were others he'd never heard of. As the names were called, each costumed hero strode out from behind the sign-bearers and took a position near Hector, each greeted by cheers from the group. The AFA members watched from behind their masks. They were silent.

"And now," said Hector, "the Cy Young Award–winning pitcher for the Los Angeles Dodgers—Fernando Valenzuela."

Roberto walked out into no-man's-land and stood next to Hector as Hector listed El Toro's accomplishments.

"And finally," Hector announced, "she who looks over all Mexico. Our patroness, she who crushes the serpent of tyranny

—Coatlaxopeuh, better known to the world as Our Lady of Guadalupe."

Rio stepped forward, moving into position between the two men as Hector narrated.

"The virgin comes here today as our protector, so that those who speak bigotry and hate will be shamed by their actions upon the innocent."

"America for Americans!" someone shouted from the AFA line. He shouted again. Another voice joined in. The rest of the AFA line began chanting, turning it into a chorus.

"America. For Americans!" they shouted in three-over-four cadence. Hector raised his voice, soloing over the beat.

"Today we come for justice," he said. "Today we come for *la gente*."

Roberto handed Hector a sheaf of paper. Hector raised it over his head.

"Tomorrow, on behalf of the virgin, in federal court, we will file a civil suit against the AFA, charging your members with sexual trafficking, kidnapping and harassment."

A large man stepped out of the line of AFA men and moved toward them.

"Fuck you," he said.

Hector stood his ground.

"Hate has no place here," he said.

The man raised his gun.

"Hate on this, Pancho," he said and shot Hector in the face.

Hector screamed and raised his hands to his face. A shock of silence came over the crowd, like a punch to the gut. The earth and ocean seemed to pause as Hector dropped the paper, turned back to the crowd and stumbled onto his knees. His hands and face dripped with red.

"Get 'em!" a voice screamed. Both sides of the crowd fell in on the middle, a swirling vortex sucking them in. Picket signs swung and paintballs flew as icons of Chicano culture wrestled with camouflaged storm troopers. Rolly retreated. He'd seen enough bar fights. He tried to stay out of them.

A break in the crowd caught his eye. A large man, in camouflage, separated himself from the scrum. It was the man who'd shot Hector, trudging toward the edge of the parking lot, where the road led back down the hill. He carried a paint gun in one hand, a bundle of something under the opposite arm. The bundle squirmed. It was Rio.

Rolly ran toward the crest of the road, taking an angle to cut the man off. He didn't know what he'd do when he got there, but he had to do something. He reached the spot ahead of the other man, then reached down to pick up a fist-sized rock that lay on the ground.

"Stop!" he yelled, turning to face the man. "Let her go."

The man stomped on toward him, dragging Rio under his arm.

"Stop, Jimmy," said Rolly. "I know it's you."

The man stopped and looked up. He pointed his gun at Rolly.

"Get out of the way, Rolly," he said.

"I know about the game," Rolly said. "I played it with Sayer Burdon. The Pallbearer."

"This isn't a game, Rolly."

"You're in it. I've seen you."

"What're you talking about?

"You were down here Friday night, weren't you?"

"I didn't kill that girl, Rolly."

"What happened?"

"I had to stop him."

"Who?"

"That little Mexican guy."

"The doctor? Ramoñes?"

"It's him, Rolly. I know it's him."

"He killed the girl?"

"He's the guy who stabbed me. At Pelicans."

"What?"

"It's him, Rolly."

"That was a long time ago. Are you sure?"

"Yeah, I'm sure. That little beaner fucked up my dick, Rolly. I remember. He fucked me all up. And the doctors. I gotta pee all the time now, 'cause of him. I always gotta be near a toilet or carry a bag."

"I'm sorry, Jimmy."

"You don't care. You didn't even remember it happened."

"I don't remember a lot of things, Jimmy."

"The Border Patrol wouldn't take me, 'cause of the peeing thing."

"What're you going to do with her, Jimmy?"

"You heard what Pancho said back there. They're gonna sue us."

"What happened Friday night?"

"I didn't do any of that stuff he said."

"Let's go to the police, then. You can tell them what happened."

"I didn't kill that girl, Rolly."

"I believe you."

"That little Mexican shit's living here like a king, Rolly. He's got his own swimming pool and a house full of tinglers."

"It's not what you think."

"I'm just a dumb-ass security guard, Rolly. They won't even give me insurance, 'cause of my condition."

"We'll tell the police about him. They'll arrest him."

"So they can send him back to Mexico again? What good will that do?"

"Let the girl go, Jimmy."

"They're running us over, Rolly. They're taking our jobs."

"Let her go," Rolly said. He raised the rock to his shoulder.

Jimmy fired the gun. Rolly felt a sharp sting against his forehead, then another against his left cheek, as if someone had slapped him. He dropped the rock, put his hands to his face. Oily liquid dripped into his eyes as he staggered. The ground gave way under his feet. He fell backwards and rolled down the embankment.

33

———————

EL ASESINO (THE KILLER)

The sky appeared once as he rolled down the hill, then a second time, mixed with clouds of dust and a view of his feet. His left foot was shoeless. He stopped rolling and came to rest on a sandy patch at the bottom of the hill. His eyes stung from the paint. There was a stabbing pain in his back. He rolled over onto his stomach, pushed himself up to his knees, grabbed the tail end of his shirt and wiped it across his face. He blinked a few times, then wiped again with a clean part of the shirt. The sting faded.

"Let her go, *el gordo*," a voice said from above, on the road.

"Fuck off, you little beaner," came Jimmy's reply.

"Give me the whore."

Rolly crawled up the embankment to the edge of the road, where he found Ramoñes and Jimmy locked in a Mexican stand-off, staring each other down. Ramoñes had his scalpel out. Jimmy pointed his gun.

"Be careful, Jimmy," said Rolly.

Ramoñes glanced over at Rolly. He laughed.

"Amigo, you don't look so good," he said.

"You know who this is, Rolly?" Jimmy asked.

"His name's Zildjian Ramoñes," said Rolly.

"He's the guy who fucked me up," Jimmy said. "That's who he is. That little Mexican, from Pelicans, the one who cut me."

"Are you sure? How do you know that?"

"I been watching him and his little operation over there on the canyon."

"You were there, weren't you, Jimmy? Friday night?"

"It had to stop, Rolly."

"Let the girl go, Jimmy. Let's take her back to the group."

"This I cannot allow," said Ramoñes, taking a step closer. Jimmy wiggled the gun at him. Ramoñes stopped.

"You heard that Pancho guy, Rolly," said Jimmy. "She's gonna sue us. They're gonna crucify me."

"What're you going to do with her?"

"It wasn't supposed to turn out like this, Rolly."

"What happened to the other girl, Jimmy?"

"She ran away. Into the ocean. I tried to stop her. It wasn't supposed to turn out like this."

"What about the other ones?"

"What other ones?"

"The other girls, from before. The ones The Pallbearer took away."

"I don't know what you're talking about," Jimmy said. "Why don't you ask him?"

"Señor," Ramoñes said, inspecting his fingernails, scraping under them with the scalpel. "This gun you are pointing, it does not frighten me."

"You wanna try it?"

In his effort to keep both Rolly and Ramoñes engaged, Jimmy had loosened his grip on Rio, letting her slip to the ground. Rolly saw Rio's face change. A dark resolve came into her eyes.

"No! Wait!" he cried, but it was too late. With as much force as her little frame could muster, Rio stomped down on Jimmy's foot.

"Oooh," Jimmy grunted, turning toward her. Rio swept in with her knee, nailing Jimmy in the crotch.

"Ahhh!" he screamed, dropping the gun. Rio twisted away from him, then ran back up the hill. Ramoñes had seen her eyes too. He moved faster than any of them, lunging forward, shoving the scalpel under the front edge of Jimmy's helmet, swiping it across Jimmy's neck with a sickening snick as he raced by, running to catch Rio. A spray of blood erupted from Jimmy's throat, raining over the dusty dirt track. Jimmy gurgled and clutched at his throat, then toppled onto the ground like a deflating beach ball.

"Rolly," someone yelled, "get out of the way!"

Rolly turned to see a police officer crouched in position at the bottom of the road, her gun pointed toward him.

"Bonnie," he said, shuffling toward her like a zombie.

"Goddammit, Rolly!" she yelled at him. "Get out of the way."

Rolly flattened himself on the ground next to Jimmy and turned his head to look back up the hill. Ramoñes had captured Rio. He held her in front of him, using her body as a shield. Another twenty feet up the hill, two TV cameramen filmed the whole thing. A crowd had gathered behind them, remnants of the diminishing riot.

"I am sorry, Officer," said Ramoñes, "but I must ask you to drop your gun and allow us leave."

"Don't let him do it, Bonnie."

"Shut up, Rolly. Just shut up and stay down."

"Yes," said Ramoñes. "No one moves, not you or your boyfriend. Or I kill the girl."

"Put the knife down," said Bonnie. "Let her go."

"I cannot do that," said Ramoñes, shoving Rio in front of him, inching his way down the hill. "It is you who must put down your weapon, Officer. My vehicle is parked down there, behind you. I will take her there. And then we will leave. No one will follow, or the whore will die."

"You're not going anywhere," Bonnie replied, not moving an inch from her cocked position.

Ramoñes looked down at Rolly. He smiled.

"Your *novia* is a tough bitch, amigo. But the handcuffs, they are not for me."

"Let her go," Rolly groaned.

"Officer, you will let me through now or I will cut the whore. I will drain all the blood from her degenerate body."

Ramoñes flicked his wrist. Rio screamed. A tiny flower of blood bloomed behind her left ear.

"Stop it," Rolly pleaded.

"Rolly, pipe down!" yelled Bonnie.

"He cut her!" Rolly shouted.

Bonnie glanced up the hill toward the TV crews. Rolly could almost see her running through her training, checking which chapter of the manual covered this situation.

"All right, sir," she relented, pulling her arm back to a semi-cocked position and stepping back down the hill, "I'm backing away. You can move down the hill."

Ramoñes smiled, pushing Rio farther down the road. The cameramen stepped forward at the top of the hill. Bonnie raised her other hand.

"You, at the top of the road, all of you. Don't move. Stay where you are."

As Ramoñes edged past, Rio looked down at Jimmy's body, then over at Rolly. There was no fear in her eyes. She looked back toward Jimmy. Rolly followed her eyes and spotted Jimmy's paint gun. He reached for the gun, watching to see if Ramoñes noticed him, but the little doctor only had eyes for Bonnie. Rolly wasn't a threat. Rolly touched the butt of the gun and moved his hand up to the trigger. He looked back up at Rio. If he'd learned anything from all the women he'd been with, it was how to read their eyes, when they were with you and when they weren't. He waited for Rio to make the next move.

She closed her eyes and went limp, drooping her head forward as if she'd fainted, abandoning all resistance. Ramoñes grunted as he moved to recover his grip, dropping his shoulder and pulling the knife away. Rolly raised the paint gun.

"Zildjian," he said. Ramoñes turned his head. Rolly pulled the trigger.

The first shot caught the doctor flush in the eye, splattering blue paint across his face. He staggered backwards. Rio uncoiled herself and pushed away, scratching at Ramoñes's face like an insane cat. He swung back at her with his scalpel but only gashed at empty air.

"Whore!" he screamed. "Filthy bitch whore!"

Rolly fired the paint gun, again and again, splattering the little doctor in explosions of red, white and blue. Ramoñes wobbled. He turned toward Rolly. Red paint poured from his mouth, flooding over his lips. It wasn't paint, though.

Rolly looked down the hill to see Bonnie back in her crouch, firing her gun. Ramoñes took another wobbly step toward him. The little doctor jerked right, then stumbled back to his left. He swung the scalpel in a weak arc of desperation and dropped to his knees. He stared down at Rolly, a dimming hate in his eyes.

"Fuckeen guitar players," he gasped.

The last color of life went out in the doctor's pupils. He tilted over and came to rest against Jimmy. The scalpel clattered to the ground an inch from Rolly's nose.

Rolly jumped to his feet. Rio ran to him, sobbing. He closed his eyes, put his arms around her and held on to her quivering body. Then he pushed her away. He leaned over the edge of the embankment and barfed.

34

LA FAMILIA (THE FAMILY)

A black hearse sat in the driveway of the house on Smuggler's Canyon. Rolly tapped the brakes on Jaime's truck, turned across the road and spun a U-turn into the dirt shoulder. He stopped the car at the edge of the road and stared up at the house on the hill. The gate was open.

Ramoñes was dead. Jimmy was dead. Rio was missing. At some point in the jagged aftermath of the riot and shooting, among the police cars and ambulances, the crowds and TV crews, she'd just disappeared. No one knew where she'd gone. Not Rolly. Not Roberto or Hector. Not the paramedic who bandaged her neck. Bonnie was livid.

"The captain'll give me hell about this," she muttered as they waited for the coroner's crew to clean up the mess.

"I'm sorry," said Rolly.

"What're you sorry about?"

"Everything. It's an all-purpose sorry."

"Yeah, well, you had your chance. I told you to drop this case."

"You think he killed Jaime?" asked Rolly, looking up at the hill where the coroner took pictures of the bodies.

"The doctor guy?" said Bonnie. "I expect it's him. Cut his throat, just like Mr. Bodeans."

Rolly felt his stomach twinge, a dry heave. It seemed like he'd thrown up everything he could possibly have in there.

"I was lucky," he said.

"Damn lucky," said Bonnie. She massaged her gun hand. "That guy was fast."

"You couldn't have saved him. Jimmy, I mean."

"What the hell was Bodeans doing anyway? How's he involved in this mess?"

"He told me Ramoñes was the guy who stabbed him. At Pelicans."

"You mean that club in IB?"

"Jimmy was a bouncer there, remember? He said this little Mexican guy stabbed him."

"When was this?"

"A long time ago. Twenty years, I guess. Moogus remembered it."

"You mean Bodeans has been looking for this guy for twenty years?"

"No. At least I don't think so. I don't know. He must've seen him somewhere recently and recognized him. I think it was at that house, on Smuggler's Canyon."

"The one with that Tangerine woman?"

Rolly nodded.

"The Honey Trap."

"You think she's part of this?"

"She knows Ramoñes."

"Well, we can probably work up a warrant for that house now. What was Bodeans doing with the girl, anyway? Trying to play hero or something?"

"Ask her lawyer. He can explain."

"She's got a lawyer?"

"That guy you talked to earlier, in the Dodger uniform," Rolly said, pointing at Roberto. "Standing next to Pancho Villa. He's going to sue the AFA, on her behalf."

"What for?"

"Assault. Sexual harassment or something like that. I didn't get the whole story. While you're at it, you should talk to this Nuge guy."

"Who's that?"

Rolly searched the area.

"There," he said. "AFA guy with the black truck."

"What about him?"

"He's a jerk."

"I can't arrest him for that."

"He's got a radio in the truck. He's got the Border Patrol radio codes."

"You think he made that call Friday night?"

"I think he's hiding something."

"We'll make sure to talk to him."

"Can I go home now?"

"No. Not yet."

"I can meet with you tomorrow."

"You'll have to talk to somebody else tomorrow. I'll be on leave."

"Oh."

"Standard procedure when there's a shooting. Just sit tight for a while."

It was another hour and a half before they cleared the scene. Rolly spent most of that time sitting by himself in Jaime's truck, trying to get warm. Everyone who'd parked in the upper lot had to stay until they'd taken the bodies away, cleared the road. It was the only way for the cars to get out. As soon as Jimmy and Ramoñes were placed in the ambulances, everyone left, including the television crews, anxious to get back to the studio and edit their footage into a tight story for the six o'clock news. If Rolly got home soon, he could watch the whole thing on TV.

He didn't want to go home. He didn't want to watch it on TV. He didn't want to do anything but play guitar all night for lonely women in some worn-out dive. Have a drink or two. Maybe a bottle. If there was ever a day when he could allow himself to start drinking again, this was it. Four people were dead, and he still wasn't sure who had driven a car through the least tern preserve Friday night. That was what Max had hired him to find out. The driveway gate was open. He couldn't go home. The game wasn't over yet.

He climbed out of the truck, walked across the road, through the gate and up the driveway to the front door where Tangerine had first appeared in blazing orange—half-stoned, fully loaded. He turned the doorknob, pushed the door open and entered the house.

A shallow foyer led into a dingy living room, lit by the big-screen TV on the wall. The late-afternoon sun streamed in through the sliding glass door. Sayer Burdon sat at one end of the living room sofa, headphones over his ears, flicking the buttons on a game controller. Rio sat at the other end of the sofa, curled up like a cat, watching him play. She glanced up at Rolly as he entered the room, then returned to the game. Sayer Burdon took even less notice. Rolly walked to the back of the couch and looked down at Rio.

"Why did you leave?" he asked.

Rio shrugged her shoulders.

"Did he bring you here?" Rolly asked, nodding at Sayer.

"*Deseo mi dinero,*" Rio said.

"Who brought you here?" Rolly asked. "*¿Que va aqui?*"

"*Recorrí aquí.*"

"I don't understand. *Hable inglés.*"

"*No hablo,*" she said.

Rolly pulled his phone out of his pocket.

"Tell me in English or I call the police," he said.

"*No policía.*"

"It's your choice," said Rolly, scrolling through his contact list. "*¿Inglés o policía?*" He found Bonnie's number, then looked back at Rio.

"Last chance," he said. "How did you get here?"

"I walk," she said. "I walk here."

"Why?"

"He will give me the money," she said, indicating Burdon.

"El Portador?"

"*Sí*. He is El Portador."

"Where is Señora Tangie?"

"She is asleep. In her room."

"Is there anyone else here?"

"El Padre," said Rio. "He is in the bedroom with Señora Tangie."

Rolly looked down the hallway where Rio pointed. If she used the names Sayer had created for the characters in the game, there was only one person it could be. Had the pastor come to save Tangerine's soul or to ruin his own again?

As if summoned by Rolly's thoughts, Eddie Sanchez appeared in the hallway.

"Who's there?" he said, walking out into the living room. "Oh. It's you."

"What are you doing here?" Rolly asked.

"Is the police detective with you?"

"She'll be here soon," Rolly said, lying.

"I will tell her all that I know. All that has happened since you came to my church."

"You can tell me."

"I have done nothing improper."

"Where's Tangerine?"

"She is gone. Her soul has departed."

"She's dead?"

"I have performed the last rites."

Rolly glanced over at Sayer and Rio. Neither of them responded to the information. Perhaps they both knew. Or they didn't care.

"What happened to her?"

"She went to sleep. Like the other girls."

"You know about them?"

"I do now," Sanchez replied. He looked over at Sayer. "He has told me."

"I played the game with him," said Rolly.

"Then you know too."

"It's not a game, though. They're really dead. Bonnie showed me the pictures."

"Yes."

"The doctor's dead, too."

"The man in your photographs?"

"Yes. And Jimmy. He's dead. El Gordo."

"That man was real too?"

"Yes."

"I did not know them. Only Tangerine. And Jaime. And the boy."

"He's the one who gave you the records?"

"I did not recognize him. I had not seen him for fifteen years."

The realization hit Rolly like a power chord to the brain.

"He's Tangerine's son, isn't he, the one you and your wife adopted?"

Sanchez nodded.

"Yes."

"Has he always been like this?"

"He has never been good with expressing himself. I think it is worse now."

"It's like he doesn't have any emotions. Not in the real world."

"His life has been very complicated. My wife took him to many doctors. They gave him medicines."

"Did it help?"

"A little. The money is his now to do what he wants. He does not always take the medicines."

"What money?"

"From the trust fund, the one the lawyers set up. From that record."

"He'll inherit it from Tangerine?"

"It has always been his money. He was a minor, so others could access it. His guardians."

"Like you and your wife?"

"Yes, my wife continued to receive the money while he stayed in her care. Until the time of his eighteenth birthday. Then the money became his, to control, to do what he wished. That is when his mother revealed herself to him. She convinced him to leave and move out on his own."

"He'd never met her before?"

"Yes. Many times. But not as his mother."

"I don't understand."

"She pretended to be my wife's sister."

"Aunt Tangie."

"Yes. My wife made a devil's bargain. She gave Tangerine money. To keep her quiet. So that she would not reveal herself to the boy."

"She paid her off?"

Sanchez nodded.

"I did not know about this until yesterday. After your visit, I spoke to my former wife. I called her soon after you left, when I realized who the boy was. She, too, had received some of the records. She did not know of their value."

"Why is he passing out these records?"

"I believe it is some kind of penitence. He cannot express himself as most people do. It is part of the game."

"You think he feels guilty?"

"In his way, yes."

"Did he kill those girls?"

"You have played the game. What do you think?"

"I think he tried to save them."

"Yes."

"It seems like he's working something out, a puzzle or something. That's why he's playing the game."

"He does not know God's way."

"It's like he's trying to be God, to control things. That's what it looks like to me."

"Yes. It is something like that."

"What about that black shroud thing? The Ancestor? Who is that supposed to be?"

"It is a man he never knew. It is his real father."

"One of those guys in the band?"

"You have not understood."

"Didn't you tell us Tangerine got pregnant while she was hanging out with the band? That she'd slept with all of them, that's why their lawyers set up the trust fund?"

"This is true. But the serpent had come to her before."

"You mean that story about the man who came to her out by the pool?"

"Yes."

"So, you think it was true?"

"I know it was true."

"Was it you?"

"No. I did not have carnal knowledge of her until later."

"Jaime, then?"

"No. There was only one man it could be, Mr. Waters, don't you see?"

"No. I guess not."

"Truly?"

"Well, from everything I've heard, her father had her locked up pretty tight. I don't see . . ."

Rolly stopped. He turned to look at Sayer Burdon. He saw it now. He understood. Some families were even more complicated than his.

35

EL CUMPLEAÑOS (THE BIRTHDAY)

Rolly sat on a stool in the backyard of his father's house, strumming his guitar under the shade of the awning while the caterers laid out food for the birthday party. One of the caterers walked over to him.

"Hey, amigo," said Hector, "I like that multicolor look you got going."

"Nice, huh?" said Rolly. "Looks like you got some left over too."

"Yeah. Vera says it looks like I got a rash."

"She knows it's paint, right?"

"Oh, yeah, she knows about that. She won't let me out of the kitchen, though. Thinks I'll freak out the customers."

"At least yours is a semi-natural color."

"Yeah, that blue splat you got does look kind of peculiar. Roberto says it'll be gone completely in another week."

"It's faded some already."

"That was some crazy shit that went down."

"Yeah."

"I told Vera I'm gonna take it easy for a while. I gotta rethink my priorities. I never seen guys killed like that."

"Me neither."

"Did they ever find that girl?"

"I don't think so."

"You never heard from her?"

"Did you?"

"Nah. She was a tough little girl, though, *una niña dura*. I hope she's okay."

"She'll be all right."

"Yeah. I wish we could've nailed those AFA guys, though."

"You're not going to sue them?"

"Can't without her."

"How about for yourself?"

"You mean 'cause of this?" Hector said, pointing at the paint stain on his face.

Rolly nodded.

"Roberto says it'd be hard, 'cause of the general confusion. Too much conflicting testimony. Don't forget my homies were in there swinging, too. Roberto heard there might be criminal charges."

"Against you?"

"Against the AFA guys. He said we should wait on that before we moved ahead with anything."

"I think it's just one of them."

"Oh, well, you probably know more than I do."

"I'll tell you about it sometime."

"Why don't you come down to the restaurant tomorrow? Lunch is on me. Vera'll want to hear about it too."

"Thanks," said Rolly.

"That lady, Alicia, she's your mom?"

"Stepmom."

"Oh, I was gonna say, I didn't think you had any Mexican in you."

"My mom's Dutch and Norwegian."

"You got the cold blood."

"Yeah, I guess. My dad's Irish."

"I didn't meet him yet."

"He's out with his buddies. It's a surprise."

"Oh yeah, that's right. I better get back to business. Good to see you, amigo. Drop by tomorrow."

"I will."

Hector walked back to the tables. Rolly checked the tuning on his guitar one last time, then placed it in the stand next to his seat. Some early guests had arrived. He waved at one of his father's old Navy buddies whose name he couldn't remember, then escaped through the backyard gate and walked out to the concrete path that wandered along the bay. He pulled out his phone and checked the time. Fifteen minutes until party time, ten minutes to chill.

It was a clear day. A massive cargo ship cut through the water, on its way to National City to deliver a load of Korean automobiles. It passed under the soaring blue bridge that connected Coronado to the city, second only to the Golden Gate as the most popular suicide bridge in the country. Bonnie had told him that. Police departments kept track of those things. Between the concrete towers of the bridge, far in the distance, he could see the blurry outline of the Tijuana hills. Below the hills, at the bottom of Smuggler's Canyon, stood a house with a pool in the back and a spiked iron fence around it. The house was empty now, cleared out by the police.

They found the doctor's operating room in the basement, originally designed as a storage shelter for waiting out the apocalypse. Very little was known to the police on either side of the border about Dr. Zildjian Ramoñes. He'd done a stretch at the Tijuana prison once, in his youth. When presented with his photograph by a reporter from *Zeta*, the front staff at the Chinese Embassy in Tijuana at first claimed to recognize him. Upon further consultation with higher-ups, the same front staff decided they were mistaken, and the reporter's trail ran into a wall of diplomatic immunity, although the paper did note the unexpected departure of two members of the embassy staff on a connecting flight from San Francisco to Beijing shortly after the inquiry.

No one knew what to do about Sayer Burdon. The police had little evidence against him, except for the video game. But the game didn't prove anything. Neither did the half-empty boxes of old shrink-wrapped records found in the house. There'd been no witnesses to the deaths of the four young girls with the Virgo mark whose bodies had been found across a wide swath of the river valley over the last six months. The most likely perpetrators were dead, leaving behind an idiot savant who could only communicate in monotone riddles. Two psychiatrists were called in, but they couldn't state for sure how Burdon had been involved, if he'd killed the girls, or just disposed of them, or simply absorbed the events around him, transmuting the ugliness into his video game. For now, Burdon had been released to the custody of Father Sanchez, who offered his services to the court on behalf of the young man.

As to the Friday night when someone had driven through the least tern preserve, Nuge, under duress, had provided details on his contribution to the misadventure, how he had come upon Jimmy and the hearse at Border Field Park. In Nuge's version of the story, the hearse had already been abandoned inside the least tern preserve and his only crime had been towing it out, which he'd done to help Jimmy, not wanting a fellow AFA member to provide the court system with any further reason to restrict their activities. He denied using his radio to mislead the Border Patrol. No one believed him, but no one could prove otherwise.

There was only one person still alive who knew what had happened that night, but the police couldn't find her. Some thought the girl had crossed back into Mexico, slipping through the border gate with the other pedestrians to escape the police.

Something no one had noticed, on the night after the riot, was the light that went on inside Norwood's Mostly Music, long after business hours. Soon after the light went on, a battered green pickup truck pulled in and parked nearby. Two figures climbed out of the truck and walked into the music shop, carrying something. They exited soon after, climbed into the truck and drove to the bus station. The driver pulled into the loading zone and the passenger got out of the truck. She was a pretty young woman, with long black hair, wearing a daisy-embroidered blouse. The woman walked into the bus station and purchased a ticket to Los Angeles. The man in the truck drove to the Rite Aid store in Hillcrest, left the truck in the parking lot and walked home, carrying a nylon-stringed Córdoba guitar. Two days later, if anyone noticed, a listing went up on eBay, advertising five copies of the original banned edition of *Jungle Love* by Serpent that were now available from a collectibles dealer in San Diego.

The cargo ship passed under the bridge. Rolly checked his phone again. It was time to go back to the party. He walked back to his father's house, let himself in through the back gate. More guests had arrived. With some horror, he realized his mother had decided to join the festivities. And she'd brought Max. He wondered if Alicia had any idea what she might have got herself into. He hoped his father wasn't too drunk when he arrived.

"He's here!" someone whispered.

Rolly took a seat and picked up his guitar. He looked for Alicia, who was supposed to give him his cue. His father appeared around the back corner of the house. Alicia nodded at Rolly. He strummed the first chord, then sang the first line of the birthday song. The crowd joined in.

His father looked less drunk than usual. The usual disasters might be avoided. He hoped his mother would leave early.

After the song ended, the guests crowded in around his father, offering their personal condolences, approbations and jokes. Rolly stuck to his post. It was a paying gig, after all, and he was a professional. He'd have plenty of time to face up to his paterfamilias.

Max broke away from the crowd and walked up to Rolly.

"That's where the guy shot you, huh?" he said, pointing at Rolly's blue splotches.

"That's it," Rolly said. He'd talked to Max on the telephone, but this was the first time he'd seen him since the previous Sunday. "I didn't know you were coming."

"Your mom didn't tell you?" said Max.

Rolly shook his head.

"Sorry," said Max.

"I didn't know she was coming at all."

"It was kind of a last-minute thing."

"I expect it was."

"You doing okay?" asked Max.

Rolly looked down at the nylon-stringed Córdoba resting on his thigh, then looked back at Max.

"I got my guitar back," he said.

ACKNOWLEDGMENTS

A bouquet of thanks to my wife, Maria, for her willingness to read and critique poorly formed chapters until they got better and became a book, and for being a damn fine partner in life.

ABOUT THE AUTHOR

"A powerful new voice on the crime-fiction scene" (ForeWord Reviews), Corey Lynn Fayman has done hard time as a musician, songwriter and interactive designer, but still refuses to apologize for it. His hometown of San Diego, CA, provides the backdrop for his mystery novels, including the award-winning *Border Field Blues* and *Desert City Diva*.

"As an independently published author, I rely on the recommendations of enthusiastic readers to help spread the word. If you enjoyed this Rolly Waters mystery, please consider posting a review on Amazon or Goodreads. A couple of sentences and a good rating are much appreciated!"

Sign up on my website or follow me on Facebook for updates, giveaways and drawings.

www.coreylynnfayman.com

facebook.com/coreylynnfayman